Every parent wants a perfect child. These parents are ready to correct a mistake and start over. . . .

An unhappy husband might kill his wife once—unless he's lucky and can do it again and again. . . .

Dirty cops, dynastic blackmailers, geriatric vigilantes—

Shamus-winner Ed Gorman, master of the dark mystery, serves up an "undertaker's dozen" bleak stories in Noir 13.

Praise for Ed Gorman:

"One of our finest contemporary short story writers regardless of genre."

Jon Breen, *Ellery Queen's Mystery Magazine*

"He seems to have, in the words of Robert Frost, 'A lover's quarrel with humanity.'"

Richard Laymon

Noir **13**

Other Books *by* Ed Gorman

Stranglehold
Ticket to Ride
The Midnight Room
Fools Rush In
Sleeping Dogs
The Day the Music Died
Everybody's Somebody's Fool

ED GORMAN

Noir 13

PERFECT CRIME BOOKS
Baltimore

Library of Congress Cataloging-in-Publication Data
Gorman, Ed
Noir 13/Ed Gorman
ISBN: 978-0-9825157-5-4

First Edition: October 2010

Contents

The Baby Store

"You know how sorry we all are, Kevin," Miles Green said, sliding his arm around Kevin McKay's shoulder and taking his right hand for a manly shake. "It's going to be rough and we know it. So whenever you need some time away, take it. No questions asked. You know?"

"I really appreciate it, Miles. And so does Jen. Everybody here has just been so helpful to us."

Miles smiled. "If you're not careful, you're going to give us lawyers a good reputation, Kevin." He checked the top of his left hand where the holo was embedded. "Time for me to head out for LA. The rocket leaves in three hours."

The Miles incident had occurred at the top of the day, just as Kevin had been about to settle himself into his desk chair for the first time in two months. The firm of Green, Hannigan & Storz had been generous indeed with one of its youngest and most aggressive lawyers. But no amount of good will could quite take away the guilt he felt for the death of his son. No amount of time off could erase the blame he felt.

By day's end, Kevin had been consoled by fourteen different members of the staff, from the paralegals to the executive secretaries to the firm's reigning asshole, Frank Hannigan himself.

Hannigan had said: "I know Miles told you to take all the time you need. But if you want my advice, Kevin, you'll get back in the game and start kicking some ass. And not just for the sake of your bonus this December. But for your mental health. You're a gladiator the same as I am. The battle is what keeps you sane." Hannigan frequently spoke in awkward metaphors.

As Kevin was leaving the office, he heard a brief burst of applause coming from one of the conference rooms. As he passed the open door, David Storz waved him in. "C'mon in and celebrate with us, Kevin. My son just graduated at the top of his class at his prep school."

Reluctant as he was to listen to even ten minutes of Storz's bragging, Kevin stepped into the room and took a seat.

Storz, a balding enthusiastic man with dark eyes that never smiled, said, "This is quite a week for this firm, I'd say. Phil's son jumped from second grade to fourth after taking a special test. Irene's daughter wrote a paper on George Gershwin that's going to be published. And now my boy is at the top of his class."

The people Storz had cited were sitting around the conference table, pleased to be congratulated by one of the firm's founders.

No one seemed to understand that inviting Kevin in to hear people bragging on their children was a bit insensitive given what had happened to him and his wife. But then nothing ever seemed to deter the lawyers here from bragging on their kids.

More than winning cases, more than accruing wealth, more than performing as talking heads on the vidd networks, the greatest pleasure for these men and women came from congratulating themselves on how well they'd designed their children at Generations, or what the populist press disdainfully called "The Baby Store." Of course it wasn't just this law firm. Designer children had become status symbols for the upper classes. An attractive, bright child obviously destined to become a prominent citizen was now the most important possession you could boast of.

These parents were unfazed by the media criticism insisting that the wealthy and powerful were creating a master race by genetically engineering their progeny. After all, as Miles had once said, "You design the child yourself. And it's no sure thing. Every once in a while somebody designs a dud."

Kevin was able to leave before the liquor appeared. It would be a long session. Six fathers and mothers bragging on their children took some time.

"May I help you, sir?"

Only up close did the woman show even vague evidence of her actual age. The plastic surgery, probably multiple surgeries in fact, had been masterful. In her emerald-colored, form-fitting dress, with her perfectly fraudulent red hair, she looked both erotic and efficient.

"Just looking, really."

"Some very nice ones. And feel free to read their biographies. Some of them are pretty amazing."

"I don't have much time today. I think I'll just look at the holos."

"Fine." A smile that would have seduced a eunuch. "I'll just let you look. If there's anything you need, just let me know."

He spent equal time with male and female holos. They were all so perfect they began to lose individuality after a time. As Miles had said, people did, of course, design duds. The looks didn't turn out quite right; the intelligence wasn't impressive or even, sometimes, adequate; and then there were personality flaws, sometimes profound. Most of these problems resulted from parents who wouldn't listen to the advice of the scientists and programmers. But their arrogance could be tragic.

Given what had happened, he settled on looking at the girls. These were finished products, used to guide the buyers in creating their own girls. He was particularly taken with a dark-haired girl of sixteen whose fetching face was as imposing as the amused intelligence that played in her blue-eyed gaze. Yes, good looks—and intelligence. Requisites for a leadership role later on.

He doted on the girl, imagining the kind of boasting you could do in a session like the one he'd just left. Even up against the likes of Storz and the others, this girl would undoubtedly triumph. Whoever had designed her obviously had known exactly what they were doing.

But then it was time to catch the bullet train home. He just hoped Jen was free of her depression, at least for a few hours.

He was never sure how to characterize the sounds she made—"crying" was too little, but then "sobbing" was probably too much. He usually settled for "weeping."

She was weeping when he got home that night. He went upstairs immediately to knock softly on the door of the master bedroom. "Is there anything I can do, honey?" he asked, as he'd asked every night since the death of their five-year-old son two months ago.

"Just please leave me alone, Kevin," she said between choked tears. "Just please leave me alone." Even given the loss they'd suffered, could this tragedy alone fuel so many endless days of bitter sobbing sorrow?

Dinner alone. By now he was used to it. An hour or so in front of the vidd with a few drinks. And then bringing her a tray of food. Otherwise she wouldn't eat. He'd come to think of all this reasonably enough as The Ritual.

After eating—she'd lost fifteen pounds from an already thin lovely body—Jen usually went into the bathroom and showered for bed. Afterward was when they talked.

"Somebody at the office told me about a very good doctor. Very good with depression."

"Please, Kevin. No more shrinks. I couldn't take another one."

"I wish you'd take the meds."

"The headaches they give me are worse than the depression."

Sometimes he wondered if she wasn't purposely punishing

herself. Maybe her depression was her way of dealing with what she saw as her negligence in the death of Kevin, Jr.

"You know the doctor said he'd never heard of anybody getting headaches from this particular med."

"That's what I mean about doctors. They say things like that all the time. *They* don't take the drugs. *We* do. We're their guinea pigs. And when we complain about something, they tell us we're just imagining it."

And so on.

The best part of the night was when she lay in his arms in the darkness, responding finally to his patience and kindness, trusting him once more as she had always trusted him in their young marriage. Sometimes they made love; sometimes the day-long siege of depression and tears left her too shattered to do much more than lie next to him.

Tonight he was afraid. He didn't know if he should tell her what he'd done. He certainly didn't want to set her off. But maybe the idea would appeal to her. Maybe she was ready now to talk about the rest of their lives. Maybe a talk like this was exactly what she needed to hear to make her forget—

He'd tell her about his impulsive visit to the Baby Store and—

But then he smiled to himself, for there, her regal blond head on his shoulder, came the soft sweet sounds of her childlike snoring.

In the next few weeks he stopped at the Baby Store three times after work. On the second visit he asked if he could talk with one of the consultants. He kept assuring the doctor that he was only asking questions while he waited for his train. The doctor kept assuring him in turn that he understood that quite well.

On the third visit, his words seeming to come unbidden, Kevin explained how five-year-old Kevin, Jr. had drowned in the small lake that came very near the front porch of their summer cottage and how Jen blamed herself for it. She'd been on the phone when he walked into the water. Kevin had been in the backyard dealing with some particularly aggravating gopher holes.

The doctor, a middle-aged man with kind blue eyes, said, "It's especially traumatic when you lose a child you designed yourself. It's a double loss."

"I guess I hadn't thought of that. You're right. And we spent so much time making sure he'd be just right."

The doctor, whose name was Carmody, spoke gently. "I know why you're coming here, Kevin. And I think you've got the right idea. But what you're worried about is convincing your wife."

Kevin smiled. "You're a mind reader, too."

"Oh, no. It's just that I've been through this process with a number of people over the years. Something unfortunate happens to the child they've designed and they're not sure if they can deal with designing another one."

"That's right. That's exactly right."

"Usually the man is the one who suggests it. The woman is too lost in her grief. And he knows that she won't like the idea at all. Not at first. And her feeling is perfectly natural. You'll both feel guilty about designing another child. Kevin, Jr. is dead and here you are going on with your lives—and replacing him."

"I'm already feeling guilty. But I think that's what we both need. A new child. While we're still in our early thirties. With our lives still ahead of us."

Dr. Carmody nodded. "But it won't be easy. She'll resist. She'll probably even get very angry. And she'll feel even more isolated than she does now. She'll think you don't understand her mourning at all."

"So maybe I shouldn't suggest it?"

"Not at all, Kevin. All I'm saying is that you should prepare yourself for some very heated discussions. Very heated."

"I don't know how you could even *think* about another child now," Jen said at dinner that night. "We loved him so much. It's not like buying a new pair of shoes or something."

"Honey, all I said was that it's something to think about. You're so sad all the time—"

"And you aren't?"

"I guess I don't have *time* to be sad most of the time. I'm always rushing around with work and—" He knew he'd said the wrong insensitive thing. He eased his hand across the candlelit dinner that the caterers had prepared so nicely. He'd wanted the right mood to introduce the subject. He knew that convincing her was somewhere in the future. "Why do you think I don't sleep well? I'm thinking about Kevin, Jr."

By the look in her blue eyes he could see that he'd rescued himself. And what he'd said hadn't been untrue. He couldn't sleep well these nights. And a good deal of the time during those uneasy hours, he thought of his son, his dead son.

"I don't even want to talk about it now," she said. "Or think about it." Her smile surprised him. One of the old Jen smiles, so girlishly erotic. "Tonight I want us to drink all three bottles of wine and just be silly. It's been awhile since we've been silly."

He slid his hand over hers, touching it with great reverence. His one and only love. He missed her. The old her. "Well, if you want silly, Madame, you've come to the right guy. Nobody's sillier than I am."

And they toasted his silliness. In fact, before they managed to stagger into bed and have some of that old-time sex of theirs, they'd toasted a good many things. And every one of them had been silly. Very, very silly.

Then came the day when he got home from work and found Jen's personal holo filled with images of children from the Baby Store. Jen often forgot to turn the holo to FADE when she was done with it. His first inclination was to rush up the stairs to the exercise room and congratulate her for beginning to show interest in designing another child. But then he realized it would be better to let her interest grow at its own pace.

He was disappointed that she didn't mention the holo that

night at dinner. But the fact that she'd come down to dinner at all told him that the old Jen had not been lost to him after all. The old Jen was slowly returning to the shining presence he loved so much.

She didn't mention anything about the holo—or subsequent viewings of the Baby Store holos—for the next eight evening meals. And when she brought it up, the reference was oblique: "Sometimes it's so quiet here during the day. Bad quiet, I mean, not good quiet."

It had rarely been quiet when Kevin, Jr. had been alive.

Dr. Carmody said, "I think a little nudge might be appropriate here, Mr. McKay."

"What kind of nudge, Dr. Carmody?"

"Oh, nothing confrontational. Nothing like that. In fact, something pleasant. I had a patient who was having a difficult time getting her husband to visit us. They'd only recently come into some money and her husband still had some of his old attitudes about designer babies from the days when he'd been not so well off. But she surprised him. Invited him to his favorite restaurant, which just happened to be near here, and after the meal she just happened to steer him in our direction—and four days later, he came in and signed the papers and started creating not one but two children. Twins."

"Well, one of Jen's favorite restaurants is near here, too. We go there for our anniversary every year."

"When's your next anniversary?"

"Two weeks from tomorrow."

Dr. Carmody smiled his Dr. Carmody smile. "That's not very far off, is it?"

She was late getting into the city and for a frantic half hour Kevin was afraid that Jen had known that this would be more than an anniversary dinner. He couldn't contact her on her comm, either. Maybe she'd decided not to meet him. Maybe she was in the bedroom, weeping as she once had. He stood on the street corner lost in the chill April dusk and the shadow crowds racing to the trains and the freeways.

And then, golden and beaming, tossing off an explanation for her tardiness that was both reasonable and reassuring—then she was in his arms and they were walking like new lovers to the restaurant where their reserved table waited for them.

After her second glass of wine, she said, "After dinner, let's go for a walk. I don't get down here very often. And I still love to window-shop."

The center of the city gleamed in the midst of darkness, an entity constantly reinventing itself, taller, faster, more seductive in every respect, the streets patrolled by android security officers. The androids were without mercy.

The store windows Jen stopped at were alive with quickly changing holos of haute couture. He was happy to see her interested in her appearance again. She even talked about making one of her shopping trips.

He made sure that they kept moving in the direction of the Baby Store. As they turned a corner, entering the block the store was on, she said, "I think I've got a surprise coming up."

"A surprise?"

She leaned into him affectionately, tightening her grip on his arm. She laughed. "You've been steering us in a certain direction since we left the restaurant."

"I have?"

"We're going to the Baby Store, as you've always called it."

"We are?"

But of course they were.

A small staff kept the three-story building open during the nighttime hours. As Kevin had arranged, Dr. Carmody had stayed late. He greeted them in the lobby and led them back to his office.

"Happy Anniversary to both of you," he said.

"Thank you, Dr. Carmody. I guess I knew somehow we'd end

up here tonight. Sometimes I can sort of read my husband's mind."

"I hope you're not disappointed, Mrs. McKay."

She shrugged in that sweet young-girl way she had. "No, maybe Kevin's right. Maybe this is what I need."

"We'll certainly do our best," Carmody said.

And so they began.

Coffee cleared their minds and numerous holos of designed girls—that was the only thing Jen knew for sure; a girl this time—sharpened their imaginations. They began to form a picture of the infant Jen would carry. And what this infant would look like at various stages of her life. And what kind of intellectual acumen the child would have. In a world as competitive as this one, superior beauty without superior intelligence was nothing.

Dr. Carmody had left them alone in front of the enormous holo console. They were so infatuated with the prospect of a new child that they became infatuated with each other, friendly kisses giving way to passionate ones; a breast touched, long lovely fingers caught behind Kevin's neck, pulling him closer. "Maybe the wine hasn't worn off after all," Kevin said. And laughed.

But Jen said, "We really should be looking at the screen now."

After forty-five minutes they stopped browsing through holos and began talking seriously about the child they'd come to create. Hair color, eye color, body type, features—classic or more contemporary? What sort of interests it would have. The level of intelligence—some parents went too far. The children had serious emotional problems later on.

Kevin asked Dr. Carmody to join them.

"Did you like any of the holos you saw?"

"They were all very impressive, Doctor," Kevin said. "In fact they were all so good it got kind of confusing after awhile. But I think we've started to have a pretty good idea of what we're looking for."

"Well, we're certainly ready to proceed with the process anytime you are," Dr. Carmody said, his perfectly modulated vidd-caster voice never more persuasive. "We just need to look over our standard agreement and get to work."

"I'm sure that won't be any problem," Kevin said. But as he spoke he noticed that Jen no longer seemed happy. The tension of the past two months had tightened her face and given her eyes a somewhat frantic look.

Dr. Carmody had become aware of her sudden change, too. He glanced at Kevin, inclined his head vaguely toward Jen. He obviously expected Kevin to deal with this situation. It wasn't the doctor's place to do so.

But as Kevin started to put his hand on her arm, she stood up with enough force to make herself unsteady. Kevin tried to slide his arm around her waist to support her but she pulled away from him. She was suddenly, violently crying. "I can't do this. It's not fair to our boy. It's not fair!"

And then before either man could quite respond effectively, Jen rushed to the door, opened it and disappeared.

Kevin started to run after her. Dr. Carmody stopped him. "Just remember. She's been through a lot, Kevin. Don't force her into this until she's really ready. Obviously she's having some difficulty with the process. There's no rush with this."

Kevin, scarcely listening, rushed out the door after his wife. She was much faster than he'd imagined. She wasn't in the hall nor, when he reached the lobby, was she there. He hurried outside.

The sidewalk was crowded with people his own age, of his own status. Drink and drugs lent them the kind of happiness you usually saw only on vidd commercials.

He didn't see Jen at first. Luckily, he glimpsed her turning the far corner. He ran. People made wary room for him. Somebody running in a crowd like this instinctively made them nervous. A running man meant danger.

There was no time for apologies, no time for gently moving

people aside. When he reached the corner, his clothes were disheveled and his face damp with sweat. He couldn't find her. He felt sick, scared. She was in such a damned vulnerable state. He didn't like to think of what going to the Baby Store might have triggered in her.

He quit running, falling against a streetlamp to gather himself. He got the sort of cold, disapproving glances that derelicts invited. While he was getting his breath back, he smelled the nearby river. The cold early spring smell of it. He wasn't sure why but he felt summoned by the stark aroma of it.

In a half-dazed state, he began moving toward the water, the bridge that ran north-south coming into view as soon as he neared the end of the block.

She stood alone, staring down at the black, choppy water. Though he knew it was probably best to leave her alone for awhile, his need to hold her was so overpowering that he found himself walking toward her without quite realizing it until he was close enough to touch the sleeve of her coat.

She didn't acknowledge him in any way, simply continued staring into the water. Downriver the lights from two tugboats could be seen, like the eyes of enormous water creatures moving through the night. In the further distance a foghorn sounded.

He leaned against the railing just the way she did. He remained silent. He smelled her perfume, her hair. God, he loved her.

When she spoke, her voice was faint. "I killed our son."

"Honey, we've been over this and over this. You were on the phone and he didn't stay on the porch like you told him. He went into the lake despite everything we'd warned him about."

She still didn't look at him. "I lied. I ran out the door in time to save him. I could have dived in and brought him back to shore. But I didn't. I *wanted* him to drown, Kevin, because I was ashamed of him. All the women I know—they were always bragging about their sons and daughters. But Kevin, Jr.—we did something wrong when we created him. He just wasn't very smart. He would never have amounted to much. And so I let him drown. I stood there and let him drown while you were in the backyard."

He'd always felt that her grief was more complicated than the death of their son. And now he knew that his guess had been correct. In addition to loss, she was dealing with a kind of guilt he couldn't imagine.

"You just thought I was in the backyard."

For the first time she turned and looked at him, her face in shadow. "But you *were* in the backyard."

"True. But only for a while. I heard him scream, too. I ran around to the side of the house. I was going to save him. That was all I thought about. But then I stopped myself. I started thinking—you know how in just a few seconds you can have so many different thoughts—I started thinking the same things you did. I loved him but we'd created a child who just couldn't compete. Who'd *never* be able to compete."

She clutched his arm. "Are you lying to me, Kevin?"

"No. I'm telling you the truth. And I'm telling you that we're both equally guilty—and that we're not guilty at all. We made a terrible mistake. We didn't listen to our counselor. We designed our son badly. It wasn't his fault and it wasn't ours. I mean, we had the best of intentions."

"But we let him die."

"Yes, we did. And you know what? We did him a favor. We'd already seen how mediocre his schoolwork was. What kind of future would he have had? He wouldn't have had any kind of enjoyable life." He drew her close to him. "But now we have another chance, Jen. And this time we'll listen to our counselor. Dr. Carmody will help us. We'll create the kind of child we can be proud of. And when Storz and everybody at the office start bragging about *their* kids, I'll finally be able to brag about *mine*."

She fell against him. This time joy laced her sobbing. He could almost psychically share the exuberance she felt knowing that he was as much to blame for Kevin, Jr.'s death as she was.

There was such a thing as the saving lie and he was happy to relieve her of at least some of her guilt. And in fact he'd sometimes wondered if he shouldn't have killed the boy himself.

A numbing wind swept up from the river. She shuddered against him.

"We need some coffee," he said. He slid his arm around her shoulders and together they started walking back toward the center of the city.

"We never did decide if we want our daughter to be blonde or brunette," he said.

"Or a redhead," she said. "I've got an aunt with beautiful red hair."

An image of an ethereal red-haired girl came into his mind. One who inspired lust and myth in equal parts. That was the kind of daughter they'd create. He couldn't wait to see the envy on Storz's face when the daughter was fifteen or so. The envy would be something to exult about for weeks.

Comeback

The morning of the birthday bash this dude with hair plugs and a black camel's hair coat and the imperious air only a big-time businessman exudes walks into Guitar City and starts looking around at all the instruments and amps.

A tourist. Most places you see a guy who looks like this you automatically think this is the ideal customer.

But in the business of selling high-end guitars and amps you don't want somebody who looks like he just drove over from the brokerage house in his Mercedes but will only spend a few hundred on his kid.

Some of my best sales have gone to guys who look like street trash. They know music.

I wandered over to him. I assumed he didn't know what he was holding. The Gibson Custom Shop 59 Les Paul cost a few thousand more than I make a month and I do all right.

When he glanced up and saw me, he said, "Hey, you're the guy I saw on the news this morning."

I smiled. "My fifteen minutes finally arrived."

"Well, you're going to the big party and everything. Sounds like you'll have some night. Nice that you all still get along."

John Temple had returned to Chicago on the occasion of his thirtieth birthday. This was at the end of his worldwide tour and his latest CD going double platinum. Some of the friends he'd met while on tour were flying in for the occasion. Names people around the world would recognize. "Too bad you had that falling-out with Temple, you and—what's the other guy's name?"

"McMurtin."

"Right. Temple, McMurtin and you. You're Rafferty, right?"

"Right."

"And you and McMurtin—went off on your own."

He was polite enough not to finish the rest. The well-known tale of how John Temple decided four years ago that it was time that he took his wounded voice out for a test run all by itself. Two double platinum CDs later, Temple was returning home for a press orgy of adulation.

I was working here at Guitar City. Pete McMurtin was one of the ghosts you saw standing on the sidewalk outside rehab houses shakily smoking his cigarette.

Even though he'd brought up an unpleasant subject, he redeemed himself by saying, "My son's graduating from Northwestern. He's very serious about his little band. I was hoping he'd grow out of it by now. But no such luck. He's coming into the firm but he also plans to keep playing on weekends. So I want something really special."

"Well, this is really special."

"Oh? What is it?"

I told him.

"So this is really upscale, huh?"

I smiled at his word. "Very upscale."

"And he'll need an amp. A good one."

"A good one or a great one?"

"What's a great one?"

"Well, you've got a great guitar so I'd go with a great amp—a Marshall. The Jimi Hendrix Reissue. Stack."

He grinned. "This could all very well be bullshit."

I grinned back. I knew he was going to go for it. "It could very well be. But it isn't."

"Well, I guess you know what you're talking about. This is your fifteen minutes, after all." He meant well but it was still painful. "So my son will know what this is and he'll like it?"

"He'll love it. He'll think you're the best old man a kid could have."

A hint of pain in <u>his</u> eyes now. Maybe this present wasn't just for graduation. Maybe this was a guilt present of some kind. "Then let's do it."

On my lunch hour I drove over to the facility where Pete was staying. I'd talked to the woman in charge. Natalie was her name. She had said that Pete was showing some progress with his cocaine problem and that she was afraid of what might happen if he went to the party. I had convinced her that I would take care of him. I reminded her that he listed me as his only friend. After years of living in a coke dream his family had bid him goodbye.

At one time the Victorian house had been fashionable. Easy to imagine Packards pulling up in the driveway and dispatching men in top hats and mink-wrapped women laughing their way to the front door fashionably late for the party.

Now the house was grim gray and the cars were those dying metal beasts that crawl and shake from one traffic light to another.

Natalie Evans answered the door herself. The odors made me wince even before I crossed the threshold. All the friends I've had in places like this—bad food, disinfectant, old clothes, old furniture, old lives despite what the calendar says.

"He's in the parlor. He got up and worked for three hours this morning helping to clean out the garage. I'm really hoping he can keep going this way. That's why I'm nervous about tonight."

Natalie was one of those sturdy women who know how to run just about anything you care to name. Competence in the blue eyes. Compassion in the gentle voice. She was probably just a few years older than me but she was already a real adult, something I'd probably never be.

I'd seen Pete only two weeks ago, but for an unexpected moment there I didn't recognize the fragile but still handsome twenty-six-year-old who sat deep in the stained arms of a busted-up couch. The smile was still there, though. John had the voice, I had the licks on the guitar. But Pete had the classic good looks of old Hollywood. Pete had been a heartbreaker since the three of us started Catholic school together in the first grade. He played a nice rhythm guitar, too.

"Hey," he said. I could see that he was thinking of standing up but decided against it. His three hours of work had apparently exhausted him.

The parlor was a receptacle for stacks of worn-out records, worn-out CDs, worn-out videotapes, worn-out paperbacks, worn-out people. An old color TV played silently; a pair of hefty cats yawned at me; and an open box of Ritz crackers and a cylinder of Cheez Whiz had to be moved before I could sit on the wooden chair facing him. Junkies and junk food.

"I don't know, Michael."

He didn't need to say any more. The apprehension, the weariness in those four words meant that I'd done the right thing by checking in with him before tonight.

"I talked to God, Pete."

He smiled again. We'd been kidding each other since we were six years old. We knew the rhythms and patterns of our words. "Yeah, and what did God have to say?"

"He said he was going to be *muy* pissed if you didn't go."

"God speaks Spanish?"

"He could be an illegal immigrant."

He rolled his head, laughing. "You're so full of shit."

"Look who's talking, *compadre*."

He leaned forward, sunlight haloing his head. He'd been the most mischievous of us. I'd never seen him turn down a dare, no matter how crazy. He wasn't tough but he sure was durable. But not durable enough to stand up to a coke habit that had taken over his life six years ago. Cost him his health, purpose, hope.

And it had cost him Kelly Keegan, the girl that both Pete and John had loved since she'd come to St. Matthew's in sixth grade. John walked away with Kelly and his career. She'd been living with Pete. After that, Pete's habit got even worse.

"You're strong enough, Pete. You look great."

"I look like shit."

"Okay, you look like shit. But you're strong enough."

"I really look like shit?"

I got up out of the chair, walked over to him and swatted him upside the head. He grinned and flipped me off. I went back and sat down. "You jerk-off. Now c'mon. I'm picking you up at seven and we're going to the party."

He lifted his right leg. Pulled an envelope free. Glanced at it. Tossed it to me. "From Kelly. Came yesterday."

It was indeed from Kelly. It read:

Dear Pete,
I made a terrible mistake. I still love you. Please come
to the party. John'll be surrounded by people. We'll be
able to talk.
    Love,
    Kelly

"Wow." I pitched the letter back to him.

"That's what I'm nervous about."

"I thought they were so happy. With the new baby and all."

"So did I. I mean I'm still in love with her. I always will be. But I've been so strung out I just never considered the possibility—" He lifted the letter from his lap and stared at it. "I almost feel sorry for John."

"Screw John. He dumped us. If he'd stayed with us we'd all be rich today."

"You really believe that?"

"You don't?"

"I don't know anymore. Maybe we didn't have what it takes—you know, the way John does."

"You know that's a crock, man." I'd had that same thought

myself, of course. But I wasn't about to admit it. "And he sure didn't worry about you when he walked off with Kelly."

He shook his head. "But she's got to be crazy. Her kid—the whole life they've got—the money and all that. What the hell would we have to say to each other?"

"Well, there's one way to find out."

"I don't know. It just wouldn't be right."

"He didn't care about you or your habit. Not the way he left and all."

He held up a halting hand. "I'm here because I'm an addict. And you're selling guitars because the little group you put together last year didn't work out. He isn't responsible for either of those things."

"No, but remember how he wouldn't meet with us? Had that new agent of his handle everything? I just want to see him face to face."

Knock on one of the parlor doors. The old-fashioned kind that rolled back into the frame. Natalie parted the doors with a deft foot and came in carrying coffee. "I had to make a fresh pot. That's what took me so long."

"She makes great coffee," Pete said.

"Flatterer." She used her foot again, this time to drag the coffee table closer to us. She set the cups on the deeply scratched wood and said, "There you go. If you want more, just let me know."

My cup had a piece missing on the lip. I wasn't worried about glass in my coffee. The chip had been missing a long time and Natalie had no doubt washed the cup dozens of times. But it made me feel like hell for Pete. For both of us, actually, I suppose. Those old days in Catholic school, high school especially. Not the best or the brightest but we did all right with the girls and the future gleamed like a new sunrise just down the road ahead of us. So much hope and so much promise. And now here we were in this busted sad place drinking out of chipped cups.

"So I'm supposed to tell her what when you don't show up?"

"You're going anyway?"

"Hell, yes, Pete. This'll be a big deal for me. And there'll be record people there. Maybe I can make a contact."

His smile was fond. He was smiling at the same memory I'd had a minute ago. The three of us in high school and all those rock and roll dreams. "You never give up, do you?"

"Not dreaming, I don't. Maybe I'll be at Guitar City the rest of my life but that doesn't mean I have to stop thinking about it."

He laid his head back and closed his eyes. "She'll look so beautiful that I won't be able to control myself. I'll probably grab her. She's all I think about. Four years later and it still hurts as much as it did the day she told me she was leaving with John."

"But she's still in love with you."

He didn't say anything for a time. I sipped my coffee. A deep sigh. He said, "I'll go but I'll probably regret it."

Even in good suits, white shirts and conservative ties the two steroid monsters at the front door of the very upscale Regency Hall were clearly bouncers. God help you if your name wasn't on the list. The usual doormen had obviously been replaced by folks more accustomed to the world of rock and roll. And rap.

If either of the killer androids knew who we were they didn't indicate it in any way. They simply consulted their BlackBerry list and waved us on through after we handed over the invitations.

The hall was the preserve of visiting artists, classical musicians, noted scholars. The lobby held a discreet Coming Attractions board. Chamber music was the next attraction. Few of the people in the lobby looked as if they'd be here for that particular event. The trendy hairstyles (female and male), the chic clothes (female and male) and the number of visible tattoos (mostly male) spoke of different musical pleasures. Dreadlocks, male rouge, cocaine eyes. Not your typical chamber music crowd at all.

Pete stood tight against me. He was the child afraid to leave his parent. I could almost feel him wanting to do a little shapeshifting.

"I shouldn't have come here," he said.

And with that the joyous evening began.

John took the stage to a standing O and then went immediately into generic humility. He thanked more people than ten Oscar winners. Nary a mention of Pete or me. No surprise there. He was saving the moment for Kelly. And it was quite a moment. Four years and a kid later she was still the pale Irisher redhead of almost mythic beauty. The emerald cocktail dress only enhanced her slender but comely shape.

John, my generation's Neil Diamond, in theatrical black shirt and tight black jeans, gave her the kiss everybody wanted to give her. I saw Pete look away.

"This is the reason I'm up here. I was going nowhere in terms of my career until my true love Kelly agreed to marry me. And that gave me the strength to break away and go on my own. I really mean it when I say I wouldn't be on this stage tonight without this woman."

I wondered how many people in the audience understood what "break away" meant. Break away from Pete and me. Bastard.

Kelly didn't reach for the stand-up mike so John leaned it toward her. "C'mon, honey, just say a few words." And as he said this, on a huge TV screen suspended from the right corner of the stage, was a sunny photograph of Kelly holding their two-year-old daughter Jen. The kid was almost as much of a beauty as the mother.

Pete tugged at my arm. "Let's get outta here, man. I can't take this."

I whispered so nobody else around us could hear. "I'm tempted to go backstage and lay him out. Just break him up a little."

"Yeah. And then I'd come visit you every weekend in jail—if they'd let me out of the halfway house."

He turned, starting toward the door but I grabbed him. "Just a few more minutes, Pete. We got nothing else to do, anyway."

"I'd rather be back at the house."

Invisible speakers boomed "Happy Birthday" so loud there was no point in trying to talk. Everybody was singing along and then this five-tiered cake was wheeled on stage. John went back into generic humility for the next few minutes as he cut the cake and served Kelly the first slice. This was when the other rock stars appeared, four of them, encased in their arrogance and privileged clowning.

Then dancing and liquor and dope of all kinds broke out. The party was officially on.

Pete managed to leave my side before I could stop him. There was a crowd at the door and he somehow eeled through it. I had to bump between two big important bellies to catch him just as he reached the front door and the androids. I could feel the belly owners glaring at me.

I grabbed him by the shoulder and spun him around. One of the androids had been facing inside. He lurched toward me.

"No problem here," I said.

Pete saw that he was eager to waste me so he said, "Everything's cool. No need for any trouble."

Disappointed, the android stopped, glared at me and then went back to his post.

I half dragged Pete into an empty corner of the lobby. "Where the hell were you going?"

"Where do you think? Watching her up there—"

"It got to me, too, Pete."

"Not in the way it got to me. You hate him and that's different from me being in love with her. You just want to hurt him."

"I want to kill him."

"That's what I mean. That's different. You don't know what

I'm going through." I'd seen him cry before, too many times, trying to kick coke. But these tears were different, not harsh but gentle, sad as only Pete could be sad.

"Aw, man, I'm sorry."

"So could we just leave?"

"Sure. We'll get a pizza."

He smiled as he brushed a tear from his cheek. "All that fancy food inside and we're going to get a pizza?"

"Yeah. Better class of people, anyway."

He saw her before I did. There was a stairway leading to the balcony. She descended it concealed by a group of much larger people. He said "God" and that was when I saw her, too.

And that was the moment when all the corny moments in all the corny movies proved to be not so corny at all. Her recognizing him; him recognizing her. It was really happening that way. Them stunned by the sight of each other. And all else falling away.

If she said goodbye to the important people around her, I wasn't aware of it. She simply left them and floated across the lobby to us. To Pete, I mean. I doubt she was even aware that I was there.

He was the old Pete suddenly. The bad drug years fell from his face, his eyes. And it was all ahead of him, the great golden glowing future. And when she reached out and took his hand, I saw that she wanted to be part of that future. That she knew now how bad a mistake she'd made taking up with John. That despite her marriage, somehow she and Pete would be together again.

She tugged him away from the corner. She still hadn't said hello to me or even let on that she knew I was there. I didn't care. I was caught up in their movie dream, happy for both of them. And happiest of all that the retribution I'd wanted to visit on John was now far more crushing than a few punches could make it. He was losing his wife. They were gone.

For the next twenty minutes I drank wine and listened to

conversations between people who were—or claimed to be—in the music industry. The anger was coming back. I wanted to hear my name instead of John's. I wanted those chart sales to be mine. I wanted the tour they were discussing to focus on me. John should be working at Guitar City. Not me.

But at least Pete was getting something out of this night. All the way back to grade school he'd been the one she'd loved. And now maybe it was finally going to happen for them.

"Are you Mr. Rafferty?" She was an officious-looking blonde in the red blazer that Regency Hall employees wore.

"Yes, I am."

"John would like to see you in his dressing room."

"John Temple?"

"Why, yes." She gave me an odd look, as if maybe I was stoned and not hearing properly. Was there any other John who mattered here tonight?

"What's he want to see me about?"

She'd been trying to decide if she found me tolerable or not. She'd just made her decision. Not trying to hide her irritation, she said, "I'm just doing what he asked me, Mr. Rafferty. I'm not privy to his thoughts."

"Aw, God. I'm sorry. I'm just a little surprised is all."

"Well, there are a lot of people here tonight who'd be happy to visit with him in his dressing room. Consider yourself lucky."

She didn't have anything more to say to me until we reached backstage and the row of three doors off the left wing of the stage. She knocked gently on the center door and said, "Mr. Temple?"

"Yes."

"Mr. Rafferty is here."

"Great. The door's unlocked."

She stood back for me. I wondered if she could tell how angry I was at hearing his voice. Four years of rage, of betrayal. I wanted to rip the knob off and flatten the door on my way inside where I'd grab him and begin beating him to death.

But he was quicker than I was. He stood in the open door, all black-clad rock star, smiling camera-big and camera-bright. He'd learned that smirking with your mouth made you enemies. Now he tucked his smirks into his dark eyes. He took a step forward and I thought he was actually going to give me a Hollywood man-hug but he obviously sensed that that might not be such a good idea so he settled for waving me in. The small room held a large closet, a make-up table with the mirror encircled by small bright bulbs and several vases stuffed with red congratulatory roses.

"Close the door, would you?" he said.

"You want it closed, you close it."

He walked over to the dressing table and hoisted a bottle of Jack Daniels Black. "I'm sure you'd rather have this than all that sissy-boy wine they're serving. You get some Jack, I get the door closed. That's how the world works, Rafferty."

I kicked it shut with my heel.

"Nice to know you've grown up," he said, not looking at me, pouring each of us healthy drinks.

"What the hell you want to see me about?"

The eye smirked as the hand offered me my drink. "We didn't leave on the best of terms. Maybe I feel guilty about things."

"Oh, man. Spare me this crap, all right? You dumped us because you knew we were going to get a contract and then you'd have to share the spotlight with us. You wanted it all your own."

The sharpness of his laugh surprised me. The contempt was bullet-true. "God, Rafferty, do you really believe that? Please tell me that's not what you really think."

But before I could say anything he went on.

"I stayed a year longer than I should have. I stayed because we went all the way back to grade school. I stayed because we were friends. But Pete's habit got worse and worse and you—" He paused.

"And me? What about me?"

I noticed that the smirk was gone. The gaze was uncomfortable. "You're not the greatest guitarist I've ever worked with."

"I was good enough to write songs with." But the whine in my voice sickened me as much as it probably pleased him.

"You'll notice I've never recorded any of those songs. Never played them on stage. Never tried to sell them."

"So you called me in here to tell me what a genius you are and what losers Pete and I are?"

"I called you in here to have a drink and to say that I'm sorry for how things were left. It's natural for you to think of me as a bad guy. But I had the right to do what I did. A lot of people leave groups and go out on their own. I didn't commit any mortal sins."

"Maybe not. But you helped destroy Pete."

"Pete was already destroyed. It was just that neither of you would admit it then. I've kept track of him. In and out of rehab. Every time the stays get longer. Every time there's a little bit less of the Pete we grew up with."

The words came out. I didn't say them. In fact I was as shocked as John had to be. "Well, right now there's enough left of him to be off alone somewhere with your wife."

There was a flash of deep pain in the eyes. "I'm well aware of that, Michael. One of my people has been keeping an eye on her for me. Kelly and Pete are in a small office off the balcony. I'm trying not to think about what's going on."

Again he spoke before I could.

"I could stop them. But she needs to get it out of her system. She thinks she's still in love with him. Her one true love. I have everything I've always wanted now but I'll never have her the way Pete had her. Maybe when she sees him tonight, sees that he's not who he once was—" He shrugged. "But that's kidding myself. She loves the idea of Pete. She knew he was a junkie and that's why she went off with me. But she can't get rid of this idea of him." He tapped his forehead. "She won't see him as he really is. He'll be the old Pete to her."

I wanted to think that this was just a performance. That way I could enjoy it as simple bad acting. But I knew better. As much as I hated him I knew that he was telling the truth.

"That make you happy, Michael?"

"Yeah. It does. The one thing you can't have. That makes me very happy."

And then the smirk was back snake-quick in the eyes. "You like it at Guitar City, do you? I'm told that you're their best salesman."

"Screw yourself."

"You didn't answer my question, Michael. Are you happy at Guitar City?"

The girls don't come as easy as I thought they would. You see all these reality shows where girls will do anything to sleep with rockers. But I do all right. A lot better than I was doing before John added me to his band. The money's pretty good, too. I own a '57 Vette and when I take it back to the old neighborhoods you'd think the Irishers were having St. Patrick's Day.

The touring was cool for the first year but now it gets to be a drag sometimes. John's letting me play on the next CD. He says that'll keep us in LA for at least six months. Cool by me.

Kelly has pretty much willed me out of existence. Even when I'm forced to stand close to her she won't acknowledge me in any way. Everybody in the band notices, obviously. I think they feel sorry for me.

She only came after me once. This was after a gig in Seattle. She'd had a few drinks and right in front of John she slapped me and said, "I know where he got the coke, Michael. You gave it to him. More than enough to kill him. And I know who put you up to it." She was staring right at John when she said it.

The word is she's staying with him because of the kid. And that may be true. But maybe she's like the rest of us. You know, the whole rock and roll thing. She's the belle of the ball, "The Nicole Kidman of Rock" as *People* called her recently. And maybe that's how he keeps her. She wouldn't be as hot if she divorced him. More number-one double platinum CDs. Not even her beauty can match that.

The last time I went back to Chicago I stopped by the halfway house where Pete had last stayed. The woman Natalie? I gave her a check for $2,500 to help with the bills for the house. I thought she'd be real happy about it but she handed it back and walked away.

Late at night I feel bad about it sometimes. But as John always says, maybe we did him a favor. I mean it wasn't like he was ever going to have a comeback or anything.

A Little Something to Believe In

by Ed Gorman and Larry Segriff

Molly disappeared sometime in the cold, gray months of winter, and Cal just assumed that one of her johns had killed her. That happened a lot to the boys and girls who peddled their runaway asses along the Square.

Of course, Cal wasn't simply a runaway. He was a changeling. He had "remembered" a year before, and by instinct had come to this vast, angry Midwestern city where even the white mayor was a junkie (an election coming up, the cokehead mayor was asking the citizens for "forgiveness and understanding").

Molly had found him—hers was the power to affect other changelings, and to recognize them. A week after he'd hit town, he'd been walking the streets late one night and had passed this beautiful young woman. Her eyes had widened slightly as he passed, and when he glanced back at her he saw her wave her hands in a familiar pattern and whisper something under her breath. A moment later, a wave of desire washed over him.

She came up to him, then, and smiled. "I'm Molly," she said.

She took him to the warehouse where the rest of the changelings crashed—well, it was a warehouse to mortal eyes; to the changelings, it was a tiny castle, but their Glamour didn't change the fact that they had to battle rats the size of small dogs for each piece of scratchy, woolen blanket, and that each of their gourmet meals came from the kitchens of the nearby McDonalds. Even though he was two years older than Molly, she took his virginity. She made it sweet, too, and tender, up on the warehouse roof one warm night when the bright wheeling stars smiled down approvingly.

He liked it so much, he couldn't leave her alone. Even without her Glamour, he wanted to make love day in, day out, every time he saw her.

He hated the fact that she hooked for a living. But he didn't hate it so much that he refused to eat the Big Macs her hooking bought them. She'd tried other jobs, but they always asked questions about her age and stuff, questions that would lead to cops, and cops would lead right back to the Chicago adoptive parents she'd run away from.

She kept up a great, glad front of liking herself and her situation—who could complain about anything after escaping that stifling home of hers—but in her bitten fingernails, and odd twitches, and frequent, inexplicable crying jags, he saw and sensed a misery and fear that no enchantment could cure.

Then he told her he loved her and she said, "Aw, shit, Cal."

"What's wrong?"

"You went and spoiled it."

"I did?"

"Yeah, you did."

They were naked and lying in each other's arms, but then all of a sudden she was sitting up Indian-style, so she could explain things to him.

"We shouldn't be doing shit like that."

"Shit like what?"

"Like falling in love."

"How come?"

She was so much more sophisticated than he was—she'd been here in the city since she was seven; he was still a hayseed through and through—and so she explained patiently.

"We're changelings, right?" she said.

"Right."

"Which means we have only one goal, right?"

"What goal?"

"What goal!" she laughed. "You really are a dweeb sometimes, Cal, you know that?"

She reached out, placed her hands along his face, and drew him closer to her, her eyes locked with his. She didn't speak, she made no gestures, but still she wove a powerful illusion, calling up in his mind's eye the wonders of Arcadia.

She showed him the Dreaming, the collective unconscious of the entire human race that gave birth to every dream, every miracle, and every wonder the world had ever known. She showed him the glory of the *fae*, from the noble houses of the *sidhe* to the mischievous *pooka* to the learned *sluagh*. And she showed him the dark side, the Endless Night that had resulted when humanity turned away from the Dreaming and sundered the realms.

She showed him his home, and when she allowed the vision to fade he found that he was shaking.

"That's the goal," she said, "a gateway back to the Dreaming. That's the only thing that matters, and love just gets in the way."

"It does?"

"Sure it does. You get all caught up in it and you start to forget about the Dreaming." She looked at him and shook her head. "You look so sad."

"I am sad."

"That's just what I'm saying."

"It is?"

"*Sure* it is. When you're in love, you're either so happy or sad, or a little bit of both, that you don't care about anything else." She pointed a finger at him. "Tell me, why'd you come here to the city?"

"To find some answers, I guess. Once I remembered, I knew what I had to do, but I had no idea how to go about doing it."

"So you came here and you found us and then what?"

"Then I started really thinking about the Dreaming. You know, like I actually could get back to it."

"All right, then, when's the last time you thought about the Dreaming?"

He felt himself blush. "I see what you mean."

"You haven't been thinking about it, you've been thinking about me, haven't you?"

He barely whispered, "Yeah, I see what you mean."

So, the rest of their time together he wasn't allowed to tell her he loved her or to express any anger or jealousy over the fact that she went with other boys and men to make money.

And then one night, when she came in especially late, one night when he especially wanted to tell her he loved her, him feeling so lonely and all with his nowhere job as a truck unloader at the local Pepsi plant—this one night she said, "God, Cal, I heard the weirdest thing tonight."

"Yeah? What?"

"That there's this rich guy who lives in the city and everybody thinks he's this stocks-and-bonds guy, but he's actually one of us."

"A changeling?"

"Yeah, but you know how he makes his money?"

"How?"

"He sells the secret to changelings."

"What secret?"

"What secret? God, Cal, *think* about it."

"You mean how to get to the Dreaming?"

"That's it. That's what he sells."

"Man, that's incredible."

"I've been saving."

"You have?"

"Yeah. And I got me five hundred dollars. That's what he charges."

"You gonna see him?"

"Yeah. Tonight. After I see this one john. He told me he'd give me two-fifty if I did this one thing that I really hate. But I figure it's worth it."

"He wanna get rough?"

"Yeah. But not *real* rough. I mean, he won't *kill* me or anything."

"You sure?"

"Pretty sure. Anyway, there's no other way I can earn that extra two hundred fifty."

"You know what, Molly?"

"What?"

"Sometimes I think you're more naïve than I am. Somebody selling secrets to the gateway? No way, Molly. No way."

"That's because you have no faith."

"No faith?"

"You know how bad it is out there, Cal? What I let all those guys do to me? How sick I get when they touch me sometimes? And you know the only thing that keeps me going? It's knowing that I'll reach the Dreaming someday. And now, here's a guy who's going to show me how to do that."

That was his last conversation with Molly. She went out that night and . . .

Either her john killed her or she found the rich man who was willing to sell her the secret to the gateway.

□

In her vanishing, he was hobbled with grief.

He could not eat, sleep, think clearly, or remain civil. He got into fights at work; he got into fights with other changelings at the warehouse. Nothing magical; he avoided Glamour completely, turning his back on his fae side, and instead got into purely mortal, and very bloody, fistfights.

There was talk at the warehouse about forcing him to leave. On occasion there was a changeling who didn't fit in there, and maybe, the others said, Cal was one of them.

John, the eldest of the changelings, approached him one day and said, "They want you to pack and leave."

"I know."

"You know and you still act the way you do?"

"I'm sorry."

"Yesterday you pushed Michael into the wall."

"I know."

"And hit Stephen in the face."

"I apologized to him for that."

"We're supposed to be a brotherhood and a sisterhood here."

All Cal could do was hang his head.

"I have to find her," he said. "If she's still alive."

"You never told me what happened."

And that was true. Cal had spoken to nobody about his last conversation with Molly.

When he told John about the rich man selling the secret to the gateway, John whooped with laughter.

"Oh, shit! She didn't really believe that, did she? Five hundred dollars?"

"You know how she was."

"Poor Molly."

"You ever heard of this before?"

"No. But it sounds like a pretty good scam. A lot of us are pretty naïve people. We believe what we want to believe." He shook his head. "The secret to the gateway. What a crock."

"I don't know what to do," Cal said.

"You want to know what I'd do?"

"What?"

"I'd find him."

"The guy with the secret?"

"Yeah. I'd find him and I'd make him tell me where Molly is."

"How do I find him?"

"Just start walking the Square. Listening. If Molly heard about this, then somebody else did, too. Nobody here at the warehouse, apparently, but a lot of us live all over the city. Start asking questions."

Spring rains.

Six gray days, six black nights of them.

He didn't go to work, he didn't worry about meals, he didn't sleep more than a few hours a night.

He asked questions.

He asked so many questions that at first a lot of people on the Square wondered if he hadn't maybe become an undercover cop.

He asked so many questions that, finally, a lot of people on the Square thought he was some kind of drug casualty . . . one of those sad creeps whose brain got burned up on crack or something.

He asked questions but he got no answers.

He was so down, he couldn't crawl out from beneath his blanket for days on end.

The others, the same ones he'd punched and insulted, brought him food and understanding words, and he accepted them with great shame, remembering the way he'd treated these people.

And then one night one of the girls knelt down next to Cal's place on the floor, scooted away a rat, and said, "There's a guy on the Square tonight. He told two different girls about this guy with the secret to the gateway."

She gave Cal the guy's description and twenty-one minutes later, Cal was right in the guy's face.

"You want somethin', pal?"

Slick, he was, this guy, with an expensive suit and an expensive haircut and an expensive tan.

"I want to know about the guy with the secret."

The way the guy blinked, Cal knew he'd nailed him.

"What secret?"

"To the gateway."

"I don't know what gateway you're talkin' about, pal."

"You're lying."

"Hey, I don't dig bein' called a liar, pal. You understand?"

Cal knew there was no way he could coerce the guy into telling him anything. The guy was too big, too dangerous. A hood of the modern, more polished variety, and Cal had no power over humans.

At a safe distance, Cal followed the guy around the Square the rest of the night.

The guy seemed to be looking for a very special type of girl. He had no interest in boys.

In two hours, the hood spoke to three girls.

Only one of them appeared interested.

The hood took out a small notebook, clicked his ballpoint into action, and wrote her name down.

By midnight, the Square was its usual clamorous self, the night alive with rock music and country western music and reggae music; the air scented with greasy hamburgers and pizzas and tacos; the darkness lit by neon and headlights and the blood-red of police emergency lights as the gendarmes busted kids for hooking and peddling dope and suspicion of various crimes committed off the Square.

The hood moved through all this, gazing, assessing. Predatory.

He found one more girl, the hood did, and wrote her name down.

Ed Gorman

Then he went back to his car in the parking lot, which was just what Cal hoped he would do.

Right after the hood unlocked the driver's door, Cal created an illusion of a young punk who threw a rock against the hood's windshield and then ran off down an alley.

The hood cried out a curse, ripped his piece from his shoulder harness, and gave chase to the phantom rock thrower.

Perfect.

The hood was big and lumbering.

By the time he was halfway down the street, Cal had crawled into the back of the hood's car and hid himself on the shadowy floor. Then he let his illusion slip away, becoming once again stray bits of dust and shadow.

Cal had no idea where the hood was going.

Freeway lights; dark streets. Stops; starts. Heavy traffic; no traffic. Brick surface; asphalt surface; concrete surface.

A driveway.

The hood cutting the engine and the lights.

Chunking the heavy Oldsmobile door shut.

Walking away; heavy footsteps.

After a time, Cal sat up.

Filling the windshield was a vast Second Empire Victorian house complete with cupola silhouetted against the full golden moon and a patterned roof just like the original Victorians back in London.

In there.

Cal sensed that Molly was in there.

He eased himself out of the car and ran down the driveway to the side of the house.

Had to be careful. *Very* careful.

But he couldn't resist sneaking up to the bay window and peeking inside.

Careful . . .

The sweet May grass was wet with dew the moon had turned into beads of liquid gold.

Cal stood on tiptoes and peered inside.

And couldn't believe what he saw.

There was Molly and she had this weird black thing, like a spidery insect, crouched on her head and she . . .

"You little changeling prick," the hood said behind Cal. "You really thought you were puttin' somethin' over on me, didn't you?"

With that, the hood escorted Cal inside.

Mr. Fenady, that was his name, wore a red velvet smoking jacket and drank brandy from an imposingly large snifter. He was silver of hair and friendly of gaze and he spoke in the fashion of an erudite but unpretentious professor.

There was a fire in the fieldstone fireplace, the shadows cast by it flickering across the books that filled the walls of this huge mansion.

The shadows also played across Mr. Fenady's face as he paced back and forth in front of the deep leather chair where Cal sat.

"You sell dreams?" Cal said, after listening to Mr. Fenady speak for twenty minutes.

"Not dreams, Cal. Hope. Hope that dreams are worth having." He nodded to the tall double doors that led to the rest of the mansion. "There are a dozen young changelings out there right now and they've never been happier in their lives."

He walked over to the desk and sat on the edge of it. "Don't forget, Cal, I'm a changeling, too. I know the whole process. How you feel like a freak once you realize what you are. How you have to run away from home to find other changelings. And then how you begin to feel despair that you'll ever reach the Dreaming. You even begin to doubt that there is any such thing as the Dreaming."

He drank from his snifter.

"So I decided to give a few changelings some real hope . . .

the ones who were just naïve enough and desperate enough to believe me. I pretended that I had this secret to the gateway . . . and you know what? As soon as I told them that I had the secret . . . their whole lives changed. They became optimistic and productive and quit doing things that were bad for them— they had hope."

"But you don't *have* the secret," Cal said.

"Not in the sense you mean, no. But I have the secret of hope, Cal. And that's to believe in something. All those changelings who work for me—all I've told them is that I have the secret and that someday the faerie realm will call all those with the secret back home . . . and when it does . . . all of us in this mansion will be ready."

He smiled.

"And now they're helping other people find hope, too."

"How?"

"A nine hundred number. Even people who aren't changelings dial it, and for two dollars ninety-eight cents a minute they hear stories of the Dreaming . . . and it makes their lives tolerable. Think of it, Cal . . . men and women who work all day for almost nothing . . . men and women who are sick with disease . . . men and women who are lonely . . . who are addicts of some kind . . . who live in the midst of unimaginable violence . . . now they can call this nine hundred number and one of our changelings tells them about the Dreaming . . . and how wonderful it is. And then the callers have hope, too. They believe that someday they'll have a better life . . . that we're all just waiting here to be called home. That's what organized religion used to do, Cal. But who can believe in organized religion these days, after all those scandals? But the Dreaming is perfect in their minds . . . a heavenly home that is uncorrupted by lust or greed or ambition. You see?"

The spidery black thing sitting atop Molly's head . . . a telephone operator's headset.

"So why do you charge them?" Cal asked.

"Charge who?"

"The changelings. Molly said you charged five hundred dollars for the secret. If you don't have the secret, why do you charge them?"

Fenady smiled. "It's a form of therapy, Cal."

"Therapy?"

"Exactly. Making them pay for something makes that something valuable to them. It's the first step toward giving them hope."

Hope. It was then that Cal thought he understood. Either Fenady was mortal and, as John had said back at the warehouse, nothing more than a scam artist, or he was a changeling as he claimed. If so, then Cal suspected he was up to much more than making money.

If Mr. Fenady was a changeling, then Cal suspected he was doing exactly what he said he was doing: building people's hopes.

Hope was the basis of dreams, and so it was the basis of the Dreaming. More, it was the very foundation of changelings' lives and their magic. He who controlled hope controlled power.

Listening to his smooth words, Cal was certain that Mr. Fenady controlled an awful lot of power.

And none of that mattered. The only thing that mattered was Molly.

"Is she happy?" Cal said.

"Happier than she's ever been in her life."

"And healthy?"

"She runs five miles a day."

"Is she lonely?"

"She has a special friend now, Cal. A satyr named Bob."

Cal thought of how unhappy Molly had always been—despite her protestations to the contrary—nothing like the girl Fenady was describing.

"Could I see her?"

"If you really want to," Fenady said. "I mean, if you think it's really in *her* best interest."

"Meaning you don't think it is?"

Fenady set down his brandy snifter and said, "Sometimes the best thing we can do for people we really love is to leave their life." He smiled sadly. "If it's real love, I mean. Unselfish love."

"Could I just look at her, then?"

"I think I could arrange that."

In five minutes, Cal and Fenady stood in another room, one with a one-way mirror. "The previous owner had this installed for reasons I don't like to think about. But it does afford us a look at our phone operations."

Twenty cubicles on the floor below, each busily staffed by a smiling operator.

When he saw her, Cal was startled by how radiant she looked. Her hair was longer, and her teeth a brilliant white, and in her smile was all the happiness in the world. On the desk of her cubicle was a framed photograph of a handsome young man Cal knew was her "special friend" Bob.

He felt emptier and more isolated and more frightened than he'd ever felt in his life.

"I don't suppose you'd consider . . . taking me, would you, Mr. Fenady?"

Mr. Fenady put a fatherly hand on Cal's shoulder and said, "Don't think I wouldn't want to, Cal. But you don't have it in you to be a believer . . . or to feel the kind of hope we do here. You're a fine young man, Cal, but an awfully cynical one, I'm afraid."

He patted Cal on the shoulder again. "I'm sorry, Cal."

Cal nodded, and took his last look at Molly, and left.

When he got back to the Square, everything was dark. Only the winos and the worst of the perverts could be found skulking in the gloom. The streets and grass were littered with beer cans and wine bottles and fast food wrappers.

He stood in the same spot where Molly first approached him that day so long ago.

He thought of how she'd looked that day, so much energy and enthusiasm, and yet the sorrow had been there, too . . . the sorrow that Fenady and his "secret" passage to the gateway had banished.

Just before dawn, he laid his body down on the same warehouse blanket where he'd made love to Molly so many times, and let the tears come hot and free.

Oh, Molly, he thought, and the thought was not unlike a prayer.

Oh, Molly.

Flying Solo

"You smoking again?"

"Yeah." Ralph's sly smile. "You afraid these'll give me cancer?"

"You mind rolling down the window then?"

"I bought a pack today. It felt good. I've been wanting a cigarette for twenty-six years. That's how long ago I gave them up. I was still walking a beat back then. I figure what the hell, you know. I mean the way things are. I been debating this a long time. I don't know why I picked today to start again. I just did." He rolled the window down. The soft summer night came in like a sweet angel of mercy. "I've smoked four of them but this is the only one I've really enjoyed."

"Why this one?"

"Because I got to see your face."

"The Catholic thing?"

"That's right, kid. The Catholic thing. They've got you so tight inside you need an enema. No cheating on the wife, no cheating on the taxes, no cheating on the church. And somebody bends the rules a little, your panties get all bunched up."

"You're pretty eloquent for an ex-cop. That enema remark. And also, by the way, whenever you call me 'kid' people look at you funny. I mean I'm sixty-six and you're sixty-eight."

Ralph always portrayed himself as a swashbuckler; the day he left the force he did so with seventeen citizen complaints on his record. He took a long, deep drag on his Winston. "We're upping the ante tonight, Tom. That's why I'm a little prickish. I know you hate being called 'kid.' It's just nerves."

I was surprised he admitted something like that. He enjoyed playing fearless.

"That waitress didn't have it coming, Ralph."

"How many times you gonna bring that up? And for the record, I did ask for a cheeseburger if you'll remember and I did leave her a frigging ten-dollar tip after I apologized to her twice. See how uptight you are?"

"She probably makes six bucks an hour and has a kid at home."

"You're just a little bit nervous the way I am. That's why you're runnin' your mouth so hard."

He was probably right. "So we're really going to do it, huh?"

"Yeah, Tom, we're really going to do it."

"What time is it?"

I checked my Timex, the one I got when I retired from teaching high school for thirty years. English and creative writing. The other gift I got was not being assaulted by any of my students. A couple of my friends on the staff had been beaten, one of them still limping years after. "Nine minutes later than when you asked me last time."

"By rights I should go back of that tree over there and take a piss. In fact I think I will."

"That's just when he'll pull in."

"The hell with it. I wouldn't be any good with a full bladder."

"You won't be any good if he sees us."

"He'll be so drunk he won't notice." The grin made him thirty. "You worry too much."

The moon told its usual lies. Made this ugly two-story flat-roofed cube of a house if not beautiful at least tolerable to the quick and forgiving eye. The steep sagging stairs running at a forty-five degree angle up the side of the place was all that interested me. That and the isolation here on the edge of town. A farmhouse at one time, a tumbledown barn behind it, the farmland back to seed, no one here except our couple living in the upstairs. Ken and Callie Neely. Ken being the one we were after.

We were parked behind a stretch of oaks. Easy to watch him pull in and start up those stairs. I kept the radio low. Springsteen.

When Ralph got back in I handed him my pocket-sized hand sanitizer.

"You shoulda been a den mother."

"You take a piss, you wash your hands."

"Yes, Mom."

And then we heard him. He drove his sleek red Chevy pickup truck so fast he sounded as if he was going to shoot right on by. I wondered what the night birds silver-limned in the broken moonlight of the trees made of the country-western song bellering from the truck. A breeze swooped in the open windows of my Volvo and brought the scents of long-dead summers. *An image of a seventeen-year-old girl pulling her T-shirt over her head and the immortal perfection of her pink-tipped beasts.*

"You know what this is going to make us, don't you? I mean after we've done it."

"Yeah, I do, Tom. It's gonna make us happy. That's what it's gonna make us. Now let's go get him."

I met Ralph Francis McKenna in the chemo room of Oncology Partners. His was prostate, mine was colon. They gave him a year, me eighteen months, no guarantees either of us would make it. We had one other thing in common. We were both widowers. Our kids lived way across the country and could visit only occasionally. Natural enough we'd become friends. Of a kind, anyway.

We always arranged to have our chemo on the same day,

same time. After the chemo was over we both had to take monthly IVs of other less powerful drugs.

Ralph said he'd had the same reaction when he'd first walked into the huge room where thirty-eight patients sat in comfortable recliners getting various kinds of IV drips. So many people smiling and laughing. Another thing being how friendly everybody was to everybody else. People in thousand-dollar coats and jackets talking to threadbare folks in cheap discount clothes. Black people yukking it up with white people. And swift efficient nurses Ralph Francis McKenna, a skilled flirt, knew how to draw in.

Once in awhile somebody would have a reaction to the chemo. One woman must have set some kind of record for puking. She was so sick the three nurses hovering over her didn't even have time to get her to one of the johns. All they could do was keep shoving clean pans under her chin.

During our third session Ralph said, "So how do you like flying solo?"

"What's 'flying solo'?"

"You know. Being alone. Without a wife."

"I hate it. My wife knew how to enjoy life. She really loved it. I get depressed a lot. I should've gone first. She appreciated being alive."

"I still talk to my wife, you know that? I walk around the house and talk to her like we're just having a conversation."

"I do pretty much the same thing. One night I dreamed I was talking to her on the phone and when I woke up I was sitting on the side of the bed with the receiver in my hand."

Flying solo. I liked that phrase.

You could read, use one of their DVD players or listen to music on headsets. Or visit with friends and relatives who came to pass the time. Or in Ralph's case, flirt.

The nurses liked him. His good looks and cop self-confidence put them at ease. I'm sure a couple of the single ones in their forties would probably have considered going to bed with him if he'd been capable of it. He joked to me once, shame shining in his eyes: "They took my pecker, Tom, and they won't give it back." Not that a few of the older nurses didn't like me. There was Nora who reminded me of my wife in her younger years. A few times I started to ask her out but then got too scared. The last woman I'd asked out on a first date had been my wife forty-three years ago.

The DVD players were small and you could set them up on a wheeled table right in front of your recliner while you were getting the juice. One day I brought season two of *The Rockford Files* with James Garner. When I got about two minutes into the episode I heard Ralph sort of snicker.

"What's so funny?"

"You. I should've figured you for a Garner type of guy."

"What's wrong with Garner?"

"He's a wuss. Sort of femmy."

"James Garner is sort of femmy?"

"Yeah. He's always whining and bitching. You know, like a woman. I'm more of a Clint Eastwood fan myself."

"I should've figured on that."

"You don't like Eastwood?"

"Maybe I would if he knew how to act."

"He's all man."

"He's all something all right."

"You never hear him whine."

"That's because he doesn't know how. It's too complicated for him."

"'Make my day.'"

"Kiss my ass."

Ralph laughed so hard several of the nurses down the line looked at us and smiled. Then they tried to explain us to their patients.

A nurse named Heather Moore was the first one. She always called us her "Trouble Boys" because we kidded her so much about her somewhat earnest, naïve worldview. Over a couple of months, we learned that her ex-husband had wiped out their tiny bank account and run off with the secretary at the muffler shop where he'd been manager. She always said, "All my girlfriends say I should be a whole lot madder at him but you know when I'm honest with myself I probably wasn't that good of a wife. You know? His mom always fixed these big suppers for the family. And she's a very pretty woman. But by the time I put in eight hours here and pick up Bobby at daycare, I just don't have much energy. We ate a lot of frozen stuff. And I put on about ten pounds extra. I guess you can't blame him for looking around."

Couple times after she started sharing her stories with us, Ralph made some phone calls. He talked to three people who'd known her husband. A chaser who'd started running around on Heather soon after their wedding day. A slacker at work and a husband who betrayed his wife in maybe the worst way of all—making constant jokes about her to his coworkers. And she blamed herself for not being good enough for him.

Then came the day when she told us about the duplex where she lived. The toilets wouldn't flush properly, the garbage disposal didn't work, both front and back concrete steps were dangerously shattered and the back door wouldn't lock. Some of her neighbors had been robbed recently.

The landlord was a jerk—lawyer, of course—named David Muldoon. Despite the comic book surname he was anything but comic. Ralph checked him out. A neo-yuppie who owned several income properties in the city, he was apparently working his way up the slumlord ladder. Heather complained to the city and the city did what it did best, nothing. She'd called Muldoon's business office several times and been promised that her complaints would soon be taken care of. They weren't. And even baby lawyers fresh from the diploma mills wanted more than she could afford to take Muldoon on.

We always asked her how it was going with Muldoon. The

day she told us that the roof was leaking and nobody from his office had returned her call in four days, Ralph told her, "You don't worry about it anymore, Heather."

"How come?"

"I just have a feeling."

Heather wasn't the only one wondering what the hell he was talking about. So was I. He said, "You got the usual big night planned?"

"If you mean frozen dinner, some TV, maybe calling one of my kids who'll be too busy to talk very long and then going to bed, yes."

"Maybe watch a little James Garner."

"Yeah or put on Clint Eastwood and fall asleep early."

"Glad you don't have plans because we're going on a stakeout."

"I go to bed at nine."

"Not tonight. Unless we get lucky. Maybe he'll get laid and get home before then."

"Who?"

"Muldoon, that's who."

"You know for a fact that he's got something going on the side?"

"No. But I always listen to my gut."

I smiled.

"I say something funny?" Sort of pissed the way he said it.

"Do all you guys watch bad cop shows before you graduate? Your 'gut'?"

"Most of these assholes cheat."

I thought about it. "Maybe you're right."

"Kid, I'm always right." Grin this time.

Turned out it was the secretary in the law firm on the floor below Muldoon's. Not even all that attractive. He was just out for strange in the nighttime.

We waited leaning against his new black Cadillac.

"Who the fuck are you two supposed to be?"

"We're supposed to be the two guys you least want to hear from." I was happy to let Ralph do the talking.

"Yeah?" All swagger.

"Yeah. You're taking advantage of a friend of ours."

"Get the fuck out of my way. I'm going home."

"It's a bitch getting rid of that pussy smell on your clothes, isn't it? Wives like to pretend they can't smell it."

Dug out his cell phone. Waggled it for us. "I don't know who you two assholes are but I'll bet the police won't have any trouble finding out."

"And your wife won't have any trouble finding out about the snatch in that apartment house behind us, either."

I didn't realize what had happened until I saw the counselor bend in half and heard him try to swear while his lungs were collapsing. He fell to his knees. Ralph hit him so hard on the side of the head Muldoon toppled over. "Her name's Heather Moore. She's one of your tenants. She doesn't know anything about this so don't bother trying to shake her down for any information. You've got two days to fix everything wrong in her apartment. Two days or I call your wife. And if you come after us or send anybody after us then I not only call your wife I start looking for any other bimbos you've been with in the past. I'm a retired homicide detective so I know how to do this shit. You got me?"

Muldoon still couldn't talk. Just kept rolling back and forth on the sandy concrete. He grunted something.

That was how it started. Heather asked us about it once but we said we didn't know anything about it. Heather obviously didn't believe us because two weeks later a nurse named Sally Coates, one neither of us knew very well, came and sat down on a chair next to the IV stand and told us about her husband and this used-car salesman who'd sold them a lemon and wouldn't make it right. They were out seven grand they hadn't been able to afford in the first place but they had to have a car so her husband could get to the VA hospital where he was learning to walk again after losing his right leg in Afghanistan. The kind of story you watch on TV and want to start killing people.

All innocence Ralph said, "Gosh, Sally, I wish we could help you but I don't see what we could do. There isn't any reason he'd listen to us."

"I can't believe it," Sally said the next time we saw her. "Bob got a call the day after I told you about this salesman. The guy said to bring the car in and they'd get it fixed up right so we wouldn't be having any trouble with it. And there wouldn't be any charge."

"I'll bet you did a lot of praying about it, didn't you, Sally?"

"Of course. We have two little ones to feed. Keeping that car running was breaking us."

"Well, it was the prayers that did it, Sally."

"And you didn't have anything to do with it?"

"Ask him."

I shook my head. "What could we have done, Sally? We're just two old guys."

After she left, Ralph leaned over from his leather recliner and said, "The only good thing about dying this way is we don't have to give a shit about anything. What're they gonna do to us?" That grin of his. "We're already dead."

I developed a uniform. A Cubs cap, dark aviator glasses and a Louisville Slugger. According to Ralph I was "the backup hood. They're scared enough of me. Then they see this guy with the ball bat and the shades—they'll do anything to cooperate." He didn't mention how old we were.

The nurses kept coming. Four in the next three months. A nurse who was trying to get a collection of family photographs back from an ex-boyfriend she'd broken up with after he'd given her the clap, spurned boyfriend stealing the collection and keeping it for her breaking up with him; the nurse whose daughter's boyfriend was afraid to visit because two bully brothers down the block always picked on him when he pulled up; and the nurse who liked to sit in on poker games with five guys who worked at an electronics discount house and thought it was pretty damned funny to cheat her out of forty to sixty dollars every time she sat down. It took her four months of playing twice a month to figure it out.

No heavy lifting, as they say; no, that came with a tiny, delicate young nurse named Callie. We noticed the bruises on her arms first then the bruises on her throat despite the scarf she wore with her uniform. Then came the two broken fingers and the way she limped for a couple of weeks and finally the faint but unmistakable black eye. A few of the other nurses whispered about it among themselves. One of them told us that the head nurse had asked Callie about it. Callie had smiled and said that "my whole family is clumsy."

It was during this time that both Ralph and I realized that we probably wouldn't be beating the prognoses we'd been given. With me it was a small but certain track of new cancer suddenly appearing on my right thigh; with Ralph it was the return of heart problems he'd had off and on for two decades.

We didn't talk about it much to each other. There isn't much to say when you get to this point. You just hope for as much decent time as you can get and if you've been helping people here and there you go right on helping them as long as you can.

We followed Callie home one night, found out that she lived in a tumbledown farmhouse as isolated as a lighthouse. The next night we followed her home and when she stopped off at a shopping center we waited for her by her car.

She smiled. "My two favorite patients. I guess you don't get to see me enough in chemo, huh?" The cat green eyes were suspicious despite her greeting. She'd developed another one of those mysterious limps.

"That's right. Tom here wants to ask you to marry him."

"Well," the smile never wavering, "maybe I should talk that over with my husband first. You think?"

"That's what we want to talk to you about, Callie," I said. "Your husband."

The smile went and so did she. Or at least she tried. I stood in front of the car door. Ralph took her arm and walked her about four feet away.

He said something to her I couldn't hear, but her I heard clearly: "My personal life is none of your damn business! And I'm going to tell my husband about this."

"He going to beat us up the way he beats you up?"

"Who said he beats me up?"

"I was a cop, remember? I've seen dozens of cases like yours. They run to a pattern."

"Well, then you weren't a very *good* cop because my husband has never laid a hand on me."

"Three restraining orders in five years; six 911 calls; the same ER doctor who said he's dealt with you twice for concussions; and a woman's shelter that told me you came there twice for three-night stays."

The city roared with life—traffic, stray rap music, shouts, laughter, squealing tires—but right here a little death was being died as she was forced to confront not just us but herself. The small package she'd been carrying slipped from her hands to the concrete and she slumped against her car. She seemed to rip the sobs from herself in tiny increments, like somebody in the early stages of a seizure.

"I've tried to get away. Five or six times. One night I took the kids and got all the way to St. Joe. Missouri, I mean. We stayed in a motel there for two weeks. Took every dime I had. The kids didn't mind. They're as scared of him as I am. But he found us. He never told me how. And you know what he did? He was waiting for us when we got back from going to a movie the kids wanted to see. He was in our room. I opened the door and there he was. He looked down at Luke—he's eight now; he was only four then—and he said, 'You take care of your little sister, Luke. You two go sit in my truck now.' 'You better not hurt her, Dad.'

Can you imagine that; a four-year-old talking like that? A four-year-old? Anyway then he looked at me and said, 'Get in here, whore.' He waited until I closed the door behind me and then he hit me so hard in the face he broke my nose. And my glasses. He forced the kids to ride back with him. That way he knew I'd come back, too."

This was in the food court of the mall where we'd convinced her to come and have some coffee with us. You could reach up and grab a handful of grease from the air. I'm told in Texas they deep-fry quarter sticks of butter. If it ever comes up here this mall will sell it for sure.

"But you always come back."

"I love him, Ralph. I can't explain it. It's like a sickness."

"It's not 'like' a sickness, Callie. It *is* a sickness."

"Maybe if I knew I could get away and he'd never find me. To him those restraining orders are a joke." Then: "I have to admit there're sometimes—more and more these days I guess—when I think maybe it'd be best if he'd just get killed driving that damned truck of his. You know, an accident where he's the only one killed. I wouldn't want to do that to anybody else." Then: "Isn't that awful?"

"It is if you love him."

"I say that, Tom. I *always* say that. But the woman at the shelter had me see a counselor and the counselor explained to me what she called the 'dynamics' of how I really feel about him. We had to take two semesters of psych to get our nursing degrees so I'd always considered myself pretty smart on the subject. But she led me into thinking a lot of things that had never occurred to me before. And so even though I say that, I'm not sure I mean it." Then, shy: "Sorry for all the carrying on in the parking lot. I attracted quite a crowd."

"I collected admission from every one of them."

She sat back in her curved red plastic chair and smiled. "You guys; you're really my friends. I was so depressed all day. Even with the kids there I just didn't want to drag myself home tonight. I know I was being selfish to even think such a thing. But I just couldn't take being hit or kicked anymore. I knew he'd be mad that I stopped at the mall. Straight home or I'd better have a damned good excuse. Or I'll be sorry. It's no way to live."

"No," I said, "it sure isn't."

"Now let's go get him."

Callie had mentioned she was taking the kids for a long weekend stay at a theme park which was why we'd decided on tonight.

Neely didn't hear us coming. We walked through patches of shadow then moonlight, shadow then moonlight while he tried to get out of his truck. I say tried because he was so drunk he almost came out headfirst and would have if he hadn't grabbed the edge of the truck door in time. Then he sat turned around on the edge of the seat and puked straight down. He went three times and he made me almost as sick as he was. Then of course being as drunk as he was he stepped down with his cowboy boots into the puddle of puke he'd made. He kept wiping the back of his right hand across his mouth. He started sloshing through the puke then stopped and went back to the truck. He opened the door and grabbed something. In the moonlight I could see it was a pint of whiskey. He gunned a long drink then took six steps and puked it all right back up. He stepped into this puke as well and headed more or less in the direction of the stairs that would take him to his apartment. All of this was setting things up perfectly. Nobody was going to question the fact that Neely had been so drunk it was no surprise that he'd fallen off those stairs and died.

We moved fast. I took the position behind him with my ball cap, shades and ball bat and Ralph got in front of him with his Glock.

Neely must've been toting a 2.8 level of alcohol because he didn't seem to be aware of Ralph until he ran straight into him. And straight into the Glock. Even then all he could say was, "Huh? I jush wan' sleep."

"Good evening, Mr. Neely. You shouldn't drink so much. You need to be alert when you're beating the shit out of women half your size. You never know when they're going to hit back, do you?"

"Hey, dude, ish tha' a gun?"

"Sure looks like it, doesn't it?"

He reeled back on the heels of his cowboy boots. I poked the bat into his back. I was careful. When he went down the stairs it had to look accidental. We couldn't bruise him or use any more force than it took to give him a slight shove. If he didn't die the first time down he would the second time we shoved him.

"Hey."

"You need some sleep, Neely."

"—need no fuckin' sleep. 'n don't try'n make me. Hey, an' you got a fuckin' gun."

"What if I told you that I've got a pizza in the car?"

"Pizza?"

"Yeah. Pizza."

"How come pizza?"

"So we can sit down in your apartment and talk things over."

"Huh?"

"How—does—pizza—sound?"

Ralph was enunciating because Neely was about two minutes away from unconsciousness. We had to get him up those stairs without leaving any marks on him.

"Pizza, Neely. Sausage and beef and pepperoni."

I allowed myself the pleasure of taking in the summer night. The first time I'd ever made love to Karen had been on a night like this near a boat dock. Summer of our senior year in college. We went back to that spot many times over the years. Not long before she died we went there, too. I almost believed in ghosts; I thought I saw our younger selves out on the night river in one of those old rented aluminum canoes, our lives all ahead of us, so young and exuberant and naïve. I wanted to get in one of those old canoes and take my wife down river so she could die in my arms and maybe I'd be lucky and die in hers as well. But it hadn't worked out that way. All too soon I'd been flying solo.

Neely started puking again. This time it was a lot more dramatic because after he finished he fell facedown in it.

"This fucking asshole. When he's done you take one arm and I'll take the other one."

"I thought we weren't going to touch him."

"That's why you shoved those latex gloves in your back pocket same as I did. You gotta plan for contingencies. That's why cops carry guns they can plant on perps. Otherwise we'll be here all night. Clint Eastwood would know about that."

"Yes, planting guns on people. Another admirable Eastwood quality."

"Right. I forgot. Tender ears. You don't want to hear about real life. You just want to bitch and moan like Garner. Now let's pick up this vile piece of shit and get it over with."

He'd worked up a pretty good sweat with all his puking. It was a hot and humid night. His body was soggy like something that would soon mildew. Once I pulled him out of his puke I held my breath.

"We don't want to drag him. They'll look at his boots. Stand him upright and we'll sort of escort him to the steps."

"I just hope he doesn't start puking again."

"I saw a black perp puke like this once. I wish I had it on tape."

"Yeah, be fun for the grandkids to watch at Christmastime."

"I like that, Tom. Smart-ass remarks in the course of committing murder one. Shows you're getting a lot tougher."

We took our time. He didn't puke again but from the tangy odor I think he did piss his pants.

When we were close to the bottom step, he broke. I guess both of us had assumed he was unconscious and therefore wouldn't be any problem. But he broke and he got a three or four second lead while we just stood there and watched him scramble up those stairs like a wild animal that had just escaped its cage. He was five steps ahead of us before Ralph started after him. I pounded up the steps right behind him. Ralph was shouting. I'm sure he had to restrain himself from just shooting Neely and getting it over with.

Neely was conscious enough to run but not conscious enough to think clearly because when he got to the top of the stairs he stopped and dug a set of keys from his pocket. As he leaned in to try and find the lock his head jerked up suddenly and he stared at us as if he was seeing us for the very first time. Confusion turned to terror in his eyes and he started backing away from us. "Hey, who the hell're you?"

"Who do you think we are, Neely?"

"I don' like thish."

"Yeah, well we don't like it, either."

"He got a ball bat." He nodded in my direction. He weaved wide as he did so, so wide I thought he was going to tip over sideways. Then his hand searched the right pocket of his Levi's. It looked like he'd trapped an angry ferret in there.

Ralph materialized Neely's nine-inch switchblade. "This what you're looking for?"

"Hey," Neely said. And when he went to grab for it he started falling to the floor. Ralph grabbed him in time. Stood him straight up.

But Neely wasn't done yet. And he was able to move faster than I would have given him credit for. Ralph glanced back at me, nodded for me to come forward. And in that second Neely made his sloppy, drunken move. He grabbed the switchblade from Ralph's hand and immediately went into a crouch.

He would have been more impressive if he hadn't swayed side to side so often. And if he hadn't tried to sound tough. "Who'sh gotta knife now, huh?"

"You gonna cut us up are you, Neely?"

All the time advancing on Neely, backing him up. "C'mon, Neely. Cut me. Right here." Ralph held his arm out. "Right there, Neely. You can't miss it."

Neely swaying, half-stumbling backward as Ralph moved closer, closer. "You're pretty pathetic, you know that Neely? You beat up your wife all the time and even when you've got the knife you're still scared of me. You're not much of a man but then you know that, don't you? You look in the mirror every morning and you see yourself for what you really are, don't you?"

I doubt Neely understood what Ralph was saying to him. This was complex stuff to comprehend when you were as wasted as Neely was. All he seemed to understand was that Ralph meant to do him harm. And if Ralph didn't do it there was always the guy in the ball cap and the shades. You know, with the bat.

Neely stumbled backward, his arms circling in a desperate attempt to keep himself upright. He hit the two-by-four that was the upper part of the porch enclosure just at the lower part of his back and he went right over, the two-by-four splintering as he did so. He didn't scream. My guess is he was still confused about what was happening. By the time he hit the ground I was standing next to Ralph, looking down into the shadows beneath us.

There was silence. Ralph got his flashlight going and we got our first look at him. If he wasn't dead he was pretty good at faking it. He didn't land in any of those positions we associate with people who died crashing from great heights. He was flat on his back with his arms flung wide. His right leg was twisted inward a few inches but nothing dramatic. The eyes were open and looked straight up. No expression of horror, something else we've picked up from books and movies. And as we watched the blood started pooling from the back of his head.

"Let's go make sure," Ralph said.

It was like somebody had turned on the soundtrack. In the moments it had taken Neely to fall all other sound had disappeared. But now the night was back and turned up high. Night birds, dogs, horses and cows bedded down for the evening, distant trucks and trains all turned so high I wanted to clap my hands to my ears.

"You all right, Tom?"

"Why wouldn't I be all right?"

"See. I knew you weren't all right."

"But you're all right I suppose. I mean we just killed a guy."

"You want me to get all touchy-feely and say I regretted it?"

"Fuck yourself."

"He was a piece of shit and one of these nights he was gonna kill a friend of ours. Maybe he wouldn't even have done it on purpose. He'd just be beating on her some night and he'd do it by accident. But one way or another he'd kill her. And we'd have to admit to ourselves that we could've stopped it."

I walked away from the edge of the porch and started down the stairs.

"You doin' better now?" Ralph called.

"Yeah; yeah, I guess I am."

"Clint Eastwood, I tell ya. Clint Eastwood every time."

Turned out Neely wasn't dead after all. We had to stand there for quite awhile watching him bleed to death.

I was visiting my oldest son in Phoenix (way too hot for me) when I learned Ralph had died. I'd logged on to the hometown paper website and there was his name at the top of the obituaries. The photo must have been taken when he was in his early twenties. I barely recognized him. Heart attack. He'd been dead for a day before a neighbor of his got suspicious and asked the apartment house manager to open Ralph's door. I thought of what he'd said about flying solo that time.

Ralph had experienced the ultimate in flying solo, death. I hoped that whatever he thought was on the other side came true for him. I still hadn't figured out what I hoped would be there. If anything would be there at all.

The doc told me they'd be putting me back on chemo again. The lab reports were getting bad fast. The nurses in chemo commiserated with me as if Ralph had been a family member. There'd been a number of things I hadn't liked about him and he hadn't liked about me. Those things never got resolved and maybe they didn't need to. Maybe flying solo was all we needed for a bond. One thing for sure. The chemo room hours seemed a lot longer with him gone. I even got sentimental once and put a Clint Eastwood DVD in the machine, film called *Tightrope*. Surprised myself by liking it more than not liking it.

I was sitting in my recliner one day when one of the newer nurses sat down and started talking in a very low voice. "There's this guy we each gave five hundred dollars to. You know, a down payment. He said he was setting up this group trip to the Grand Canyon. You know, through this group therapy thing I go to. Then we found out that he scams a lot of people this way. Groups, I mean. We called the Better Business Bureau and the police. But I guess he covers his tracks pretty well. Actually takes some of the groups on the trips. Five hundred is a lot of money if you're a single mother."

The chemo was taking its toll. But I figured I owed it to Ralph to help her out. And besides, I wanted to see how I did on my own.

So here I am tonight. I've followed him from his small house to his round of singles bars and finally to the apartment complex where the woman lives. The one he picked up in the last bar. He's got to come out sometime.

I've got the Louisville Slugger laid across my lap and the Cubs cap cinched in place. I won't put the shades on till I see him. No sense straining my eyes. Not at my age.

I miss Ralph. About now he'd be working himself up doing his best Clint Eastwood and trying to dazzle me with all his bad cop stories.

I'm pretty sure I can handle this but even if it works out all right, it's still flying solo. And let me tell you, flying solo can get to be pretty damned lonely.

Aftermath

1

Not even the other cops much liked Frazier. He was too angry, too bitter to spend much time with. And he enjoyed the dirty aspects of the job too much. Hurting people. Shaking down shopkeepers and pushers and the richer variety of junkies. Getting freebies from the hookers and then beating them up afterwards and daring their pimps to do anything about it. In Vietnam, it had been called fragging, a grunt shooting his superior officer in the back and blaming it on the Cong. There'd been more than one boozy cop-bar conversation about good old Frazier getting fragged some night.

Josh Coburn managed to get the split pea soup off Lisa's face but not her white shirt. Oh well, what ten-month-old didn't walk around with part of her latest meal on her blouse?

"All right, honey," he said, down on one knee, steadying the home video camera so he could capture her walking toward him. "C'mon to Daddy."

Josh was babysitting his daughter tonight while Elise went shopping for their Christmas gifts. She'd laughed and said that Josh was more of a baby than Lisa about wanting to know what she was going to get them.

The living room of the Tudor-styled home sparkled with

decorations. This year's tree was so tall they'd had to cut off the top to fit the angel on. Blue, red, yellow and green lights played off the glass doors of the fireplace, and imbued everything in the room with an air of festivity.

"Daddy! Daddy!" Lisa giggled as she toddled toward Josh.

The camera was last year's Christmas gift. Elise had said that it was guaranteed idiot-proof, meaning that even a mechanical dunce like Josh could operate it.

And then he was on his feet, shooting straight down on her as she danced around in something resembling a circle, waving her tiny hand at Harold the Cat as he strode into the living room. "Hi Harral!" she shouted.

And then she was running toward Josh, arms spread wide. He swung her around and around. Daddy's girl. And neither of them would have it any other way.

He'd done this before.

It was an odd thought to have at this moment when her fists were smashing his face and her knee was trying to find his groin.

But she couldn't help but notice that for all the violence of his sudden assault, he was careful not to tear her clothes or bruise her. He was thinking of afterward. He did not want to mark up his victims.

And almost ludicrously—he was already wearing a condom. He'd probably put it on before he'd come to work. Ready. Knowing he was bound to run into somebody he could lure away as he'd lured her.

And then he was inside her. And she was sobbing. But she was no longer hitting him or trying to knee him. She was spent now. She just wanted it over with. She knew he wouldn't kill her. If that had been his intention, he wouldn't have been so careful not to mark her up.

He finished quickly and that gave her a strange surge of pleasure. He probably thought of himself as a swaggering macho man. And he couldn't even last two minutes.

Lisa wasn't old enough to say prayers. So there in her in pink crib, he said them for her. He prayed for Mommy and Daddy and

Grandma and Grandpa and Harold the Cat and Princess her doll. Then he thanked God on her behalf for all the good things they had in their lives, and said a prayer for those who weren't so fortunate and asked that they be similarly blessed.

He gave her a kiss, checked her diapers a final time, and then turned out the light and left the room.

Downstairs, he fixed himself a light scotch and water and sat in the TV room watching the last of an NBA game. He kept the sound down so he could hear Lisa if she called out. He routinely checked her every fifteen minutes. He would have checked her every five but Elise had finally broken him of that neurotic habit.

Not until ten o'clock did he begin to worry. The malls were open an extra hour this last week leading up to Christmas. Maybe she'd stayed till ten. But if she had, why not call him? There were plenty of public phones around and she had a cell phone besides.

He thought of looking over the storyboards one more time. Early tomorrow morning they'd be pitching the Chuck Wagon fast food account. As the TV producer on the potential account, he'd be responsible for approximately a fourth of the whole dog-and-pony show. But, no. He'd looked them over three times earlier tonight. They were fine. He was proud of them. They were classic hard-sell ads and that's just what the account—which had lost 16 percent market share in the past two years—badly needed. Their present agency relied too much on whimsy. Chuck Wagon needed a whole new approach.

At eleven o'clock, he was in Lisa's room, changing her. She'd developed a diaper rash and so he was powdering her when he heard Elise come in. He called downstairs to her but there was no answer. He wondered why not.

When he finished with Lisa, he rolled her on her back, kissed her forehead, and then went downstairs.

Elise was not in the kitchen. Or the living room. Or the bathroom. Or the den. Or the TV room.

And then he heard the faint noise from the basement. Elise was one of those women who liked instant contact when you came home. She always wanted a hug and kiss from you; and always returned the favor as soon as she got home. So why the basement? And why hadn't she responded when he'd called out to her from Lisa's room?

He opened the basement door. "Elise?"

No answer.

They had yet to finish the basement. It was a huge concrete bunker that housed furnace and washer and drier and assorted boxes with stuff they'd probably never use again.

He smelled gasoline. Smoke.

He rushed down the stairs so fast, he started to slide. He grabbed the slender wooden railing.

Elise stood, completely naked, in the center of the basement floor. Before her, in a pile, were the clothes she'd worn tonight. She'd set them on fire with the help of a small can of gasoline she'd apparently brought in from the garage.

She spoke only once. "I want you to go upstairs and not ask me any questions. Do you understand?"

The sensible, sensitive gaze of his good wife was gone, replaced by the kind of despair and frenzy one saw in the eyes of people who had just suffered some vast trauma.

"Elise. Please tell me what happened."

She shrieked at him. In the eight years of their marriage, the perfect suburban couple, she'd never once shrieked at him before. "Get out of here and leave me alone, you son-of-a-bitch!"

She'd never called him a name before, either. There was nothing to say. Do.

He went doggedly up the stairs, like a man dragging himself to his own execution. What the hell was going on with her, anyway?

Four showers.

Twenty, thirty minutes apart.

Four different showers. What was she trying to scrub off her?

He lay in bed in the darkness, listening to the guest room shower down the hall. She didn't even want use their own shower. It was as if he'd alienated her in some irrevocable way. Every half-hour, he'd check on Lisa. He wanted to ask her what was going on with mommy.

He finally fell asleep near dawn.

Earl Frazier had made a bad mistake. It was one thing to rape hookers, as he sometimes did. It was another to rape women who lived in rich subdivisions.

She was beautiful in a slender, almost ethereal way. But it hadn't been about sex. . . . She was the kind of woman who'd snubbed him all his life. Who'd made him feel stupid and cheap and unmanly. She was so sleek and polished and perfect. He wanted to ruin that perfection for life. Feel his dirty hands ripping away her purity, her beauty, her money, her privilege.

But she would have access to power. And she could destroy him. Why in God's name hadn't he been able to stop himself? After his shift, he hung up his uniform neatly and lay in the shadows of his bedroom, sipping whiskey and smoking Pall Malls and praying—actually praying that God spare him this time. That he would never do it again. Whores, yes, because nobody cared about them. But not women of so-called virtue. That was just too damned risky.

Elise was in a white terrycloth robe and slippers when he came down for breakfast. The smells were good. Bacon, eggs, toast. This was much more than the usual mid-week breakfast.

One look at her and he knew not to ask any questions. He felt awkward, bursting with doubts and dreads and curiosity, but unable to give them voice.

He was just finishing up when she sat down across from him in the breakfast nook.

"Isn't your big presentation this morning?"

He nodded.

"I'm sorry. You probably didn't get much sleep and it's my fault." She started to put her hand out, to touch his, but then pulled it back abruptly. As if she'd suddenly recognized that touching him might contaminate her in some way.

He couldn't help himself any longer. "What the hell's going on, Elise?"

She said it simply. No dramatics. "I was raped last night."

"Raped? My God. Did you go to the police?"

She shook her head. "I couldn't."

"Why not?"

"It was a cop who raped me."

The Chuck Wagon presentation went pretty well. The two women in charge of the account from the client side laughed in all the right places and expressed enthusiastic interest in the coupon program the agency had come up with. The competition was killing Chuck Wagon with aggressive coupon programs.

Josh did well, too. It was one of those moments when a person stands aside and lets his doppelganger take over. Yes, it looks like me and sounds like me. But actually the real me is off somewhere else.

In this case, Josh was mentally stalking the cop who'd raped his wife. Josh did not embrace the adolescent beer-commercial machismo of so many advertising men. But he had a bad temper. And he also owned a .38 Special he'd bought at a gun show a few years ago. It was kept in the bedroom nightstand in case of prowlers.

All the way home on the freeway, he kept glowering at cop cars, wondering if this could be the one carrying Elise's rapist. Several times, he wished he had the family gun.

Elise left a note on the kitchen table.

TOOK TWO SLEEPING PILLS.
LISA NEXT DOOR. SHE'LL NEED
DINNER. LOVE, ELISE.

After retrieving Lisa from the neighbor's, Josh fed her dinner and then spread out some of her toys on the floor of the TV room. He tried to concentrate on the Seven O'Clock News but it was impossible. All he could think about was Elise being raped. He didn't kid himself. He knew that her pain and degradation were his main concern. Some women never psychologically recovered from being raped. But he also knew that his own ego was involved here. He felt that he'd failed her, hadn't sufficiently protected her, must now defend her after the fact.

He got Lisa to bed around nine. Around ten, Elise came down in a Northwestern sweatshirt—Northwestern being their mutual alma mater—and went into the kitchen and put on a pot of coffee.

They sat in the breakfast nook. All she'd had time to tell him this morning was that a cop had raped her. He'd had to hurry into the city and his pitch to the Chuck Wagon folks.

He said, "Tell me."

She said, "He pulled me over for speeding. I was out in the boonies. That new mall? I'd taken a wrong turn and was trying to get back to civilization. I was on some country road."

"He was a city cop?"

She nodded, sipping at her coffee. "He pulled me over for speeding. Told me to come back to his squad car and get in. I figured he was just going to give me a speech about my driving. Instead, he drove up the road to a grove of trees and then told me to get out of the car. He took me behind the trees and raped me." She looked tired but certain of herself. "That's all I'm going to say."

"Why didn't you report it?"

"God, Josh, are you forgetting Sandy Lewin?"

Sandy Lewin was a classmate of theirs. In their senior year, she'd been raped by a very trendy broker who'd earlier interviewed her for a job. By the time his lawyers got done with her, the impression had been left with the public at large that Sandy Lewin was a very sleazy young lady. Sandy was not only Elise's best friend, she was also one of the most respectable people Elise had ever known. But not anymore. Not to anybody who'd watched the rapist's lawyers destroy her on the Seven O'Clock News every night. Sandy had finally left town, relocated to LA. The broker went free.

"You have to report it, Elise."

"It's too late anyway. All those showers I took last night. I've destroyed the kind of evidence they'd need."

"You don't know that for sure."

She sighed. "I'm not going to the police, Josh. I couldn't handle what Sandy went through." She stared at her coffee. "I wasn't exactly an angel in college, you know."

He'd met her when she was still trying to get over the senior who'd dumped her. She hadn't dealt well with her heartbreak. Drank, smoked, slept around. Had something of a reputation there for a while. The kind of thing defense lawyers get down on their knees every night and pray for.

"I don't want Lisa to ever have to hear about me that way. And if there was a trial, she'd eventually hear about it. About me. And this isn't exactly the kind of news Dad needs either."

Right now, her seventy-eight year old father's cancer was in remission. But news like that certainly couldn't be good for him.

He reached across the table and took her hand. She pulled it away as if he'd electrocuted her. "I love you so much, Elise. But to just let this thing go—"

"Now it'd just be my word against his."

They stared out at the night. It was just warm enough tonight for the raccoons to put in an appearance. He loved sitting here in the nook with the lights off, watching the raccoons play on the white snow in the blue moonlight. He liked it especially when the baby raccoons came along.

He said, "Do you remember what he looked like?"

"Sure."

"Do you remember any identifying marks?"

"No. But I remember the number of the squad car he was driving. Number 93."

"That's great."

"It is? For what? We're not going to do anything about it. So what's so great about remembering it?" She looked sad and weary. "I'll just have to work through this myself. Just please don't ask me any more questions about it."

The next two nights, Josh went looking for car 93. He had an approximate sense of which precinct the car was from, and what part of the city it would be cruising.

He didn't spot it.

He came home late, exhausted, Elise asleep in the guestroom. She still didn't want to be in the same bed with him.

On his lunch hour, he walked to a nearby Barnes and Noble and found a book on the aftermath of rape.

Elise was following the general pattern the book outlined. Rage, shame, depression, anger, an inability to make any kind of physical connection even with her husband, even if that connection was as unchallenging as a hug.

There was one other terrifying piece in the book. One he'd already thought of because he'd heard it somewhere before. Some men, after their wives had been raped, blamed the women themselves. And no longer wanted to be intimate with them. The same way some men responded to their wives' having a mastectomy. Rationally, none of this made sense. The women were the victims, not the men who loved them. But then given the male ego, he could see how some men might see the rape as some kind of abstract challenge to their own masculinity. He prayed to God that his male vanity never got that far out of control.

He was thinking of all this when, a few nights later, he spotted city police car number 93. The place was a strip mall. The police vehicle was parked in front of a shoe repair shop with a large front window. The car was empty. The cop was inside at the cash register.

Josh had pictured a hulking man. This one was tall but sinewy and slim. He was losing his hair. The way he was laughing with the shoe repairman, he looked like one of the many Officer Friendlys they had on TV to talk to kids. He was even just a tad nerdy.

When he came out and got in his car, Josh realized that he might be looking at the wrong man. Maybe the rapist was in another car tonight. Or it was his day off. Or he'd called in sick. He just couldn't imagine that this was the man. He picked up his cell phone and hit the proper speed-dial button.

"I know you don't want to talk about it, honey," he said. "I just want you to describe him for me."

"I thought we had an agreement."

"We do. I just want you to describe him."

"I thought you were at the office."

"I am."

"No, you're not. And you haven't been at the office the others nights either, have you?"

"Just please describe him?"

"Why?"

"I'm—working on something."

"Working on something? Just leave it alone, Josh! Leave it alone!"

"Just tell me if he's tall and slim and balding."

"Yes but—"

"I'll talk to you later."

He followed number 93 for nearly twenty minutes. He stayed a couple of cars back, the way detectives always do on TV. The .38 was in the glove department.

He didn't have any sort of plan. He'd just wanted to actually see the man. He'd told himself that that would be enough for him. But it hadn't been enough. Now he just wanted to follow him around. Hopefully, that would be enough.

But number 93 burst away from him suddenly, siren screaming. Probably a traffic accident somewhere. Or a tavern shooting. This was the kind of neighborhood for it, long, shabby, dying blocks.

At home, Elise accosted him as soon as he came through the kitchen door. "Where is it?"

"Where is what?"

"You know what I'm talking about. That gun you bought a year ago."

"Oh."

"God, Josh, that's all you've got to say is 'Oh?' Now where is it?"

"In my pocket."

"I want it. Now." She put her hand out, palm up. He put the gun in it. She slipped it into the pocket of her jeans. "If I can handle this whole thing, so can you."

Lisa started crying upstairs. Elise hurried to find out what was troubling her little girl.

After dinner, he thought of a good excuse to leave the house. He was low on computer supplies for his home machine. Office One was at a mall twenty miles away.

"You couldn't wait till Saturday?"

"I'm just going to the mall."

"I don't believe you."

"You've got the gun. What're you worried about?"

"You. That's what I'm worried about. Doing something crazy." She slid her arms around him. Pulled him close. "I know you love me, sweetheart. But it doesn't help me if I have to worry about you as well as deal with this thing myself."

"So he just gets away?"

"Sandy Lewin's rapist got away, too. And she got destroyed in the process."

"He'll do it again, you know. Rape somebody else. Maybe even kill them sometime."

"We have a life that I love. I'll learn to live with this. It'll take some time and some patience but if we really love each other we can put it behind us. I want another baby, Josh. And I thought you did, too."

"You know I do. It's just the idea of him getting away—"

He kissed her more passionately than he had since she was raped. She surprised him by responding. No mad surge of passion. But her lips parted and she moved her hips gently against his. The mention of babies had brought back his favorite mental photo of her. There in the delivery room. Being shown Lisa for the first time. Thinking about it, he teared up.

"I love you so much," he said.

Office One was crowded for a weeknight. He bought more than $400 worth of supplies. He knew he should have gone straight home. Instead, he headed for the cross-town. And for the precinct where car 93 prowled the streets at night.

He found the squad car parked in front of a video store close to the strip mall where the cop had been the other night. He sat in the car looking into the store. He wished he would've found the cop in the XXX section. Instead he found him in the comedy section.

He was very conscious of the clock. He knew that if he was gone long, Elise would be suspicious. What was he doing here anyway? What good did it do to just follow the bastard around?

He put the car in gear and drove out of the video store lot. He was seven blocks away when the emergency light bloomed blood red in his rearview mirror.

2

He pulled over to the curb. Waited for the cop to appear. A few cars went past, surveying the scene. Wondering what he'd done.

No swagger. Unassuming walk. Flipped open his ticket book as he approached.

Josh had his window rolled down. The night smelled of distant rain and cold. It was in the low forties.

"Evening, sir."

"Evening."

"May I see your license?"

"Sure."

Showed him his license.

"The information here correct?"

"Yes; yes, it is." It was a good thing she'd taken the gun from him. He wanted to kill this man right here.

"Was I speeding, officer?"

"No."

"Taillight out or something?"

"One thing about a silver gray Saab. Brand new one."

"Oh? What's that?"

"There aren't very many of them."

"No, I don't suppose there are."

The cop handed him his license back. "Why're you following me, Mr. Madison?"

"Following you? You were behind me."

"The other night it was the shoe repair shop. Tonight it's the video store. And then you just follow me around in general sometimes. What's going on?"

"Gosh, I wish I knew what you were talking about."

For the first time he saw anger in the cop's face. "I catch you following me again, something bad could happen, Mr. Madison. You understand?"

Put the bullet right in the center of his throat. Watch the life choke out of him as he grabbed and clawed at the wound.

"You keep that in mind, Mr. Madison."

Josh woke up around two o'clock. A light rain haloed the streetlight outside. Elise was awake, too. They made love. He surprised them both with the power of his ardor. He could have killed him. He knew now he was capable of it. It gave him new strength. He didn't tell Elise about seeing the cop. The next night in bed when he approached her she pushed him away.

Three weeks later, they were having after-dinner brandies in the TV room when Elise said, "My God, it's him."

Nine O'Clock News on WGN.

"Patrol officer Earl Frazier has been accused of rape by South Side resident Oreila McGee."

Frazier's photo was a color close-up taken some years ago.

"While McGee's lawyer, Jefferson Hardin, freely admits that his client is a prostitute, he insists that Officer Frazier beat and then raped his client this past Thursday night. Police spokesperson Donald Thomas said that the department will issue a statement tomorrow morning. But that as far as he knew, Officer Frazier would stay on his regular duty at full pay."

"Earl Frazier," Josh said. Now he knew the bastard's name.

"They'll laugh her out of court," Elise said, "a prostitute accusing a cop like that." Then, quietly, "He's just going to keep on doing it, isn't he?"

"Yeah," Josh said. "Yeah, he is."

"That poor woman," she said.

At breakfast, Lisa decided to decorate herself for the holidays. She got most of her Gerber's pureed carrots all over her face, hands, arms and hair. The carrots looked especially fetching dangling from her left ear lobe. She looked intensely, radiantly pleased with herself.

Josh fed her. He loved feeding her. "I think I'll run her through the car wash this morning," he said. "That'll clean her up." He'd almost cleaned out the small glass jar.

He glanced at Elise. She looked drained, tense. "You all right, honey?"

"I should've gone to the police that night. I should've told the truth. But it's way too late, now. It'd be just my word against his."

"Yours and a prostitute."

"God, I really want to see him in prison."

"So do I."

"But how can we do it now?"

He was glad that Lisa chose this moment to smear more of the carrot puree all over her face. "Gee, look, honey," he said, not answering her question. "An orange baby."

It was two days later when Josh got the idea.

He was in a TV studio producing a commercial for a car security system. Everything was wrapped up except the final sequence, which showed a shadowy burglar trying to break into a new Buick. The set was carefully lighted to effect a film noir look. The actor, dressed in dark clothes and a fedora, was hulking and ominous as he leaned into the car and glanced first right then left. Resembled a shot from a horror movie.

The sequence took on a more urgent meaning suddenly. He

imagined that the burglar was actually Frazier the cop and that he was forcing Elise out of the Saab. He didn't want to imagine any more. He'd tried to avoid thinking of the actual rape itself. Doing so literally made him sick to his stomach.

"You all right?" the director said. They were in the control booth, a spaceship-like panel of knobs and buttons stretching out before them. Sixteen small monitors filled the dark wall in front of them. They could see the sequence being shot in both color and black and white. "Man, you're really sweating. Maybe you're getting that flu that's going around."

But it wasn't the flu. It was glimpses of the rape filling his mind. Her eyes. Her small fists hammering on him. The brutal way he'd taken her. And it was his idea. It had happened before, so why couldn't it happen again? An unseen private citizen with a home video camera out for a night's amusement when he accidentally stumbles on. . . .

"Yeah," he said, finally answering the director. "Must be the flu."

Elise's first response was negative. She didn't think it would work. But the more he showed her the unedited video from the car security commercial, the more she got drawn in. There was a lot that needed to be done. And it wouldn't be cheap. He'd have to pay a lighting director, a camera operator, a makeup person, a costumer, two actors and an art director who could find the right car and fit it out accordingly.

The first night they were scheduled to shoot was canceled. Rain. The second night was also canceled. Fog. The third night, they actually got down to business. They drove out to the lonely, deserted spot where the rape had taken place and then everybody went about his job. They did every sequence over three or four times. He was afraid that reliving the experience would be too much for Elise. But her anger kept her sane. She'd been able to match the outfit she'd worn the night of the rape. She looked beautiful.

They didn't get home till midnight. Terri, the babysitter, was asleep on the couch, her senior History book over her face. Conan O'Brien was talking to her but she wasn't listening. Josh ran her home. By the time he got back, Elise was in the kitchen, microwaving them hot cocoa with tiny bobbing marshmallows. They sat in the breakfast nook. She raised her cup. They toasted. Everything was ready to go.

Frazier had lived in an apartment complex ever since his divorce. He liked summers best because he had most of the day to hang around the swimming pool and size up the ladies. A lot of them were stewardesses. Being politically correct, the airlines had started using older women these days. The image of the vacuous but deadly-beautiful stew had changed. You now often found middle-aged ladies serving you on your flights. Still, there was plenty of young flesh around the pool, many of whom didn't mind coming over to his apartment for a gin and tonic and some afternoon delight. It was the cop thing. They'd deny it of course. But they — the type of women he attracted anyway — liked the authority thing. Even the women he raped. A few of his victims had even had an orgasm while he was raping them. Even against their will they'd responded to the uniform, the badge, the nightstick, the gun. One of them, he'd even used his nightstick on a little bit. He could still remember the way she'd shuddered.

He was still worried about the guy in the new Saab. Following him around like that. It was too late for the bitch to come forward with any evidence. So what was the use of following him around? The only answer was that the guy planned to kill him. Maybe he was just working up his nerve. He didn't look like the type who'd have the balls to do it face-on. He should never have raped the Coburn woman. He hadn't been able to control himself. Usually he stuck to the hookers. Stupid bitch that turned him in, she wasn't going to get anywhere. A hooker challenging a sworn officer of the law? Give me a break.

But the Coburn woman. What the hell was her husband following him around for?

These were his thoughts the morning of the day the tape arrived. The mail came at one o'clock. Just after an argument with his mother. Bitch

*had cost him two marriages, the way she was always horning him. She'd
never liked any of his girlfriends and absolutely detested his wives. His old
man had dropped dead of a heart attack at forty-two. Frazier knew why,
too. So he could escape. Whatever was on the other side of life—extinction
or folks with wings or pitchforks—had to be preferable to life with his
mother. He'd thought that moving away from her—leaving St. Louis and
picking up his cop's life here in Chicago—would help. She was very tight
with a dollar. She wouldn't let herself spend all that money on long
distance. But she got in one of those cut-rate calling programs and now
she was calling him all the time again. Sometimes, twice a day.*

*The first piece of mail he opened was a birthday card from his
eight-year-old daughter. Today being his birthday. He smiled. She was
his pride, his one true love. Carrie. She signed it with a big heart and a
lot of XXXXs for kisses.*

*He knew something was wrong the moment he felt the video mailer.
just had some kind of foreboding.*

Who'd be sending him a video?

He went upstairs and plugged it into the VCR.

*And started shaking immediately. Five minutes later, he was
gunning down a couple drinks of bourbon and chewing on Tums. The
tape—he couldn't see himself on it particularly well . . . shadowy and
shot from the back . . . but you could see what he did to the woman
grabbing her wrist the way he had that night . . . dragging her into the
copse of trees. And then the camera moved in closer for a final shot of he
and the woman disappearing into the woods . . . and held for a moment
on the back fender of the squad car. Car 93. No doubt about that at all.*

Josh called Frazier from a pay phone. All the afternoon traffic
made for nice ambient sound. A blackmailer probably would call
from a pay phone.

"Good afternoon, Mr. Frazier." He tried to make his voice
sound like a happy phone solicitor. After working with actors all
these years, he had no trouble disguising his voice.

"Who's this?"

"A friend of yours." Pause.

"Yeah? What's your name?"

"What's more important is my occupation, Mr. Frazier. Or pre-occupation, I guess I should say. I spend most of my nights driving around and finding interesting things to shoot with my home video camera."

"Yeah? What's that got to do with me?"

"You're too modest, Mr. Frazier. You're the star of my last video. And my best, too, if I may say so. In fact, I think I remember sending you one."

He said nothing.

"It's a little out-of-focus, I'll admit. But you can see the number of the squad car pretty clearly. And you can see the woman pretty well, too. Sorry all we could see was your back. And that was pretty close up." They'd shot the sequence so that you could only see his shoulders and the back of his head. Jumpy, jerky shots, barely in focus. But ominous.

Silence. Then Frazier said, "We need to meet."

"All right."

"How about my apartment?"

"Fine."

"And alone. Tomorrow night at ten."

"You don't work then?"

"I'll worry about work. You just worry about yourself."

It happened more and more often these days. Private citizen with a home video camera. Roaming the night. Never knew where they were gonna show up. One had shown up the night of the rape. The son-of-a-bitch. Too late for the Madison woman to do anything. And the hooker's lawsuit wouldn't go anywhere. But a man with a videotape.

Frazier cursed himself again for ever letting go of himself this way. Nice, respectable woman. That was not the kind to rape and push around. He must've been crazy.

And the longer he thought of killing the video man right here in the apartment, that sounded crazy too.

There had to be a better way. Had to.

The store sold everything from guns to tiny microphones you could hide in a tiepin. It was the world of subterfuge and intrigue and it was fascinating to both Josh and Elise.

The chunky man with the crew cut and the American flag pin on the lapel of his sport jacket led them to what they were looking for. "They always make it look real complicated on cop shows. But actually it's pretty easy."

Elise laughed softly. "Can an idiot operate it?"

"An idiot can operate it fine," the salesman said.

"Then we're in good shape," she said.

At home, they spent two hours testing the equipment out. It operated simply, just the way the salesman had said it would.

Toward dinnertime, Elise took a nap with little Lisa. Josh used the time to go down in the basement and check over the .45 he'd bought a few days earlier. He'd known that eventually he would confront Frazier and he wanted to be ready. He was hoping the cop would force his hand. He very much wanted an excuse to kill Frazier. He took the .45 out to the Saab and put it in the glove compartment. He spent a moment looking at the decade-old black BMW Elise usually drove. It had been the first symbol of their success, of Josh moving from a small, factory-like art studio to one of the country's major advertising agencies. He'd drive it tonight. Frazier wouldn't recognize it.

He couldn't relax. He kept pacing in the basement. Thinking of Frazier. The Rape. The .45.

Finally, it was time to go. He went to the den and knocked back a drink of bourbon.

Elise watched him from the doorway. "Remember, you're not there to do anything more than we planned."

"I remember." But the harshness of his tone contradicted his words.

She came over to him. Slid her arms around him. "This hasn't been easy for either of us, honey. I know that. I wish I could tell you when I'll feel like being intimate again but—"

He turned around and took her carefully in his arms. "All I care about is that you get better. That you come out of your shell. All the sleeping. Rarely leaving the house. Never calling your old friends—"

"Just don't do anything that makes things worse, Josh. You know your temper."

"Don't worry. Everything'll be fine. We'll nail the bastard. And I won't do anything stupid."

Then it was time to leave.

3

The parking lot of Frazier's apartment house told its own story. All the cars were wannabes, knock-offs of this or that sports car. Josh knew the place by reputation. The last bastion of middle-aged swingers. A number of divorced ad people lived here. A cop could do well for himself here. A certain kind of woman liked authority figures a lot.

He found the building he wanted and went inside, glad for a respite from the numbing cold. It was only a few degrees above zero and the clouds hiding the moon forebode more days of similar freezing.

Dance music filled the lobby from a nearby apartment. Some kind of updated disco number. It was a well-kept place. New carpeting recently vacuumed. Fresh paint. Window casings in good repair. He found Frazier's apartment and knocked. No answer.

Down the hall two fifty-year-old women emerged from another apartment. They were nice-looking. They smiled at him. "You're cute," one of them said. "You want to come along?"

"Maybe some other time."

"You a cop, too?" the other one said.

"No, just a friend."

"Well, that story about him raping that hooker—he'll need all the friends he can get. It's too bad when some old whore can make trouble for a man like Frazier."

"He's very nice to everybody," the other one said. "And—no offense—but some cops are pretty hard to deal with. Especially after they've had a couple of drinks." The other one giggled. "Remember Larry?"

Her friend returned the giggle. "After a couple of drinks, he'd always haul out his bass guitar and take his pants off and walk around in his boxers."

"I guess he thought he was turning us on," the lady laughed. "Well, toodles, and if you see Frazier, tell him Kitty and Candy said hi."

After they were gone, he knocked again. What the hell was going on? Where was Frazier?

He tried knocking again. Then he started jiggling the doorknob. A man came out of an apartment down the hall and stared at him. Josh left.

In his car, starting the engine, he wondered what kind of game Frazier was playing.

He drove away, preoccupied. He didn't notice, as he reached the slippery nighttime street, that a blue Chevrolet was following him.

The leak was slower than Frazier had figured. He'd slashed Josh's right rear tire deeply. He'd also taken the spare. By now, the car should be limping along, giving Josh particular trouble on the ice-glazed streets. Trucks were out all over the city, spewing sand on the worst of the main-traveled streets. Cops had already given up on the idea of responding to fender-benders. There were just too many of them.

Then it happened quickly. The black BMW slumped to the right and the car started bumping toward a stoplight. He wouldn't be going much further on that tire.

He was beginning to lose it.

The tension of the whole situation. Frazier not being home. And now a flat tire.

He pulled the BMW over to the curb and pulled on the emergency lights. He got out of the car, slip-sliding on the ice, doing a couple of silent-movie arm-waving gags while he was at it. He walked back to the trunk.

Great. No spare.

He remembered passing a Sinclair station a few blocks back. There'd been a service garage as well as gas pumps.

Then he remembered the .45 in the glove compartment. He could lock the car but that wouldn't stop any real dedicated pro. They'd take everything, including the weapon. Better stick it in his pocket.

He got back in the car and opened the glove compartment and the gun wasn't there and he knew, of course, what had happened.

Elise had found it. Removed temptation from him. He spoke a few nasty words to himself.

He was just getting out of the car when he saw Frazier standing there. Nobody had taken Frazier's gun. It was right in his gloved hand.

"Let's go back and get in my car," he said. "And be sure and bring that videotape."

Josh glanced wildly around the street. Mercury vapor lights exposed a small convenience store, a tattoo parlor, a fingernail boutique, an ancient Catholic Church, three bars, a dry cleaners, a real estate office. The rest of the block, on both sides, were filthy giant houses that had long ago been divided up into filthy tiny sleeping rooms and so-called apartments. The legion of the lost plied these streets. Only the bars and the church had any succor to offer them.

Nobody was paying any attention at all to the two men standing by the downed BMW.

"You bring the tape?"

"Yeah."

"Let's see it."

Josh held up the videotape cartridge.

"Good. Let's get going."

Again, no swagger, no macho posturing on Frazier's part. He didn't have to impress anybody. He had a gun and Josh had no doubt he would use it.

"You drive," Frazier said.

Josh had to fight to control the car. It was a big, lumbering beast and tended to skid.

"The guy who took the home video, how much does he want?"

Josh almost smiled. Not only had Frazier bought the video as authentic, he was assuming that Josh was working with some nameless person who'd shot the footage. "Thirty-five thousand."

"I want to meet with him."

"I have the tape."

"You ever heard of copies?"

"He claims this is the original."

"I don't give a damn *what* he claims. I want to meet him. But first I want you to go over on the Avenue and pull into where all those deserted warehouses are."

"For what?"

"Just do what I said."

Driving was still treacherous. They saw a couple of fender-benders on the way to the warehouses. Then Josh saw that the icy streets could help him. What if he plowed into a parked car? Maybe he'd have a chance to get away. It was his only hope.

"Slow down," Frazier said.

Josh saw an opportunity half a block ahead. A car just now pulling out. Perfect timing to ram into him. And in the confusion, run.

Then he felt cold steel against the side of his neck. "I'm not afraid to kill you, Coburn. Not at all. You try and pile us up, the first thing I do is put a bullet right in your heart."

Ten minutes later, Josh eased the car down a narrow alley between dark, looming warehouses. This had been a vital section of the shipping business until two large importer-exporters moved away. Now maybe as many as fifteen warehouses stood dark and empty.

"I still don't know what the hell you want with me," Josh said.

"Pull over there and kill the lights."

What choice did Josh have?

"Now kill the engine."

Josh switched off the key.

"The key."

Josh handed it over.

"Get out."

Josh was reduced to silent-movie sight gags again. He slipped and nearly fell on his back.

"I'm going to give you something to remember," Frazier said. "And something for your wife to remember, too."

He drove his fist into Josh's stomach so hard, all time, all sensory data stopped. There was only pain. His entire body, his entire mind, his entire soul was pain. He wanted to scream, he wanted to throw up, he wanted to lash out at Frazier. But he was momentarily, and completely, immobilized. He just crouched in half there, his mouth open in a sound he didn't have strength enough to make.

Then the same fist smashed into the side of Josh's face. He remembered how, in *The Exorcist*, the girl's head had turned all the way around. Surely his head had just done the same thing.

"I don't want you or that bitch wife of yours botherin' me anymore, Coburn," Frazier said. "You understand me? We speaking the same language here?"

"You—you raped my wife," Josh managed to say. "I'll never stop bothering you."

"You ask her if she enjoyed it, Mr. Advertising Executive? You ask her how many times she came when I was inside her? Huh? You ask her that, you piece of shit?"

He started to move on Josh again.

And that was when the bullet tore through Frazier's left

shoulder and he was turned leftward and slammed against the exterior wall of the warehouse next to him.

Moonlight shone on the ice-glazed tarmac of the warehouse area. Fog was setting in from the nearby Lake. The bullet had come from the fog. And now something else came from the fog, too. A familiar shape. Familiar except for the .45 she was holding.

"You try and hurt my husband again, I'll kill you right on the spot, Frazier," Elise said.

Josh was forcing himself past his pain so he could function again. Two of his ribs, his lungs and his head pounded with agony.

"You think you got it, honey?" Elise said.

"I was just afraid," Josh said, still out of breath, "when he hit me in the stomach he'd feel the wire."

"The wire?" Frazier said. "What the hell you talking about?"

"It's all been recorded," Josh said. "And it'll be on your commander's desk tomorrow."

Elise reached in and took Frazier's gun from him.

Then she moved a step closer and brought her knee straight up the middle of his crotch. He screamed and doubled over.

"That was for both of us," she said.

Then she led her hobbled husband away from Frazier and to the gray Saab parked three warehouses back.

Later, in bed, there in the sweet shadows, she said, "I'm sorry I still don't feel like it, honey. But I'm getting better all the time. If you can just hold out—"

He took her tenderly to him and kissed her. And gave her the answer they both wanted to hear.

Loose Ends

Bryce had checked his watch twice so Rafferty assumed their meeting was over. He'd peed into a cup, he'd given Dick Bryce a rundown on what he'd been doing and he'd listened as Bryce had told him that he, Rafferty, was getting good reports from the Valu-Mart, the job Bryce had arranged for him after Rafferty had been released from prison.

"So that's about it for today, Seth. You keep up the good work, all right?"

Rafferty nodded. During his four and a half years in prison he'd heard horror stories of all kinds about various officials. Parole officers were particularly bad guys. They were usually portrayed as sadists who couldn't wait to return you to the high gray walls of incarceration. Bryce could be a prick but generally he seemed decent enough.

Rafferty started to get up from his chair when Bryce said, "His daughter would like to see you."

"Conroy's daughter?"

"Yeah. She called me the other day. Said she'd appreciate it if I could arrange a meeting."

Rafferty smiled. "Wasn't she at the parole hearing? She was pretty nasty."

"That was Karen Conroy. Her brother Michael was there, too.

This is Linda Conroy. The other sister. She didn't go to the trial or to the parole hearing."

"Well, there's no way."

"That's what I told her you'd say."

"I pushed him and he tripped and cracked his head. I didn't mean to knock him over and I sure as hell didn't mean to kill him."

Bryce shrugged. He was probably wishing that someday one of his parolees would talk about his crimes without finding excuses for them. "Well, I told her I'd ask you. Now I have. See you in a month."

The waiting room was crowded. Four parole agents and they seemed to be busy all the time.

The warm spring day was one of those small gifts that reminded Rafferty of how profound freedom was. He didn't have to be back at the store for another ninety minutes. He decided to walk over to the park and feast on a chili dog for lunch then board his city bus and head out to Valu-Mart.

The slim blond woman in the black jacket and the dark jeans fell in next to him. At first he assumed she was just another pedestrian hurrying along to the traffic light at the end of the block.

"Mr. Rafferty."

He turned to get a better look at her face. Pretty but with her youth beginning to soften and go slightly out of focus. He knew who she was of course.

She started to say something else but by then he was already glancing over his shoulder and planning his escape.

"Mr. Rafferty," she said again.

He probably startled a few of the people behind him when he plunged into their midst, fighting his way through a knot of them so that he could find an open space and start jogging away from her.

The trial, the sentence, the parole hearing. He never wanted to hear the name Conroy again.

☐

"I think it's pretty clear what happened here," the dramatic redhead said as she concluded the public's case against Seth David Rafferty. Every word was conjecture but she was clearly having an effect on the jury. "Leonard Conroy, his employer, was working late at his office as he frequently did and found the defendant doing the same thing. This was one of the rare times Mr. Rafferty ever worked late. In fact he was an unreliable employee. Mr. Conroy explained this to Mr. Rafferty and Mr. Rafferty became violent. He struck Mr. Conroy and Mr. Conroy struck him back. There is the evidence of Mr. Rafferty's black eye, which Detective Willingham noticed immediately. Then Mr. Rafferty pushed Mr. Conroy again and Mr. Conroy fell back and cracked his skull against the doorframe, killing him instantly."

She finished by noting that the character of the wealthy, powerful Mr. Conroy had been testified to during the trial by some of the most prominent people in the community, including an NFL star, a business partner and an archbishop.

And the jury, in less than an hour, agreed with the dramatic redhead's argument. Manslaughter. Three to seven years.

The calendar said that Rafferty was thirty-one years old when he entered prison. But that was the last time a calendar had any relevance to Rafferty's real age. He emerged from prison an old man in many respects. He'd been one of Conroy's many accountants. Now he was a minimum-wage worker at a Wal-Mart imitator. And his job prospects weren't likely to improve much the rest of his life.

Rafferty spent the afternoon rearranging the displays of new summer clothing. Some of it wasn't so bad. He held back a jacket in his size. With his discount he could afford to pay for it by saving up for two or three paychecks.

"We're getting up a team for some basketball," Bob Landru said to him as they had some Valu-Mart food after work. The burgers here were pretty good; the fries sucked, but with enough ketchup and salt they sufficed.

"Where do you play?"

"Phil's church has a good place in the parking lot. We usually meet there. It's not too far from where you live."

"That's probably what I need. Some outdoor time. Don't get a lot of that."

"And with the weather changing—" He paused. "There's a very nice looking woman standing by that big display of batteries. She's watching us."

"Watching me."

"Why you and not me?"

Bob knew about Rafferty's time in prison. "Daughter of the man I went to prison for. She missed the parole hearing—I told you about it—the son and other daughter started screaming at me. They had to take them out of the room. Now it's her turn."

"You sure it's her?"

Rafferty described her.

"That's her all right."

"She wants a little shrieking time of her own."

"Looks like she's going to come over here."

"Shit." Then: "Do me a favor. Go over and talk to her."

"About what?"

"About anything. Just stall her. I'm going out the front door."

"I'll give it a try."

Bob eased out of the booth and started moving toward the woman. With him doing the defensive blocking, Rafferty slid from the booth and headed straight for the front doors. Because the place was open twenty-four hours a day, there were still customers coming and going. He managed to use them as a further block before he got outside.

He started running through the night. He knew a place about a quarter mile from here where he could pick up the last of the city buses for the night. One transfer and the long ride would deposit him very near the grim gray apartment house where he lived.

☐

He'd learned one thing quickly in prison. Just pretend that he'd done what the justice system had claimed that he'd done—intentionally tried to hurt the older man. None of this accidental bullshit. Nobody would have believed him, anyway, and he'd have just sounded like a wuss.

Of course he'd learned a few other things in prison, too. There were a few decent people among the convict population. That had come as a surprise. He'd never thought much about the penal system. He assumed, like most citizens, that they'd put themselves here and to hell with them. But he knew now that there were some convicts who still managed to be reasonably decent people. And he also learned that prisoners' rights groups didn't exaggerate the kind of brutality visited on the men by prison guards.

That was the most frightening lesson of all. Between the brutality of the guards and the brutality of many of the inmates, just waking up in the morning was a perilous undertaking. Danger from both sides.

Mrs. Raines was in the hallway when he came in. She was talking to Mr. Johansen who had the tiny apartment next to Rafferty's tiny apartment. Johansen had the decency to look embarrassed when he saw Rafferty.

They had obviously been talking about him—or Mrs. Raines had been, anyway. There were six efficiency apartments in this ancient house and each renter was constantly treated to her suspicions about Rafferty. She didn't bother to look embarrassed. She watched him as he walked to the stairs. She might have been watching a dangerous animal. One of the renters had told Rafferty that she only rented to him because she was rarely able to fill Apartment D. The heat didn't work so well and the only window lacked a screen. And it was the only apartment without a window air conditioner.

He went on up. He would never get used to the mixed feelings of anger and odd shame he felt being treated as a pariah. But tonight he was too damned weary to worry about it.

He let himself into his room, went to the elderly refrigerator, grabbed himself a generic beer, turned on the black-and-white TV that had come with the "furnished" apartment and dropped his ass on the sprung couch. A very pretty black-and-white cat he called Jenny had also come with the apartment. She'd been hiding in the closet the day he moved in. She sat on his lap now. Petting her calmed him down.

An hour later he lay on his single bed, Jenny snoring softly at his feet. He tried not to think of prison. He tried not to think of the woman. He tried not to think of his life.

When he came in the following night, Mrs. Raines was spreading some more tabloid trash about him in the hallway. By now she was probably pitching him as Jack the Ripper. This time it was to Mr. Freholt. One thing Mrs. Raines didn't seem to understand was that Freholt, well into his seventies and living on Social Security like most of her renters, was damned near deaf.

But it wasn't Freholt who surprised him. It was Mrs. Raines. Instead of the cold face and the harsh eye, she was smiling tonight. He couldn't ever remember her smiling at him. He wasn't sure what to do. All he did was nod and walk over to the stairs.

He saw a string of light along the base of his apartment door. While putting the key in, he realized who was waiting for him inside.

He pushed the door wide and said, "I want you out of my apartment right now." Then he yelled: "Mrs. Raines! Get your ass up here!"

Linda Conroy had been sitting on the couch. Jenny, the traitor, had been on her lap. She gently set Jenny on one of the cushions, stood up and straightened her dark green jersey dress and the black jacket she'd been wearing the other day.

"All I want to do is talk to you for a few minutes."

When he realized how his hands had become fists, how his heart slammed against his chest, he understood what this was about. He would get angry and say something—maybe so angry that he'd smash something—and she'd report him to the police and then the parole board would be brought in. Guess who'd be going back to prison? The Conroys were clever people. The perfect trap.

He never wanted to be alone with this woman. Alone, she could say anything she wanted and would be believed.

"Mrs. Raines!" he shouted again.

But the bitch was already on her way up the stairs. Given her age, each step was a chore. When she reached them, her face was red, slick with sweat.

"You had no right to let this woman into my apartment."

"You're a fine one to be talkin' about rights. Men like you got no rights as far as I'm concerned."

"But if you'd only let me talk to you a few minutes—"

"Get out of here," he said. "And quit following me. I served my time and it's over. Now leave me alone."

The woman frowned, glanced at Mrs. Raines. She sighed, gathered her jacket around her and then started to leave.

"I ain't givin' you back that twenty," Mrs. Raines said. "I said I'd let you in. I didn't make no guarantees that he'd see you."

Rafferty hurried in and locked his door. He couldn't afford to tell Mrs. Raines what he thought of her. This place was close to work and it was cheap.

He thought about not picking Jenny up as he usually did because he'd found her in the lap of the Conroy woman. How was that for irrational anger? But one sweet little yawn made it impossible for him not to scoop her up and sit down with her in his lap.

On Saturday of that week, one of those splendid warm May afternoons when most people felt immortal, Rafferty ate lunch at a Taco Bell. He took his food outside to one of the tables. A few minutes after he sat down a pair of uniformed cops, one man and one woman, sat down at a table directly across from him.

As a middle-class white boy, he always thought of police officers as the good guys. But prison had made him see them as the enemy; people who could help put him back into prison on a mercenary whim.

Even though they only glanced at him, he felt that they knew who and what he was, as if they had computer chips in their brains that could allow them to identify all ex-convicts on sight.

He leaned over to the table next to him and grabbed the newspaper lying there. He feigned great interest in it. He couldn't sit there and watch them as he ate. Their presence spooked him.

He managed to get interested in an article about new jobs in the computer field. Jobs you could do from your home. He knew that the local community college offered computer courses. It was worth looking into.

The tables had filled up. Chatter competed with birdsong, traffic noise and the squawky metal voice of the drive-through speaker.

So when he raised his head from the article and saw her standing behind the seated policewoman and talking to her, the shock paralyzed him. He wanted to run, shout, anything to express his fear and anger. But when he did begin functioning again, it was only to knock over his soda.

As he took his napkin and started to mop up the spill, he knew she was telling the officer about him. Maybe she was lying about him. Maybe the female cop would come over and start asking him questions.

As she did—

He sat there and watched how she rose up from the table—in good old slo-mo, just like the movies—and how she and the woman came for him.

Damn, he wanted to run. To run for miles, to run into night, to run into the world he'd known before prison.

But he knew how stupid it would be to run. How dangerous. So all he could do was sit there and wait till they reached his table.

"Excuse me, Mr. Rafferty. My name's Officer Malloy."

The taco he'd eaten burned in his stomach, firing flame all the way up into his throat. Cold sweat made him shudder.

"This nice lady tells me that she'd like to talk to you but that you won't let her have just a few minutes of your time. She thinks you're afraid of her." She smiled. "I'm not sure but I think what we've got here is something to do with two people who really should have a talk about what's bothering them. And if you think she's going to do something illegal to you—" here she smiled at the Conroy woman—"I'll be sitting over there with my partner and we promise to protect you."

"I really appreciate this, Officer. Thank you so much."

"Don't hurt him now," the officer laughed. "He doesn't look all that delicate but you never know."

He sat. He watched her. He waited.

"I'm sorry I had to resort to this."

"What did you tell her about me?"

"That we had a rough breakup and you wouldn't talk to me."

"You didn't mention what I did?"

"No. Nothing about it."

"Then what the hell do you want?"

He knew instantly that he'd spoken too loudly. Both cops and two young women at the table next to his looked at him.

In the sunlight he saw that she was older than she'd seemed before. Probably mid-thirties, maybe even a bit older. Still pretty but somber, sad somehow.

"I want to thank you for killing my father."

He started to object to what she said but she added quickly, "It was an accident. I believe that. You just happened to have an accident with one of the most powerful men in this city. And you paid for it." She paused. Tapped two long fingers against her temple. "Headache."

"You may have a headache but I'm going to have a heart attack. Those cops could throw me right back in prison."

"Not unless I make up some lie about you. And I don't plan to do that. I meant what I said. Even though it was an accident, I appreciate that my father is dead."

"But your brother and sister—"

"They idolized him. They'd never believe me when I told them he killed our mother."

Was this some kind of setup? He searched her face for any hint of betrayal but found none.

"When I was fourteen, I went on a boating trip with my father and mother. They were arguing the entire time. My mother had found out about my father's mistress. One night we went out on the boat. I was supposed to be asleep below deck but I heard them arguing even more violently than before. Then I heard my mother scream when my father pushed her overboard. He'd murdered her. I attacked him. I told my brother and sister what happened—I told the police the same thing—but nobody believed me. Or wanted to believe me. He was a powerful man. That was when he started putting me in psychiatric hospitals. I had so many shock treatments over the years I was in a daze a lot of the time. I even began to doubt my own memory sometimes. But I know he killed her and got away with it. And that's why I want to thank you. He should have died a long time ago. When he murdered my mother.

"I just got out last week—my latest stay. I've been in the hospital so often it feels strange to be out. I got so used to it I put myself back in even when my father was gone. But this time I plan to stay out." And then she said it and then, for the first time, he relaxed. She had a beautiful forlorn smile. "I just got out of my prison a little later than you did."

"Then you believe me? That it happened that night just the way I said it did? He was drunk and he came into my office and started yelling at me. Told me what a terrible worker I was. That much I could handle. But he started calling me names. I tried to walk out but he shoved me. And then he hit me. I hit him back. And then I pushed him and . . . then it happened."

"I knew you were telling the truth. I followed the trial from the hospital. I knew all about his temper. Especially when he was drinking."

He felt himself slump forward. His hands were still shaking. He felt drained from all the terror, the images of returning to prison.

"Down the street there's a very nice outdoor grill where they serve drinks. Why don't we go there and talk?"

"You must have really hated him."

"I did. I wish I felt guilty about saying it but I don't. I really don't."

Behind her the two police officers stood up. Officer Malloy came over and put her hand on Linda Conroy's shoulder. "Looks like you're finally having that talk. Hope it works out for you two."

"Yes," Linda said in that wan voice of hers, "so do I."

Killing Kate

One night, after he learned what was going on, he got into bed with Kate and they made love. Inside, she was cold. Always before, and quite normally, her body temperature inside had been warm. But this night and for many nights after, she was cold inside, cold against his sex, cold even during orgasm.

That's one of the ways he learned about the man Kate was sleeping with. For the other man, her insides were undoubtedly warm. Juicy. He could imagine her moans.

Shortly after this he actually saw them together. He was eating in the park across from the building where she worked—thinking he might surprise her in the good sense—when he noticed them. Throwing bread on the tranquil surface of the sunny duck pond. The man had his big hand over hers. Up near the playground part of the park, where cute little innocent kids made the swings groan from fervent use, the man took her in his arms and kissed her.

Sitting there watching them—stunned, ashamed for himself and ashamed for Kate, all their plans for a good marriage and children seemingly dashed now, wanting to die but alive in a terrible irrevocable way—he knew then he'd kill her.

Oh, yes; oh, yes, he'd kill her.

In the afternoon, he called Myrna.

"Yeah?"

God, he wished she weren't so crude. Over the past two months, he'd tried to teach her some manners. Little things. Not smacking your gum. Crossing your legs in a ladylike way. And answering the phone by saying, "Yes" instead of the grating "Yeah."

"This is Robert."

"Oh. Hi."

"Wondered if you were busy tonight."

"Uh, lemme think." Smacking her gum as she riffled through pages. "Earlier I'm busy. Like five till five-thirty."

"How about six then?"

"Yeah. Great."

But he sensed it wasn't so great with her. Sensed some reluctance in her voice. Was she getting tired of it?

"Is another time better for you?" he asked.

"Six's fine."

"Myrna, I thought we were honest with each other."

"Well, actually I wish it could be seven."

"Seven would be fine with me."

"Really?"

"Really."

"Great. Then I won't have to miss the match."

He said nothing. What could you say? You tried to help a young woman refine and reform her ways and she spends her time exulting over professional wrestling.

"You're, uh, still being careful?"

She sighed, suddenly a little girl being chastised by her father. "I always make 'em wear a rubber, if that's what you're asking."

"I'm just trying to be your friend."

Again, a sigh. "Oh. I got the package."

"You did?" He couldn't keep the excitement from his voice.

"Weird stuff."

"It's called a Poet's shirt."

"It just looks like this weird sleep shirt."

"It's real silk."

"Oh, yeah?"

Grating with the "yeah" again.

"Well, anyway, I got it. You want me to wear it, huh?"

"If you would."

He could hear the smirk in her voice—it was always there when she addressed this subject—as she said, "We're gunna do the same stuff, huh?"

"Yes. If you wouldn't mind, I mean."

"I'm in the shower again?"

"Yes."

"So you want me to leave the front door open?"

"Please."

"And then you come in and—"

"Yes. Then I come in and—yes."

The sigh again. "You're the boss."

God, he hated it when she used that cliché, so dutiful and contemptuous at the same time.

"Seven?" she asked.

"Seven," he said.

He kept the knife in a drawer of his big mahogany desk in the center of his big mahogany law office where he was the most senior of partners in a resolutely successful firm that specialized in criminal law. It was a chef's knife with an eight-inch blade and a walnut handle. It had once belonged to a client of his, a gigantic Hispanic who had used it to lob off the breasts of six different women, after, that is, he was done strangling them. Somehow, through bureaucratic confusion, the knife had come back to him after the trial and after the Hispanic (a well-heeled drug dealer) had been sent upstate for a minimum of thirty years.

Now the knife—cleaned and stropped carefully with a piece of sharpening steel several times a month—rested in his hand. Ready.

For some reason, he always ate a huge meal before he did his deed. Nothing fancy, usually a McDonalds or a Hardee's. Greasy fries and greasy burger and fake milk shake and imitation cherry pie. The staple American repast.

It wasn't the food that attracted him to such places, it was the suspense. He liked it when mommies and daddies burdened with screaming kids took a moment to glance over at him. The solitary middle-aged male. There was always something vaguely threatening about such a man in a family place (is he queer? does he molest children? is he wife-dumped and lonely?) and he enjoyed their contempt, wondering if in fact they suspected what he was all about.

Black turtleneck, black jeans, black Reeboks, black gloves and a black hairpiece to cover his balding dome.

Myrna's apartment house.

Up the back stairs.

Smells of fish, pizza, marijuana.

Sounds of television, heavy metal record, domestic argument.

Sight of hallway walls in need of paint, apartment door numbers hanging askew, kid's red trike sitting unused.

Look left. Look right.

All clear.

He put his gloved hand to the doorknob. Unlocked. He let himself in.

The place, as always, smelled acridly of a vague gas leak she always claimed not to notice. The place, as always, was a mess, cheap furniture covered with cigarette burns and stains, and littered with magazines that ran to *Soap Opera Stars* and *True Detective.* She claimed she picked the place up frequently. He'd never seen any evidence of that.

He stood in the darkness of the tiny living room, right in front of a plastic crucifix that glowed when the lights were off, listening to the shower run. Yellow light outlined the bathroom door.

She was inside waiting.

The knife came up in his hand from the sheath attached to his belt.

He took four steps to the door. He was beginning to smell the dampness from the shower. The scent of steam.

He opened the door, pushed inside.

If anything, the bathroom was a bigger mess than the living room. Half-empty jars, bottles, tubes, and spray cans of deodorant, hair gel, hair spray, toothpaste and much more covered every available surface. The toilet bowl was rusty and the once-white sink a gritty gray. The mirror in which his face appeared was cracked right down the center and the petite pink wastebasket overflowing with tampon boxes and used Kleenex.

The shower curtain was plastic and white. He could see the silhouette of her body against it. She soaped her bountiful breasts and then let her hand drop to the thatch of pubic hair she kept neatly trimmed.

His loins ached.

But this was not his mission tonight. It never was on the final night. "You're out there, right?" shouting so she could be heard above the blasting water.

"Right."

"This kinda scares me. You know, the way it usually does."

He said nothing.

"I guess it's just when you throw back the curtain and I see that phony rubber knife in your hand. Once I get over that part, it's OK."

"How was wrestling tonight?"

"The Cowboy won. He's a real stud."

"Did you wear the Poet's shirt?" he asked.

"Yeah."

"Did you like it?"

"It's all right. Kinda tight around the boobs, though."

"You ready?"

"Just like usual, huh? I mean, you throw back the curtain and then pretend to start stabbin' me and then we go into the bedroom and get it on, right?"

"More or less."

She was quiet for a time. "You sound kinda—funny tonight."

"Long day at the office."

"I'm gettin' scared." Pause. "I don't know if I want to do this."

He said nothing.

"You hear me?"

"I heard you, Myrna."

"I think I'd like you to leave. Like right now, all right?"

He said nothing.

"You're scaring the hell out of me. In about ten seconds, I'm going to start screaming."

But he was faster than that. Much faster.

Before she could even form a scream, he had the curtain thrown back and the knife plunged deeply into the flesh between her sumptuous breasts.

For a moment, he allowed himself the luxury of a look at her face. Even wet and without makeup, the resemblance was startling.

He stabbed her thirty-eight times.

In bed that night, they watched the late news. Kate, rumpled from a hard day with her two sons but as always still beautiful, said, "Listen." She sat up, her breasts loose beneath the silk of her Poet's shirt.

"What?"

"Sssssh." She nodded to the TV set.

He put down his Tom Clancy novel and stared at the screen. Another prostitute had been found brutally slain in her apartment shower. This was the third such killing in three years. The newscaster finished the story by saying, "Police are intrigued by the resemblance of Myrna Tomkins with the other victims, all of whom bore a very strong likeness. A police psychiatrist speculates that the murderer is killing the same woman again and again."

Myrna's photograph flashed on TV. He looked at it and then looked over at Kate. The two women could have been sisters, maybe even twins. It was not easy, finding prostitutes who looked so much like his wife.

But he had no choice. Five years ago, shortly after he saw Kate and her lover in the park, Kate surprised him by dropping the man and devoting herself entirely to their relationship. A fling, really, nothing more. How badly he wanted to forgive her but he couldn't, not quite—until he got the idea for the surrogate killings.

Now, whenever his rage and jealousy at the remembered affair got very bad for him, he began his search for a look-alike hooker.

He spared Kate and their two fine sons the ugliness that he knew still to be within him.

Kate said, "God, it's so scary, knowing somebody like that is out there."

He leaned over and kissed her tenderly. "You don't have anything to worry about, Kate."

She looked at him skeptically. "I wish I was as sure of that as you are."

He kissed her on the cheek again, patted her hand, and went back to his novel.

Favor and the Princess

Thursday, finally, something happened.

Favor had been tailing David Carson for two days, and they had each been equally dull days. Back when he was a city detective, there were two jobs Favor hated most: telling parents that their child had been killed, and tailing people. Favor's ass always went to sleep.

For two days, Carson, a slender and handsome man, went to work, played squash, stopped by his country club for two quick drinks, and then drove on home to the wife and kids. Home being a walled estate complete with large gurgling fountain on the front lawn, and a pair of Jags in the three-stall garage.

Thursday, Carson was nice enough to do something different.

As CEO of the electronics firm he had recently inherited from his father-in-law, Carson didn't have any problem sneaking off in the middle of the afternoon. He stopped first at a branch of the Federal National Savings bank. Favor figured this was going to be another nowhere tail. But Carson parked and went inside, and stayed inside for nearly half an hour. When he came out, he carried a manila envelope.

From the bank, he drove straight to the bluffs out in Haversham State Park. On a weekday May afternoon, the birds and the butterflies frolicking in the warm air, the park was empty. Carson angled his shiny black Lincoln Town Car into a spot near the log-cabin restrooms, and got out carrying the manila envelope. There was another car already parked there, a sporty little red Mustang convertible with the top up. He then took off walking toward a path that led straight to an overlook above the river.

Favor gave him a couple of minutes and then went after him, shoving his small notebook back in the pocket of his blue blazer. He'd written down the number of the Mustang.

All Favor could think of, as he wound his way down the forest path, the damp leaves and loam playing hell with his sinuses, was that he didn't have a cap on and was therefore susceptible to Lyme disease.

Favor was a good-looking guy of forty-five who seemed competent and confident in every way. His darkest secret was his hypochondria.

Being in a room where somebody sneezed pissed him off for an hour and he could feel the jack-booted cold germs invading his body and seizing control of it. Sometimes he was so upset he wanted to take out his trusty old Police .38 Special and waste the offender. If he ever got to be President of the United States, which, he had to admit, wasn't real likely, he would make public sneezing a felony.

For a few minutes, as the path wended and wound its way through the deepest part of the forest, and possums and rabbits and raccoons lined up to look at him, he was a seven-year-old again, imagining he was Tarzan, and this wasn't a forest at all but a jungle, and it wasn't in Iowa, it was in Africa, and it wasn't the real Africa, which was actually kind of boring, it was Tarzan's Africa, which was about the coolest place on the whole planet. Favor had been a stone Tarzan freak until he was fifteen years old, when he discovered a) girls b) marijuana and c) Neil Young records. Neil couldn't sing for shit but he did stuff to a guitar that never failed to give Favor chills. But now, for a brief time at least, he was Tarzan again and seven years old again and if he wasn't careful he just might get himself attacked by an alligator. . . .

The overlook was actually a kind of stone verandah set on the highest point of a woodsy bluff. It was the kind of aerie the Indians had no doubt used for spying on intruders. Beyond, across the wide rushing river, were other bluffs, gleaming with the skins of white birch trees that struggled all the way up hill to the point where some old narrow-gauge railroad tracks could still be found. Jesse James had once robbed one of the short-haul trains that had used these very same tracks.

The man with David Carson was short, stumpy and bald. He wore a buff blue polo shirt, khaki pants, argyle socks and penny loafers. He put his hand out and Carson set the manila envelope on it.

Favor couldn't hear what they were saying. A couple of motor boats were showing off below and drowning out the words.

Then Carson was angrily jamming his finger into the smaller man's chest.

The man backed up but Carson pursued him, continuing to jab at his chest, continuing to spit angry words into the man's face.

Favor could see that Carson was starting to glance back up the trail. He was probably going to leave soon.

Favor decided this would be a good time to leave.

He hurried back along the path, got in his car, and drove up near the exit, where he parked on the shoulder of the road and took out his trusty newspaper. The paper was ten years old. He used it for every surveillance job. Someday he'd have to get a new paper.

A few minutes later, Carson came shooting up the asphalt. The posted speed limit was 15. He was doing at least 60. When he reached the stop sign at the exit, he jammed on his brakes, fishtailing a bit. Then he peeled out, laying down rubber. He was sure pissed off about something.

Favor followed him back to the manse, then drove down to the police station, where he had an old buddy of his run a check on the Mustang's plates.

"You know anybody who drives a red Mustang?" Favor said three hours later.

"I didn't know they still made Mustangs."

"Yeah, they do. This one is red."

Jane Carson shook her wondrously lovely head.

Jane Dalworth Carson had come from one of the old-money families in the city. Favor had first met her when he was ten, helping his dad in the yardwork business. He got goopy over Jane. No matter what girl he met he always compared her to Jane and found her coming up short. Jane was not only blonde and beautiful and rich and fun to be around, she knew how to make you feel like the most special guy in the known universe. None of Favor's first three wives had been able to do that.

Jane had called him three nights ago. She said her husband was acting weird. Would Favor kind of, you know, follow him around a little and see what was going on? She suspected he might have a woman. "Nobody married to you would ever have a woman on the side," Favor said.

"Oh, you haven't seen me lately. I'm looking middle-aged, Favor. I really am."

Today was the first time he'd actually seen her in eleven years, here in this fern-infested restaurant with the waiters who all wore bouncy little pony-tails and nose-rings.

Favor made a point of it to be modern. It didn't always work. As for Jane, she looked great to him. Maybe a teensy-tiny bit older. But nothing to take seriously.

Jane said, "Do you know anything about this guy?"

"He's a male nurse. Sam Evans."

"Are you serious?"

"Yeah. I was kind've of surprised, too."

"Why would he be meeting a male nurse?"

"I don't know. He handed him a manila envelope."

"An envelope?"

"I think it had money in it. He went into the bank without it, and then came out with it. There's only one thing I know you can get in a bank."

"A male nurse and an envelope with money in it."

Favor said, "Guy's shaking him down."

"Blackmail?"

"Uh-huh."

She looked stunned by a thought she'd obviously just had. "I saw an Oprah once where this woman didn't know her husband was gay till she found him in bed with another guy. I mean, a male nurse—"

For some reason, Favor was disappointed she watched Oprah. Princesses should have better things to do with their time. "I don't think he's gay."

"How can you tell?"

Favor shrugged. "I just don't."

"Then what do you think it is?"

"He drink a lot?"

"Not really."

"Take drugs?"

She laughed. "David? God, he's the most conservative man I know."

Her laugh made him mushy inside. He knew that even if there happened to be a fourth Mrs. Favor, his last thought on planet earth would be about Princess Jane. She was drinking wine and he was drinking Diet Pepsi because he was afraid he might blurt out something embarrassing if he had any booze in him. Many, many drunken nights he'd come this close to picking up the phone and calling her and telling her something embarrassing.

"I guess I wouldn't blame him if he did have a woman on the side."

"I told you. That's crazy. Nobody married to you should even look at anybody else."

She smiled. "Maybe I should've married you, Favor."

"Yeah, right. What a prize I am."

He wanted her to go on a little more, you know, kind of extol the hell out of all his virtues, but she didn't. "I haven't been much company since Dad died."

"I was sorry to hear about it. I would've been there but I was working in Chicago."

"That's all right. We just had a small family funeral. Dad wanted to be cremated. He hated big funerals." Her blue blue eyes were damp. "Things were kind of rough for him the last couple of years. All the foreign competition. Profits were way down. He didn't blame David. My two brothers, did, of course. They've always thought that they should be in charge of the company. He got so sick, the cancer and everything, he had to turn it all over to David. Actually, after the chemo didn't do any good, I expected he'd die right away. But he hung on for almost a year."

"He was a good man."

"He always liked you and your father very much. He never forgot where he came from. The west side, I mean."

Her lower lip began to tremble. He wanted to take her in his arms, hold her, comfort her, make her forever grateful for his remarkable powers of succoring. "How's the business doing now?" he said, trying to forestall her tears.

"Much better."

"Oh?"

She sipped wine, then nodded with that gorgeous head of hers.

'We were way overextended," she said. "The bank was even calling in some of our biggest notes. Then, thank God, right after Dad died, David met Mr. Vasquez."

"Who's he?"

"A very rich Argentinian. David's broker knew him. And he brought them together."

"Vasquez bought in?"

She shrugged. "You know me. I don't know much about business. And really have no interest in it. I'm really more artistic than anything."

"Right. Your painting."

"It's still the center of my life."

She was a terrible painter. Fortunately, she chose the representational mode to paint in. If she did abstract art, Favor wouldn't have been able to tell if she was any good or not. If he found a bunch of paintings by Picasso in his garage, he'd be inclined to throw them away.

"So the company's doing well again?"

"Yes. As I said, I just wish Dad were alive to see it. He spent his whole life building that company. And at the end—" Her eyes were moist again. "I'm sorry."

"No problem. I cry sometimes myself."

"You do?"

"Yeah."

"Somehow I can't imagine that. You crying, I mean."

Favor wasn't sure how to take that. Was she saying that he lacked the sensitivity to cry? Or was she saying that he was too macho to cry? Either way, he wasn't sure she'd paid him a compliment.

"The only time I ever saw David cry," she said, "when my father got on him one night and blamed him for the business going downhill."

"I thought you said your father didn't blame him."

"Just that one time."

"Oh."

"It really got to David."

"I imagine."

"Took away all his pride. So he went into the den and I knocked but he wouldn't let me in. And then I heard him crying. It was a terrible sound." More wine. "I just don't know what any of this has to do with that man in the red Mustang."

"Neither do I. But I'm going to try and find out."

She reached over and put her hand on his. He felt as if he were going into cardiac arrest.

"I really appreciate this, Favor. And I want to pay you for it."

"No way."

She gave his hand a cute little squeeze. "Maybe I really should have married you, Favor." And for one brief moment he had this wonderful thought: what if he really got something on her husband, and she really did decide to take up with Favor? What if . . .

Sitting in a car and doing surveillance allowed you certain liberties. You could pick your nose, scratch your butt, belch, pass gas, and dig the green stuff out of the corners of your eyes. While his thoughts of Princess Jane were mostly ethereal, every once in awhile thoughts of her got him right in the old libido. He kept seeing the swell of her small but perfect breasts, and smelling the erotic scent of her perfume.

This was five hours after leaving her at the restaurant. He'd started following Sam Evans right after dinner. While he waited, Favor picked up his cell phone and called a private number at the credit bureau.

"Hey, Favor."

"How'd you know it was me?"

'We got one of those deals?"

"Oh, that identifies the caller?"

"Yeah."

"I should get one of those. So what'd you find out about Sam Evans."

Paulie Daye worked at the local credit bureau. At night, from his apartment, he hacked into the bureau's computers and sold information to a variety of people.

'Well, he paid off all his bills. Had about ten different creditors really on his ass. Had a whole bunch of stuff—stereo, shit like that—repossessed in fact."

"Any idea where the money came from?"

"Huh-uh."

"When did it start showing up?"

"Eight, nine months ago. Paid everything up to date in two days."

"Cash or checks?"

"What'm I, a mind-reader?"

"He buy a lot of new stuff?"

"A lot. Bought himself a condo, for one thing, and a new Mustang and about five thousand dollars worth of clothes."

"Man, what a waste."

"Yeah?"

"Yeah, he ain't exactly a male model."

"And he took two vacations."

"To where?"

"San Juan and Paris."

"Wow. Sounds like Mr. Evans is doing all right for himself."

"He shaking somebody down?"

"Probably."

"Figures. No male nurse makes this kind've change."

"I need to see his checks for the past ten months. That possible?"

"You looking for anything special?"

"I'll know it when I see it."

"Cost you five big ones."

"Done."

"Take me till about this time tomorrow. I got a friend at his bank can help me, but not till right after work."

Just then, Sam Evans came out of Cock A Doodle Do Night Club and got into his red Mustang.

"Gotta go," Favor said.

Turned out Sam Evans was a real XXX-freak.

He hit, in the next two hours, Club Syn, Lap-Dance-A-Looza, Your Place Or Mine, and The Slit Skirt. He stayed about the same time in each one, forty, forty-five minutes, and then jumped back in his red Mustang and hauled ass down the road. At the last one, he emerged about midnight with a bottle blonde with balloon boobs and a giggle that could shatter glass. He shagged on back to the condo. And ten minutes after crossing the threshold, killed the lights.

Through the open window on the second floor, the blonde's giggle floated down. A waste of a whole night. Didn't learn one damned useful thing about Sam Evans.

"I got the print-outs," Paulie said nineteen hours later. "You want me to fax them?"

"Yeah," Favor said.

"Sounds like a pretty boring evening to me. Going through all these check print-outs."

"Yeah, but I'll be naked while I'm doing it."

"Careful, you can get arrested for stuff like that, Favor."

"Don't remind me. I used to work vice."

Couple hours later, Favor was seriously thinking about getting naked. Anything to break the monotony of poring over and over the printouts of where Sam Evans had written the checks, and in what amount. There was a Cubs game on. Every time the crowd groaned, he looked up to see a Cub player looking embarrassed. Cub fans didn't cheer, they sighed.

He went through the lists six times before he saw that there was only one really interesting name on the whole print-out: nine months ago, Sam Evans had spent $61.00 at Zenith Pharmacy. Favor wondered why a male nurse who worked for a hospital that had its own pharmacy would spend money at another pharmacy. Maybe it was as simple as the fact that the hospital pharmacy didn't stock certain things. Maybe. The Cubs lost a close one, 14-3, and then Favor went to bed.

"Good morning."

"Accounting please."

"Thank you."

This was the next morning in Favor's combination apartment

office. Favor was gagging down a cup of instant coffee while Mr. Coffee took his good sweet time about making the first real cup of the day, the sonofabitch.

"Hello. This is Ruth."

"Hi, Ruth. My name's Bob Powell and I'm a tax accountant. I've got a client named Sam Evans and we're filing a late return this year. But Sam isn't exactly great at keeping receipts. He's got a canceled check here written to Zenith and I wondered if you could tell me what he bought that day."

"I can help you if he's got an account here. Sam Evans?"

"Right."

"Thank you."

She went away and then she came back. "The check paid the balance of his old account."

"I see. Do you have a list of what the check paid for?"

"The specific items?"

"Yes."

"Let's see here. Two hypodermic needles. Looks like the large ones with very fine points. And a bottle of insulin."

The accountant Bob Powell wrote down everything she said. "Well, that's about all I need, I guess."

"He in trouble?"

"Trouble?"

"You know, the IRS."

"Oh. No, not really. Just a late file. A lot of people do that."

"We got audited once, my husband and I, I mean, and it was terrible."

"I bet. Well, listen Ruth, thanks a lot."

"Sure."

"I'm not sure there *was* an autopsy," Jane Carson said on the phone half an hour later.

"He died of what?"

"A heart attack."

"Did he have a history of heart problems?"

"No."

"Did he see a doctor within two weeks of his death for heart problems?"

"No."

"Then there was an autopsy. Had to be. Legally."

"God, how'd you ever learn all this stuff, Favor?"

"I just picked it up."

"I keep wanting to ask him about that male nurse."

"I wouldn't."

"No, I won't. But it's tempting." Then: "Why did you want to know about an autopsy?"

Princess Jane had one of those circuitous conversational styles. You never knew when she was going to circle back to the original topic.

"Because a week before your father died, Sam Evans bought some insulin at a medical supply house."

"Insulin? You mean for diabetes?"

He didn't want to share his suspicions with her just yet. "I'm not sure why he bought it," Favor said. "It may not have anything to do with this at all."

"How will you find out?"

"Talk to the medical examiner."

"He a friend of yours?"

"More or less."

She laughed. "You don't sound real thrilled about him."

"He borrowed fifty bucks from me two Christmases ago and never paid me back."

"Why don't you ask him for it?"

"Because if I asked him, he might get mad, and if he got mad then he wouldn't help me anymore."

"Maybe he was drunk and forgot about it."

"Maybe."

"Then just figure out some subtle way to ask him, if it really bothers you, I mean."

"We'll see. I'll check in with you after I talk to him."

"I just can't figure out," Princess Jane said, "why David'd pay off a male nurse."

"I think," Favor said, "we're about to find out."

Bryce Lenihan, MD, it said. He was fat, bald with a little cherub Irish face. The shoulders of his dark suit coats were invariably snowy with dandruff and his teeth were invariably clogged with bits of his most recent meal. He had been medical examiner for twelve years, as long as Mayor O'Toole had been mayor. O'Toole was his uncle. You figure it out.

Favor decided now was the time to give Lenihan the Big Hint.

"You like my tie, Lenihan?"

"Your tie?"

"Yeah. This one." He waggled the tie at him the way a big dog waggles his tongue at you.

"Yeah, I mean it's nice and all."

"Guy owed me fifty bucks for so long, I figured he'd forgotten about it. And then I open my mail box the other day, and there's a nice new fifty in an envelope. Guy said he was just walking down the street and remembered it all of a sudden, after all these years. You ever do that, Lenihan, forget you owe somebody money I mean?"

"Not that I remember."

As if on cue, so he wouldn't have to pursue the subject any more, Lenihan's phone rang and he got into this five-minute discussion about spots on a dead guy's liver, and what the spots did or didn't signify. Favor didn't see how anybody could be a doctor.

After Lenihan hung up, he said, "I gotta go down to the morgue. That's why I don't think chicks should be doctors. Dizzy bitch can't ever figure things out for herself, my assistant I mean. So what can I do for you, Favor, and make it fast."

Favor knew he could forget all about his fifty bucks. Probably forever.

"I got three things I'm trying to put together here," he said.

"First I got a guy who had a heart attack with no history of heart attacks."

"Which doesn't mean diddly. Lots of guys with no history of heart trouble die from heart attacks."

"Two, I've got a male nurse who may or may not be involved in this whole thing. And three—"

The phone rang again.

"Yeah?" Lenihan said, after snapping up the receiver. Then: "Then let him do his own fucking autopsy, he's so god-damned smart. I say the guy suffocated and if he doesn't like it, tell him to put it up his ass."

Lenihan slammed the phone. "Lawyers."

He glanced at his watch. Would Favor be able to finish his question?

"I gotta haul ass, Favor," Lenihan said, standing up. He did what he usually did when he stood up, whisked dandruff off his shoulders with his fingers.

"Number three is, four days before this guy has a heart attack, the male nurse buys two large syringes with fine points—"

"—probably 60 ccs—"

"And some insulin—" That's when the first knock came. "And I'd like to find out," Favor said, "if there's a connection between these things."

Lenihan looked as if he were about to say something to Favor when the second knock came. "Yeah?" Lenihan shouted.

The woman who came through the door literally cowered when she saw Dr. Lenihan. She looked as if he might turn on her and throw her into the wall or something.

"What the hell is it, Martha?"

A trembling hand held out a single piece of paper.

"The lab report you wanted on the Henderson case."

He snatched it from her. "Tell them they can kiss my ass. I wanted this early this morning."

The woman cowered again, and then quickly left.

Lenihan probably wasn't going to win any Boss of the Year

awards. He was scanning the lab report when Favor said, "So what do you think? Those three things I told you about fit together?"

When Lenihan looked up, his eyes were glassy. Whatever information the lab report held, it must be damned engrossing. "Huh?" he said.

"The male nurse and the syringe and the insulin."

"God," Dr. Bruce Lenihan, MD, said, shooting his cuff and glaring at his wristwatch. "I'm so fucking late I can't believe it." Then he said, "I figure a smarty-pants like you woulda been able to figure it out all by your lonesome, Favor."

"Figure what out?"

"The insulin bit. Very old trick. Thing is, it still works eight out of ten times. Last convention I went to, that was one of the big topics on the docket. It's still a problem. I mean, it doesn't happen that often, but it's still a bitch to spot."

On the way down in the elevator, Lenihan gave the lowdown on how exactly you killed a guy the way the male nurse had. Lenihan's last words, just as Favor was saying goodbye, "But a really good medical examiner would be able to spot it." He smiled. "A good one like me."

Lenihan had done the autopsy in question, of course, and he hadn't spotted it at all.

Favor had kept some of the old burglary picks he'd taken from various thieves back during his city detective days. He got into Sam Evans's condo with no problem. He went out into the kitchen and found some Jack Daniels black label and fixed himself a drink. Then he went into the living room and parked himself in the recliner. He used the channel zapper and found the Cubs game. During a long commercial break, Favor picked up the phone and called Princess Jane.

"I think I figured it out. What your husband was up to."

"Oh, God, Favor, I'm almost afraid to hear."

He told her and she started crying almost immediately.

All the time she cried, he thought, the cops're going to nail David's ass, and she's going to be free. Maybe seventh-grade dreams really do come true. You just have to wait a while. Say twenty or thirty years.

She kept on sobbing. "I'm sorry, Favor. I'd better go."

"Don't mention any of this to your husband. I've got a little plan in mind."

He could imagine how she'd feel in his arms right now, the tender slender body against his, the warmth of the tears on her cheeks.

"Just remember," Favor said, "you need anything, any time night or day, you've got my number."

"Oh, Favor, I just feel so terrible right now."

"You lie down and try to nap. That's the best thing."

He could feel the gratitude coming from the other end of the phone. It was almost tangible.

Four innings later—the Cubs losing another close one, 9-0—Favor heard somebody in the hall. Evans.

Favor took out his .38—he saw no reason to carry one of the monsters cops seemed to favor these days—and then just sat there with his drink in one hand and his .38 in the other.

When Evans came through the door, the .38 was pointing directly at his chest. He was all flashy sports clothes—yellow summer sweater, white ducks, $150 white Reeboks, and enough Raw Vanilla cologne to peel off wallpaper. Being bald and dumpy and squint-eyed kind of spoiled the effect, though.

"Hey," he said, "what the hell's going on?"

"Close the door and sit down and shut up."

"That my booze you're drinking?"

Guy's holding a gun on him and all Evans worries about is his booze. "You heard what I said."

"You're obviously not the cops."

"No shit."

Then Evans finally went over and sat down on the couch. What he didn't do was shut up.

"You're in deep shit, my friend," he said.

"First of all," Favor said. "You're the one in deep shit. And second of all, I ain't your friend."

"Who the hell are you?"

"I want you to get David Carson over here."

"I don't know any David Carson."

"Yeah, right. Now pick up that phone and call him and tell him he needs to get over here right away, that somebody's figured out what you two did."

"You're crazy, you know that? I don't know what the hell you're talking about."

"Pick up the phone."

"No."

"No?"

"Damn right, no. This is my condo, not yours."

Favor got up and went over to where Evans was perched anxiously on the edge of the couch. He brought the barrel of his gun down hard across the side of Evans' head.

"You sonofabitch," Evans said, and then kind of rolled around on the couch, holding the right side of his head, and wrinkling his pretty yellow sweater. After the pain had subsided somewhat, Evans said, "I still don't know any David Carson."

"Pick up the phone."

Evans started to protest again. This time, all Favor did was give him a good swift kick in the shin. An old playground technique.

"Ow! Aw shit! Ow!" This hurt a lot more, surprisingly, than the gun barrel along the side of the head. Evans bitched and cursed for four, five minutes and then Favor handed him the receiver.

"You sonofabitch," Evans said. He dialed the number, asked for Carson. "You need to get over to my place right away," he said as soon as Carson came on the line. "We got a problem. A big one." He looked up at Favor. "Right away." He hung up.

Favor sat down in the recliner again. "How much he pay you?"

"None of your business."

"Whatever it was, it wasn't enough, was it? You've still been shaking him down."

"Yeah? Is that right?"

"One thing about people you blackmail. They wake up one day and decide they're really sick of living under your thumb. And then they get violent."

"I'll keep that in mind."

"You're gonna get life, you know that, don't you?" Evans didn't say anything. Just stared out the window at the spring blue sky. "Unless, of course, you turn state's evidence against him. His idea, you say. He came to me with the whole plan. The County Attorney'll cut you some slack if you go that route."

Evans said, "I wouldn't get life?"

"Not if you cooperate."

"Carson's a lot bigger fish to fry. Socially, I mean."

"He sure is. The County Attorney'd rather have his scalp than yours any day."

Evans put his face in his hands. When he took them away, his eyes were moist. "God, I don't know why I ever agreed to do this."

"How'd you meet Carson?"

"He had an employee, this guy named Mandlebaum, and he had cancer and I took care of him the last couple weeks of his life. At home, I mean. So then Carson looked me up about ten, eleven months ago."

"So he offered you the deal?"

"He kept hinting at it, talking about how the only thing that could save the business was the old man's insurance policy. They had one of those key-man deals, where if one of the partners dies the business gets a lot of money. Almost three million, in this case. Enough to pay off some of the bills and keep things going."

"How much he pay you?"

"Hundred grand."

"How much more you been getting out of him?"

"Not that much."

"How much?" Favor said.

"Thirty, around there. I'm not sure exactly."

"You think it'd last forever?"

"Yeah, I guess I kinda started thinking that way. Kinda dumb, huh?"

Favor nodded. "Someday he'd either run out of money or run out of patience."

"God, does my head hurt."

"Sorry."

"And my shin."

"Sorry about that, too."

"You really get off on slapping people around?"

"Sometimes."

"That seems weird to me, hurting people I mean. I'm always trying to *help* people, you know what I mean?"

"Yeah, like you helped Carson's father-in-law."

"That was the only time I ever did anything like that." He sounded as if Favor had deeply hurt him by reminding him of the incident. Footsteps in the hallway. Coming this way.

"You going to hide?" Evans whispered.

"Huh-uh," Favor whispered back. "Just go open the door."

The footsteps came closer. Evans looked scared. Favor waved him to the door with the .38. "When he knocks, open the door and then step back and let him walk inside."

When the knock came, Evans looked back at Favor. Favor nodded. David Carson was framed in the doorway. He was a lanky, impressive middle-aged man. He looked very unhappy.

"What the hell is this, Evans?"

Evans stepped aside so Carson could get a look at Favor.

"C'mon in, Carson," Favor said.

"Who the hell are you?"

"Just get your ass in here." Favor liked pushing people like Carson around. For once, it was Carson's turn to be the pushee.

"He knows," Evans said.

"Oh, isn't that just fucking ducky?" Carson said. He walked into the living room. "How'd he find out?" Carson said to Evans.

"I told him."

"Figures. You dumb bastard." Carson looked at Favor. "You're not getting jack shit from me. You'd better understand that right up front. No more for Evans, and none at all for you."

Favor decided now was probably a good time to get out of the recliner.

"You killed your father-in-law," Favor said.

"What I did is my own business." Carson's tone made it clear that he never explained himself to peons.

"You ever think how your wife might feel about that?"

"Say," Carson said, snapping his fingers. "Favor. Now I know who you are. Your father used to be the old man's groundskeeper or something like that."

"I liked the old man," Favor said, "a lot more than you did, apparently."

Carson looked at him and smiled. "When's the last time you talked to her? To Jane."

"A while ago. Why?"

"Go down and get her," Carson said to Evans. Evans looked baffled. "My wife," Carson said. "In my car."

"What the hell're you trying to pull here, anyway?" Favor said.

"Go get her, Evans," Carson said. "I picked her up on the way over here."

Evans looked at Favor for approval. Favor nodded. "Right back," Evans said.

"You gullible bastard," Carson said after Evans was gone. "You're one of these guys who has a life-time crush on my wife, aren't you? She told me how you used to write her letters sometimes."

Favor felt his face redden.

"She may not be what you think," Carson said. He was smiling again. Smirking, actually. "You're some kind of investigator, right?" Carson said. "What'd she do, hire you to follow me around or something? That how you got into this? Stupid bitch."

The name-calling stunned him. How dare anybody call Princess Jane a name. My God, this guy must be insane. Favor was about to say something when Jane came through the door. She wore a camel-colored suede car coat, a starched white shirt, black slacks and a pair of black flats. She was, as always, gorgeous.

"I'm sorry for all this, Favor," she said.

Favor looked at Carson. "She knows what you did. To her father."

Favor expected a big scene. All that happened was Jane looked at Carson. "I need to talk with Favor alone," she said.

"Why the hell'd you have him following me around?" Carson said.

If Carson had called her a name, Favor was prepared to slug him. "Because I didn't know what was going on," she said. "You were acting so strange. I thought maybe you had a woman on the side."

"So you hire this creep?" Carson said.

"He isn't a creep, and I want to talk to him alone. Why don't you and Mr. Evans go outside for a while?"

Carson glared at him, then nodded for Evans to follow him out. Carson slammed the door behind him good and hard.

Jane said, "I really appreciate everything you've done for me, Favor. And I do want to pay you."

"You know better than that." Then: "I know some good divorce lawyers."

Jane smiled sadly. "I love him, Favor. We have two children together."

"He murdered your father."

"We talked about that, on the way over here. I told him what I knew and we talked about it." She reached out and took his hand. "This isn't a very pretty thing to say about myself, Favor, but it's true. I'm used to living a very lavish lifestyle. That's the first thing David said to me after I told him that I knew what he and Evans had done to my father. He said, 'I did it for the sake of our family. If I hadn't, we'd be broke today. He was dying anyway, he didn't have long to go. The company needed that key-man insurance payoff.' That's what he said, and you know, he's right."

"Oh, shit," Favor said. "You mean you don't mind he killed your father?"

She leaned forward on her tip-toes and kissed him on the cheek. "I knew you'd be disappointed in me."

"He killed your father. In cold blood."

"He saved our family. Me. The girls. Himself. He didn't have any choice. Daddy was dying anyway, don't forget." Done kissing him, she leaned back and said, "My father would have done the same thing in David's circumstances. They're the same kind of man, really. I'm sure that, subconsciously, I knew. That's why I married him."

"I should go the police."

"You'd destroy my life, Favor. Do you really want to do that?"

He looked at her. She was a stranger suddenly. "I guess not."

"I knew you'd say that. I said that to David on the way over here. I said Favor's an honorable man. He wouldn't let me be hurt that way."

This time, she kissed him on the lips, quickly but with real tenderness. "We just come from different backgrounds, Favor," she said. "I guess I can't expect you to understand me sometimes." She looked back at the closed door.

"Now I'd better go."

"Yeah. I guess you'd better."

"I know you're disappointed, Favor. And I'm sorry."

"Sure."

"Goodbye, Favor."

"Yeah."

"I'll always remember you. Really."

And then she was gone.

Princess Jane was gone. Forever, Favor knew.

Forever.

When Sam Evans came through the door, Favor was in the kitchen helping himself to more Jack Daniels.

"Hey, man," Evans said, sounding pissed. "That's my booze."

"This is for you," Favor said, and slapped a ten spot down on the counter. Favor knew he should be heading out but right now he didn't want to go anywhere. He just wanted to stay right here and get wasted.

"She's a looker."

"She sure is that," Favor said. "She sure is."

"But her tits aren't big enough."

"Don't talk about her that way. And I mean it."

Evans was smart enough to look scared. Favor had suddenly turned dangerous again.

"She's a princess," Favor said. "A princess." He felt like crying.

"Hey, man, I just like bigger tits is all. Sorry if I offended you. Now do you mind if I get in there and have a drink from my own bottle?"

"She's a princess," Favor said.

"Yeah, man, you said that already."

"A princess," Favor said, getting out of the way so Evans could get in there and get a drink from his own bottle. "A regular god-damned princess and don't you forget it."

AUTHOR'S NOTE

Thanks to Dr. F. Paul Wilson for supplying the medical details in this story.

Heritage

by Ed Gorman and Terence Butler

I suppose that I should have been more demonstratively grief stricken. My mother and my sister and my father's current wife certainly didn't seem to be having any trouble bringing forth tears, but I just couldn't keep my eyes off the blond assistant funeral director who had stationed herself in one of the side chapels. Cool and elegant and suitably somber in her tightly wound chignon and her nicely fitted black suit, it was the single long curl that fell at each side of her face that gave her away. I knew she would be completely abandoned once in the big bed in my uptown apartment.

I forced myself to stop looking at her for now and listen to the minister drone on about my father's virtues, which were ordinary, and say nothing of his vices, which were legendary. It did feel strange in this setting to think of how little I knew about the man, given that his secretive nature was part of my knowledge of him since I was a boy. It was true that he was always generous, always kind and even affectionate toward me, but he'd never taken me with him to work, or held gatherings of his employees at the mansion, or spoken of just what it was he did that kept us all so very, very comfortable. In the week since he'd died, I'd become more curious about that than I ever had been before.

I pictured him in wherever it is that dead people go, looking down on us with a little "gotcha" smirk on his face. I longed to find out the source of his fortune.

When at last we got outside the church, I gratefully inhaled the crisp smoky air of the September morning and looked around for the lovely undertaker. She was holding out her hand and nodding, while a Vincent Price look-alike that I assumed was her boss dangled car keys and imparted instructions to her. And then she turned on her lovely ankles and placed her lovely derriere in the seat of a plain black Ford sedan and drove away.

Another missed opportunity, another love affair unfulfilled. I realized that I felt more sadness about the loss of her than for the loss of my father. I should have been ashamed.

In the limo on the way to the cemetery my father's current wife Erika broke the silence. "He never forgot our anniversary." They'd had only two, but it seemed she wanted to say something.

"Or a birthday," my mother said, an expression of her sense of sorority with Erika.

They sniffled a bit and looked out their respective windows at the suburban lawns we were passing.

My sister Kendra, sitting between them, looked at me, sitting opposite in the facing seat, and said, "Or those monthly checks, thank God."

"Kendra!" Mother said. "This is hardly the time to talk about that."

"Now's the perfect time," I said. "We're all here. All of us who knew him well, or thought we did, at least. I'd like to ask if any of you ever learned of the source of those checks."

Erika shrugged. "I always thought it was probably oil or something."

"I know he played the stock market," Kendra said, "And he owned those awful apartment houses in the Bronx."

I looked at the three sleek blondes sitting across from me; my father's stable of thoroughbreds, and spoke to the prototype. "How about you, Mother? Where do you think Father got his money?"

She threw me a look and addressed me firmly. "Your father was a private man. He had old fashioned ideas about finance and never thought that it was appropriate to involve his family in the rough and tumble of the marketplace. I, for one, am grateful to him for that. You might do well to repay him with some of that same gratitude and, at least for today, not bother with such trivia."

She knows something, I thought.

There were about half the people from the church at the interment, still a good sized group, and the minister droned again, and then it started to rain, and Vincent Price signaled for him to wrap it up, and I found myself alone in the limo with my mother. Kendra and Erika apparently had left in another car. They were the same age after all, with many of the same friends.

Mother was looking back at the cemetery as we rode, as if watching a good portion of her life fade away, and she didn't speak until we were many blocks beyond.

"What will you do now, Richard? Now that you don't have even the slight pressure to produce that your father applied, I mean."

"I don't know. He did get me through Harvard Law, just as he had done, but since I failed the bar exam, I really haven't felt much passion for a position in some corporate law firm. I may take the exam again, or I may travel some more."

"Oh please don't bring home any more Mexican girls this time. You wouldn't have failed the bar exam if you hadn't spent so much time with her. I did like her grandfather. Such a fine military bearing."

"She's Brazilian, Mother. There is a difference, you know. And I'm curious to know if you ever wondered why the family has a German last name."

"I never thought of it. Why do they?" She is, as they say, clueless.

"It's not important. Could we discuss Father's money again? I feel I need to know something about it. There must be a will, and a trust, and one of us may have to be executor and so on."

"If I tell you what I know will you stop bothering me about it?" she said, not hiding her irritation with me.

"Promise."

"Grandfather Connelly is the man who made all the money. His father was a doctor who was poor but respectable, and your grandfather grew up with some very wealthy friends. One of them was Lucas Stewart, who was to become president of the United States. Your grandfather's wealth increased dramatically at the same time that Lucas Stewart's exploded and it's always been assumed that the Stewarts helped the Connellys. There is no shame in that; it's common among people of similar interests to bring others along, isn't it?"

"But what about Father; what did he *do*? Didn't he work at something?"

"Well, he graduated Harvard Law. You know that."

"But he never worked as a lawyer!"

"I've told you, he never wanted me to know about his money, so I never asked." She grew pensive then, and stared out the window for a bit. "I do remember that when *his* father died he changed. Actually, it was after that. After he met with the family lawyers."

"How did he change? What happened with the lawyers?"

"I don't know. He was more serious somehow, and he dropped all his old friends, Lucas Stewart II, among others. We had recently married and I thought it was something that I had done for awhile, but then gradually he came out of it, and we went on a big tour of Europe, and he spent money as I had never seen him do before." Again she gazed out the window without speaking for awhile. "And then he began to have his flings and affairs, and he told me that we were married in name only, but that he would always take care of me, and he always has. And you children. He has always taken care of us and I am sure he always will."

The limo turned into the driveway and went through the gates to Foxmoor, the big old pile of bricks and timbers that had been built at the beginning of the last century by Grandfather Connelly. Of course, each generation was expected to live in it until they could manage an escape. My father had made his after he and my mother had reached their accommodation, and my sister and I had both flown, but Mother still stayed in the old museum for some reason.

I wondered if that really sexy black girl still worked in the kitchen. I had unwrapped her by the tree last Christmas eve, when not a creature was stirring all through the house.

There were more than a hundred people there that afternoon. Most of them I knew, and so I was obligated by the rules of familiarity to stand in the parlor with Mother and Kendra until they had all spoken their condolences and remembrances and were released to start their serious drinking. In a while they stopped coming by in bunches, and Kendra and I were able to find some time to talk. We sat by the fireplace in our father's den, she with a Bloody Mary, tall, lots of ice, and me with a giant snifter of Hennessy's.

"You know, you've got me curious now," she said.

"About Father?"

"Ummm." She nodded, sipping through her straw. "If you find out anything, let me know, will you?"

"Of course, but I didn't think you cared."

She bristled, slightly insulted by my implication. "I'm not just some dumb whore, you know. I'm not happy that I've been divorced twice already and I'm only 25. I want to stop this sense of *drift* that I feel." She set her glass down, slipped off her heels and pulled her legs up into the wing chair.

"Don't laugh," she said, looking at the flames, not at me, "but I'd like to find a good husband and move back into this old house and raise kids here."

I realized right then that she was speaking for me also. Oh, I didn't want to move back to this house, or maybe not even raise kids, but I knew that feeling of drift. I'd been looking for something solid my whole life. Maybe if I'd had to work for a living I might have found it, but as it stood I was just a lost little rich kid.

Suddenly I was excited.

"I think you're on to something, Kendra. I want to find out about our heritage, why Father was so mysterious and why we're not like other families who can trace everything about their background in intricate detail. I'll try to find out what I can, and maybe we'll both feel better about ourselves."

"That would be so great, Richard. I'll help you in any way I can, just let me know."

There was a discreet knock on the half-opened door then, and Mrs. Anderson, Mother's housekeeper, leaned her upper body in and said, "Mr. Connelly? There's a person here from the funeral home to see you. They've brought the flowers."

In the foyer stood the lovely undertaker. As soon as we made eye contact she blushed and dropped her eyes. I knew she'd had the same thoughts as I had. I knew also what my evening would entail. It would involve the undoing of that chignon.

The following Monday we were informed by my father's attorneys, Darius, Grainger & Whidby, that his will would be read thirty days later at their in offices in Manhattan. They provided the name of a junior partner, Nora Lee, who would be our contact if we had any questions or a problem with the date.

My mother and sister were perfectly willing to let me handle the whole thing and it was agreed that I would keep them informed of the unfolding of the process.

I did have questions, and so I called and asked to speak to Ms. Lee.

"Good morning, Mr. Connelly, how may I help you?" she said in a pleasant, musical voice, pitched low and resonating in the erotic register that I prefer.

"Oh, hello. I've been wondering if you might have access to any of my father's files, perhaps those regarding just what his holdings are, just the names of the companies and so forth. I'd like to be somewhat prepared when I come to our meeting next month."

"I'm afraid not. Those kinds of things are handled by people far more senior than I am. I can pass your question on and get back to you, if you like."

"I see. Well, I guess that will have to do, if you don't mind. Will you call me?"

"Of course. Is there anything else?

"Just that you have a wonderful voice."

Her throaty laugh excited my imagination even further. "Well, thank you," she said, "Is there anything more?"

"Yes. What color is your hair?"

She breathed the laugh again. "I'm a natural blonde with gray, not blue, eyes."

"And I'll bet you're married."

"Hmm. Darius, Grainger & Whidby, legal services and phone sex?"

My turn to laugh. "You have a great sense of humor. Would you join me for a drink this afternoon?"

"What if I said I was married?"

"I'd still ask you for a drink."

"You're a bad boy, aren't you?"

"Marlowe's? Two o'clock? The very last booth. I'll be waiting."

"'Bye, Mr. Connelly."

☐

When she walked in I fell in love right away and I fell hard. She might have been my sister. Or my mother. Or any of my father's previous wives or lovers. The same kind of polished blonde that good breeding and tons of money produces. She was Bryn Mawr and Yale Law and we were made for each other.

She knew it right away too, but was nervous because her bosses would not approve of her fraternizing with a client. So we had our dinners at little out of the way places, and spent a lot of time at my apartment. Sometimes we even made it all the way through a video before we got sidetracked.

She began to tutor me for the bar exam, and we talked about opening a family law practice in her home town of Providence. I felt motivated by something other than a dull sense of duty for the first time in my life.

After just four weeks of bliss it was time for the will to be read. And Nora had never been able to ascertain just what my father's holdings were.

Nora came and got me at the reception area. She acted as if she had met me before and was very pleased to see me again. I teased her by making ogle eyes when the receptionist looked away, and by bumping into her in the hallway, copping a feel as she led me to the office of her boss, Scott Darius.

Once ensconced there though, I stopped my antics and got serious. We only had to wait a minute, no more, for Darius to arrive. He was past retirement age, tall, slender, tanned and fit, with a gray brush cut and steel blue eyes. He had the perfect Ivy League lawyer get-up on and almost crushed my hand when Nora introduced us. He sat behind his desk and pushed a bulging sealed manila envelope across it to me. Written on it in my father's bold hand were the words: "To be opened in private by my son, Richard, after my death," and with his unmistakable signature.

"Is this the will?" I asked.

"No," Darius said, "Ms. Lee has the will."

"What is *this*?"

"I have no idea. I do know that when I was a junior partner with this firm forty-two years ago, your grandfather left a similar envelope for your father after his death."

"Really. And you never found out what was in it?"

"No, sir."

"You were never curious?"

He made a rather prissy face, as if I'd said something distasteful.

"A firm like ours, Mr. Connelly, depends on discretion. We are the legal equivalent of a Swiss bank. Curiosity is not in our job description."

"Shall I read this now?"

"Why don't we read the will first, and then we can leave you alone to read whatever is in the envelope."

"Fine."

There were no surprises in the will. As Mother had said, Father would take care of us. All of us. I spent the whole time looking at Nora and wondering which color of matching bra and panties she had on under her tailored suit. There was a midnight blue set that was my favorite.

When Darius was finished reading he asked me if I had questions. I had only one.

"Thank you, counselor. Tell me, do you have any idea how my father got his fortune?"

The mouth moved in the unreadable face. "He inherited it from your grandfather, but as to the provenance of that fortune, this firm cannot say. Will that be all today, Mr. Connelly? If so, Ms. Lee and I will leave you to your envelope."

I looked at him for a moment, smiled at Nora, and began to tear open the envelope. I heard the door close quietly behind them.

☐

Senator Lucas Stewart III has three mansions scattered around the country; in New England, and in Palm Beach, and this one, "The Cabin", as it's called, in Wyoming. It's a working ranch set on a parcel of family-owned land within the Teton National Forest, a fantasy escape to the days when men were men and politics was whatever you could get away with, a policy Senator Stewart and his group of advisors would dearly love to implement again. He's called "Bull Rider" by his pals, but at Harvard he was just known as "that fascist, Stewart."

We knew each other then, and we were cordial because of the link our families shared, even though neither of us was clear on exactly what it was. But we ran in different circles, politically and socially, and he became the youngest governor ever of Wyoming, and now the youngest Senator ever of any state, and is on track to become, you've got it, the youngest President of the United States ever.

He certainly had the lordly bearing part down as he swept hurriedly into the room, a small den furnished with shelves of old books and heads of dead animals and the smell of leather and pipe tobacco. He was taller, thinner and more imposing than he looked on television, and his slightly long blond hair gave him a reckless air, as did his angry blue eyes. Worn Levis, boots and a western-cut shirt with the sleeves rolled up completed the picture of a busy, manly man.

He stuck out his hand for a brief shake as he muttered, "Connelly," and pointed at a leather Mission chair. "God damn Appropriations Committee deadline coming up. Hate to cut you short, but—"

I placed the manila envelope on the desk and pushed it across to him. He took out the little digital recorder from inside it and said, "What the hell's this?"

"Push the little round button, it will speak to you."

"This better be important," he growled.

"I think you'll find it riveting, sir." He was a Senator, after all, as had been his father before him.

It was his father's voice that spoke from the recorder, and from the grave.

It took him roughly half an hour to explain that my family's fortune was based on extortion from his family; that my family, through my grandfather, held unimpeachable evidence of his grandfather's murder of a business partner, which allowed him to reap millions in illegal profits and develop the base of power that put him in the White House and Lucas II in the Senate, and that he, Lucas III, was to continue this arrangement from now on, and to pass the obligation on to his heirs. He was to make the same recording when his time came.

When it was finished, he stared at me, his whole body shaking with barely contained outrage. Then he slammed his fist down on the recorder and vaulted to his feet.

"You can't do this!" he shouted, and began to pace.

I sat and watched and listened while he raged. His mission was too important to the world, he held too many lives in his hands, his career was based on honesty and transparency, and finally, his path to the White House was endangered.

"Not if you comply," I said. "Not if you just keep putting those adjusted amounts in those same bank accounts. I have documents to show you exactly how to proceed."

"I could cut your throat, you son of a bitch."

"Originals of everything, including the evidence in the murder case, are in a safe deposit box, of course."

"You son of a bitch. You rotten son of a bitch."

"It's all relative, isn't it?" I said.

I wish I could describe the blue of the lagoon where Nora and I are spending our honeymoon. It's almost a violet color and, played against the white sands, it seems to glow in the sunlight.

I haven't told Nora about what was in the envelope, and she hasn't asked. I'm working out what to say when she does. I'll never tell her about the men who follow us wherever we go, the men in the white Chevys and gray Fords that seem to be everywhere since I returned from Wyoming. My private investigator tells me that they follow Mother and Kendra and The Wives everywhere too. He's trying to find out who they are, but he doesn't think they're from the government.

I've even seen them here, two guys in black boxer swim trunks and Ray-Bans, just sitting on the beach watching us. I wonder if Father had to put up with this too. If I had their job I'd be watching that brunette in the chartreuse thong. I'll bet she's Brazilian.

The Long Way Back

Giff's new red Porsche attracted as much attention as he wanted it to. It wasn't often that a development like this one played host to a car that cost as much as most of the houses. He could've flown here, but sometimes he liked the cross-country driving. Giff Bryant knew where he was going. He'd been here before. Too many times, in fact. He'd hoped that by now his brother Michael would have been able to afford a nicer home.

As the Porsche wound its way through the narrow, confusing streets of the development, people paused to look at it. The lady raking her front lawn. The older man washing his older car. The young boy dressed up in a football helmet and jersey, running touchdowns that would fill his ears with endless applause only he could hear. This was 3:37 of an early and warm October afternoon, school having just let out.

He tried not to notice how shabby the homes were. Window cracks covered with tape. Roofs that needed new shingles. Front windows missing shutters. Hardscrabble lives were lived here, and that certainly included Michael's.

He pulled the Porsche smartly into the drive of 4216 Palmer Drive and parked the car.

A boy and a girl were standing by the garage shooting baskets. The backboard was rusty, the net gnarled.

When they saw who it was, the girl stopped shooting and dropped the ball and ran over to the Porsche.

"Uncle Giff!" she said. She was eleven and her name was Amy. She was a slight, sweet-faced girl with a perky little ponytail.

She hugged him hard.

The boy was named Karl. He was twelve. He was fleshy in the way of his father. There was also a hint of his father's sourness in his dark eyes. Giff knew why the boy seemed reluctant to hug him. Karl was his mother's son. He shared all her likes and dislikes. Giff wasn't exactly Mae's favorite.

Giff put his arm out and Karl came over and hugged him, too. Karl wore his Cubs cap backwards, the way rap stars did.

"I'll bet I know what you're wondering," Giff said to both of them.

He was a tall, gym-hardened man who was just now, at age forty-one, starting to go bald. A long time ago, he'd decided that he liked the corporate look. His suits, like the gray tweed he wore now, were invariably Brooks Brothers. "You're wondering what Uncle Giff bought you."

He saw Karl staring at a point just to the right of his shoulder.

He turned. Mae, pretty Mae, was watching him through the kitchen window. He waved to her and smiled. She waved back, though without any enthusiasm. And she didn't smile.

Amy at least had the grace to look embarrassed by her mother's attitude. Giff turned back to the kids and then reached inside his suit-coat pocket and brought out two crisp, green fifty-dollar bills.

Even sullen Karl was impressed.

"One for you," Giff said, handing the bill over to Amy. "And one for you, Karl."

"Wow," Amy said. "Is this real?"

"No," Giff said. "It's counterfeit. I have a printing press in my basement."

Amy giggled and hugged him again.

"Thanks, Uncle Giff," Karl said. The only time he ever sounded happy around Giff was when Giff was giving him things.

"We have new furniture," Amy said. "Wait till you see it." She took Giff's hand and led him inside.

"This is really nice," Giff said. "The furniture, I mean."

"We like it," Mae said. As always, she sounded slightly defensive.

Actually, he hated the stuff. It was the kind of furniture you bought by the room instead of the piece. The fabric color of the couch and two matching chairs didn't help any. Some kind of wine-red that played hell with the green carpeting.

Mae saw where he was looking. "We're going to get new carpeting next spring." Then added, "If Michael gets his promotion."

"Promotion?" Giff said, putting the kind of enthusiasm into the word a Chamber of Commerce type would. "Hey, he didn't mention that."

"Assistant manager," she said. "And they're talking about his own store within a year. They're building one in Rock Island, which'd be nice."

"Fantastic," Giff said, still making himself sound impressed.

Mae said, "You still seeing that singer?"

Giff shrugged. "Off and on."

"We saw her on Jay Leno that time."

"She's had a nice, solid career."

"Michael's always telling people about how you're going out with her."

"I haven't seen her in a while, actually," Giff said.

He'd been doing a little trophy hunting. Had spent a weekend in Vegas and met her at a blackjack table. Everybody was making a fuss over her. Her third CD, a kind of combination disco and salsa thing, was in the Top 40. And she'd not only done Leno, she'd also done a Barbara Walters interview. Barbara had asked her if she believed in God, Heather having survived a car accident two years ago, and then Heather'd had a good on-camera cry.

For a time, it had been fun and had made him feel important. A West Side kid from Cedar Rapids hanging out with a singing star.

She liked him a lot. In fact, two months into their relationship, she'd told him she a) loved him and b) was preggers. Neither one of them wanted the kid. He flew her to LA, where there was a clinic he'd used on several previous occasions. It was a private, secret clinic. You didn't run into any plump, shrieking, right-to-life housewives or stolid, lesbian nuns on the sidewalks out front.

After that, they drifted apart. It had been his experience that abortions had that effect on relationships, sometimes. He didn't know why. He didn't give it much thought, either. No broken hearts, no bitter last words.

Now, he was dating a very wealthy divorcee who drank a lot at the nightclub he was managing this year. She was actually much better-looking than the recording star, and a lot more fun in bed.

Still, it had been nice to go out with the recording star, something to work into the conversation when you met somebody new. It was like having an especially good credential on your resume.

Then she said, "He's drinking again."

"I just talked to him last week. He said everything was fine."

"He lies. You know that. Addicted people lie all the time."

"God dammit," Giff said. He didn't know what else to say.

"He made it seven months this time," Mae said. "Without a drink, I mean. I suppose I should be grateful. He's never made it seven months before."

Mae was a faded flower. She was still very pretty, she had classic facial bones, but fifteen years of marriage and motherhood had taken their toll. It was like looking at somebody in black and white who had once been in vivid color. She wore a white blouse and blue slacks. Her shoes were scuffed and needed heels. She shooed the kids outside.

She said, "He still compares himself to you."

"This is my fault?" Giff said. "That's what you're trying to tell me? This is my fault? God dammit, Mae, don't start this crap with me again. Don't start it at all."

"I didn't say it was your fault."

But of course she had. She'd always felt that Giff was a bad influence on his brother, filling Michael's head with all sorts of fanciful dreams. Eight, nine years ago, Giff had even invited Michael to be his assistant in the nightclub he was running. This was in Miami, which at the time was experiencing a new round of cocaine wars, so the scene was both exciting and dangerous. Mae had resented how Giff had taken her husband away, uprooted him from his home in Cedar Rapids. She didn't understand Giff's intention, which was to get Michael making some real money, and send for Mae and the kids once he had established himself.

But Michael didn't amount to a damn as his assistant. He drank too much and started hitting on all the waitresses. When he started hitting on the lady customers, Giff stuffed three one-thousand-dollar bills into Michael's shirt pocket, handed him a one-way on United, and sent him home to Mae and the kids.

The way they'd grown up, near the poor section of Cedar Rapids, pride was a big thing to Giff. There was nothing he liked more than riding around Cedar Rapids in an exotic car, giving the locals envious thrills. The same bastards who had busted his father's back for a pitiful hourly wage, the same people who'd snubbed him in grade school and high school, and looked right through him whenever they glanced his way.

But triumphing over these bastards wasn't easy. Took hard work. Giff was used to putting in sixty, seventy hours a week. Forty-five weeks of the year. That was how you paid them back, you worked hard. And, in Giff's case, you took some chances. Were his nightclubs merely fronts for mob guys who needed places to launder their money? Giff never asked many questions about his backers. Was a lot of coke sold in his various nightclub toilets and hallways, and did his backers get a piece of every transaction? Giff didn't ask many questions about that either. Hard work and a modicum of risk, that was how you succeeded.

All Michael ever wanted was the fun. The ladies. The dance floor. The nice suits and sports jackets. And the booze. Michael had been battling alcoholism for most of his adult life. He used to laugh about how Giff didn't drink at all.

But Giff had seen too many men in his particular calling lose everything over liquor and lines of white powder.

"What time's he get home?" Giff said.

"Six, six-thirty."

"I don't want you ever to say that again, about this being my fault."

"It was a cheap shot, Giff," Mae said. "I'm sorry. I'm just scared and all. He just keeps getting worse and worse. Now he's even gambling."

"Oh God," Giff said.

"He found this place downtown, down by the tracks where the Magnus Hotel used to be. They gamble in this basement. Two weeks ago, he lost his whole paycheck. We had to take money out of our savings account to make the house payment." Her small white hands were like animals sleeping in her lap. Every once in a while, as if they were having bad dreams, the animals twitched violently. The twitches gave Giff a sense of how close to the edge Mae was.

"He's going to blow it at the store," she said. "They're going to fire him. I'm sure of it."

"I thought you said he got a promotion."

"He did. He started there about seven months ago, when he went back to AA and stayed sober."

"But now—"

"Now he leaves early and he goes to work with whiskey on his breath. And he's kind-of out of it when he talks to customers and—" She stopped and abruptly started sobbing.

She buried her face in her hands and wept.

Giff went over and sat next to her on the ugly, misshapen couch.

Mae and he had never been close, not even when things had been good for her and Michael, and so he felt awkward about sliding his arm around her and bringing her to him. He held her as he would a child.

She seemed grateful for his strong arms, huddling herself inside them.

He became aware of her breasts against his chest. He'd never been erotically aware of her till now and he felt ashamed of himself. Giff was a decorous person. There was a time and a place for everything. You shouldn't be aware of your sister-in-law's breasts when you were trying to comfort her.

The kids slammed in the back door.

Mae jumped from his arms like a kitten jumping to the floor.

She took a Kleenex from her pocket, wiped her eyes. She was just starting to blow her nose when Amy and Karl reached the living room. They both looked at her.

"You all right, Mom?" Amy said quietly.

"Why don't you go out and play some more?" Mae said. "Uncle Giff and I are just talking."

Karl watched Giff suspiciously, as if Giff might have been beating his mother up or something.

"Everything's fine," Mae said. "Now you two go and play, all right?" When they were gone, she said, "You shouldn't have given them so much money."

"What the hell," Giff said, "I want them to be happy. You know, have the life Michael and I never had."

"You'd make a good father, you know that, Giff?" she said, still sniffling.

"Maybe," Giff said. "Maybe I would."

The dinner was the kind he remembered from his boyhood. His mother died when he was eight and Michael five. Heart disease. The family curse. The old man served the best meal he could, but it always ran to starches. The old man never remarried. He came close once, then backed out when the wedding was two weeks away. Said he felt guilty about their mother.

Dinner tonight was mashed potatoes, a hamburger patty, canned corn, a fresh spinach salad, and a modest slice of pumpkin pie. The kids said grace before dinner and afterward cleared the table for their mother.

"I'm sure this wasn't the kind of meal you're used to," Mae said. "The circles you travel in and all."

"I enjoyed it very much."

Every few minutes, Mae would look up at the kitchen clock. There had been no phone call from Michael.

"He's going to be embarrassed tomorrow," she said, "knowing you were here waiting for him and all."

"I'm going to wait for him."

"You are?"

"I want to talk to him."

He sounded angry and he didn't give a damn that he sounded angry. The kids had gone to their rooms. The only person to hear was Mae. He assumed she was just as angry as he was.

After a time, they went into the living room and watched TV.

They watched some sit-coms. Neither of them laughed, not even once. Then there was a rerun of *Chinatown* on. He never got tired of watching it.

About halfway through, Mae got up and excused herself and went in to say good night to the kids. It was now almost ten o'clock. There had still been no call from Michael.

At ten the local news came on. Cedar Rapids was still a small town, judging by the newscast. Not much happening at all.

"You sure you wouldn't be more comfortable at your hotel?" Mae said.

"You want me to go?"

"No. But I don't want to feel like I'm holding you here, either. You could be out having fun."

"I'm too mad to be out having fun."

Mae went over and sat on the couch across from his chair. She put her face in her hands and started sobbing again.

He went out into the kitchen. Earlier he'd glimpsed a bottle of Jim Beam. He poured her a big one and carried it back to the living room.

She wasn't much of a drinker. Every time she took a sip, she made a cute face, like a kid taking bad-tasting medicine.

"You know the funny thing?" she said after a time.

"What?"

"This house, this development we live in? I mean, I know you and Michael think we could do a lot better. But I love it here. I really do. I grew up in a trailer park and it was really bad. I used to walk by here when I was a little girl. I thought that the people who lived here must be rich. I really did. All I ever wanted was to live here. I love it here. I like my neighbors and the school our kids go to and I love this house. I really do."

She started crying again, much more quietly this time. "Michael's going to lose his job, and we're going to lose this house. I know you can't understand this, Giff, but this was all I ever wanted, a house like this and a family."

"I'm going to have a real hard talk with him," Giff said.

"Oh, Giff, that's sweet but you know it won't do any good. I've had so many real hard talks with him, I'm all worn out. I really am."

The local news came on and then Jay Leno. They sat through his monologue without laughing even once. Every time they heard a car, Mae looked up sharply, as if they might be under attack. But the car always went on past.

After Leno, she said, "I don't think I can stay up any more, Giff."

She nodded to the glass of whiskey. Over the past hour and a half, she'd drunk the whole thing. "I'm sort of drunk." Then: "You know when you held me this afternoon, when I was crying so hard and all? I really liked that. And I don't mean anything sexy by it, either. Michael used to hold me like that but he never does anymore. But when you held me, it was real sweet. It made me like you a lot, and you know we've never gotten along especially."

"You need some sleep."

"I'm sorry if it embarrassed you, what I said."

"It didn't embarrass me, Mae. I felt the same way. All these years we didn't like each other, and now we do."

"God works that way sometimes, you know. The nuns always told me that and I think they were right. God had you be here this afternoon so I'd have somebody to lean on. And so we'd learn to get along with each other."

She stood up. She was wobbly and it was kind of cute. Mae was very cute.

"What a cheap date I am," she grinned. She looked like a kid again. She wobbled out of the living room and down the narrow, dark hall to her bedroom.

Michael drove in a little past one o'clock. Giff had gone to sleep in the recliner with the TV still on. He woke up when he heard the car.

Michael opened the back door quietly and came in on tiptoes. Giff was waiting in the darkness of the alcove that led to the kitchen.

The first thing he noticed about Michael was the blood on his hands and the right sleeve of his cheap tan sports jacket. The second thing he noticed was how much Michael had started to resemble him, now that he was headed toward middle age. Growing up, they hadn't looked like each other much at all.

"What the hell happened?" Giff said, coming in from the alcove.

Michael's head jerked upward. "Hey, Giff." Michael smiled. "What're you doing here?" He was so drunk, he'd apparently forgotten the blood all over his hands. "Huh?"

"You stupid bastard, what the hell'd you do?"

Michael looked utterly baffled. He was that drunk. "I don't know what you're talking about, Giff."

"Your hands, you dumb bastard," Giff said. "Look at your hands." He kept his voice low. He didn't want to wake Mae.

He took Michael by the shoulders and led him over to the kitchen table and sat him down.

"Sit there and don't move," Giff said.

Michael started to get up.

Giff pushed him back down.

"Hey," Michael said. But he stayed seated. He put his head down on the table and tried to cry. But he didn't know how. A lot of men didn't know how. Giff wasn't all that good at it, himself.

Michael kept saying, "It wasn't my fault, it wasn't my fault."

When he lifted his face, some of the blood from his sleeve was now on his left cheek.

Giff microwaved some instant coffee and set the cup in front of Michael. Then he started asking Michael questions. It took two cups of boiling coffee and an hour for Michael to make sense. "You were shooting craps?" Giff said.

"Yeah.

"And after the game, you got into it with this other guy?"

"Yeah."

"The guy who had the dice?"

"Yeah."

"And you pushed him?"

"Yeah."

"Pushed him hard?"

"Yeah."

"God dammit, Michael."

"I didn't mean for him to die, Giff. I really didn't. He just banged his head against the edge of this door." Michael was starting to get coherent.

"You remember where this place is?"

"Sure. I play there every week."

"Mae tells me you blow your paycheck."

"Mae likes to exaggerate things."

"You don't deserve her, you know that, Michael?"

Michael smiled bitterly. "Now there's a switch. You defending Mae. You two are supposed to hate each other."

"Let's go.

"Go where?"

"Back to where the guy is."

"Hell, no, man. Are you crazy? The cops'll be there."

"Maybe he isn't dead."

"What?"

"You were so damned drunk, how could you know if he was dead or not?"

"I felt his pulse."

"C'mon."

"I don't think this is a good idea."

"If you need to pee, go get it over with. And while you're in there, wash yourself up and comb your hair."

"You should've seen him, Giff All the blood. I really got scared."

"Hurry up."

"I don't think this is a good idea, Giff."

"Right now, I don't give a damn what you think, Michael. Now get your ass in gear."

The Porsche seats were cold. The temperature had dipped to thirty-two. At night, moonlight and shadow lent the development a real beauty. The houses looked cozy and snug.

"I want you back in AA."

"You have been talking to Mae."

"You're an alcoholic, Michael. You're killing your wife and your kids."

"I'm not really an alcoholic, Giff."

"Right."

"I'm not. Honest to God. I just drink a little too much sometimes. There's a difference."

"Boy, what a line of crap that is," Giff said. "You're an alcoholic and you need to start going to AA meetings again."

Michael stared out the window. They had just reached the First Avenue hill and were driving down into the valley where the downtown was. Michael said, "I'm scared, Giff."

"I know you're scared. So am I."

"You know what I just did?"

"What?"

"I said a prayer. I said, God, if you help me out of this one, I'll go back to AA. I really will. You think praying does any good, Giff?"

"Can't hurt."

"The most they could get me for is manslaughter."

"Let's wait till we get there to start worrying about that kind of thing."

"You really think he isn't dead?"

"I think there's at least a chance."

"I meant what I said, in that prayer I told you about."

"Good."

"I shouldn't have gotten mad at you, Giff. You know, about AA and all. Deep down, I know I've got a drinking problem. I guess I just don't like people to remind me about it, you know what I mean?"

"Yeah."

"Manslaughter's about all they could get me for, I mean at the worst, don't you think, Giff?"

"Why the hell'd you ever start gambling?"

"I'm an addictive personality, I guess."

Giff hated talk like that. TV talk was how he thought of it. Like you didn't have any control over yourself. Like if you said you were an addictive personality then you weren't really responsible for anything you did. But Giff kept it to himself. Now wasn't the time to tell Michael what he thought of TV talk.

They passed two cop cars on the way downtown. Both sets of cops, one of them a male-female team, gave the Porsche a good look-over.

Michael directed Giff down several alleys, always moving toward the railroad tracks that ran behind Quaker Oats.

The rail yards were dark except for a couple of green signal lights here and there. Maybe ten cars stood open and empty in the gloom. The smell of engine oil lay on the cold night air. Giff had the window down to keep Michael good and awake. The tracks gleamed in the moonlight. You could smell winter tonight.

They crossed the tracks, drove up a steep hill, and then angled right. A deserted two-story brick building sat on a corner. Graffiti covered the walls. The front yard was littered with beer cans, smashed wine bottles, and dog turds. All the windows were boarded up.

Giff pulled around back. They got out and walked to a side door. This had been a tool-and-die place for decades. Michael stood in front of the door and jiggled the doorknob. Then he led the way inside and down some steep stairs to the basement.

Giff had brought his flashlight from the glove compartment. The dust made him sneeze. Another family curse. Bad sinuses.

The landlord had gutted the place. The basement echoed emptily. Even a lot of the electrical wiring had been torn out, along with phone jacks and conduits. Their shoes crunched on a variety of hardened animal droppings. Giff played the beam of his flashlight around. In the middle of the floor you could see where they'd shot craps. There were crushed beer cans, a pint bottle of Jack Daniels, and what looked to be two marijuana roaches.

A long time ago, men and machines had filled this basement. Lives had been led here, paychecks taken home to families. Like so much of the Midwest these days, the factories had been silenced, as if in the wake of a marauding army. Back in the days when this factory had been pounding out work night and day, good jobs had been easy to come by. But not today.

"Where's your friend?" Giff said.

"Far corner," Michael said. He sounded increasingly sober, and increasingly scared.

The beam found the guy a few moments later. Michael had propped him up in the corner. The guy had soiled himself and the smell wasn't nice at all. He was a bald guy, big in a fleshy way, dressed in a blue windbreaker, white button-down shirt, chinos, and Reeboks. Country-club casual. The guy looked as if he might have money.

Giff knelt down next to him. He checked neck then wrist then ankle.

"He's dead, isn't he?" Michael stood over Giff.

"Yeah."

"Oh my God." Michael sounded as if he might be getting hysterical.

"That's not going to help things."

"I killed a guy. I goddamned killed a guy. Oh, I should've stayed with AA, the way Mae wanted me to. I swear to God I should have." He started walking around in crazy little frantic circles.

Giff played the beam to the back of the guy's head. That was where the wound was. It was a good-sized wound, too. Must have hit his head very hard. The wound, purple and all bloody, looked like an exotic flower blooming. Giff stood up. His knees cracked as he did so.

"I'll go to Mexico," Michael said.

"Don't be stupid. You're not going anywhere. Now I need to ask you some questions and you give me the best answers you know."

"There're all kinds of people who saw me here tonight."

"You were alone when you pushed him?"

"Yeah."

"Think. Don't just say yeah."

Michael thought. "I'm sure I was."

"How about when you walked out to your car. Anybody see you then?"

"Not that I know of. But I was pretty drunk."

"But as far as you know—"

"—nobody saw me."

Giff shone his light in the dead guy's face again. "Who was he?"

"Conroy. Pat Conroy."

"He anybody special?"

"Downtowner. Mostly does favors for rich people."

"Favors?"

"You know. Their kid gets in a jam. Or some guy's sniffing around their wives. Stuff like that. Pat was always good at figuring out things like that."

"So he had enemies?"

"Uh, I think so."

Giff played his light around the basement again. He didn't see anything especially noteworthy.

"We need to get out of here," Giff said.

"They're going to nail my ass, aren't they, Giff?" Michael was sounding hysterical again. "I really didn't mean to kill him, Giff. I really didn't."

"Yeah," Giff said. "I know you didn't."

They followed the flashlight beam all the way up the basement steps.

Mae was waiting up for them when they got back. She was in a frayed white terrycloth robe. She sat at the table drinking coffee.

She didn't say anything when they came in.

Michael went right to the bathroom. They could hear him throwing up in there.

"There was blood in the bathroom," Mae said. "What happened to him tonight?"

Giff told her.

"Oh my God. What's going to happen to the kids?"

"We have to stay calm, Mae. We have to think this through."

Michael came back. He'd put on so much aftershave, Giff could smell him as soon as he reached the kitchen.

Michael tried to kiss Mae but she moved her face away. Michael went over and sat in the chair across from her.

"It was all an accident, Mae," Michael said. "Just a freak accident."

"They'll send you to prison."

"Maybe not, Mae. Not if I can prove it was an accident."

She looked at Giff "They'll send him to prison, won't they, Giff?"

"It's nice you and Giff got so goddamned cozy all of a sudden," Michael said.

"Keep your stupid mouth shut," Mae said. She glared at him. "They'll send him to prison, won't they, Giff?"

"Here's what we need to do," Giff said. There was no sense answering Mae's question. Yes, if the police conducted a competent investigation, Michael would be going to jail. Why make Mae feel worse by confirming it? "You need to get up and go to work in the morning, Michael, just like nothing's happened. If the police contact you, call me right away. I've still got some friends here. They'll steer me to a good lawyer. That's where we'll start."

"What'm I going to tell the kids?" Mae said.

"Nothing for now," Giff said. "Anything you say'll just scare them."

Michael was swooning again, shaking his head over and over. "I just don't know how it happened. I just don't know how it happened."

Giff stood up. "Get to bed, Michael. You'll need your rest for tomorrow."

He looked up at Giff. He looked awful. "I'm not good at this stuff, Giff. Not like you are. The cops'll ask me questions and I'll fall apart."

"You'll be fine," Giff said. But he wouldn't be, of course. Michael was never fine about anything.

Giff nodded good night to Mae and then went quietly out the back door.

In his hotel room, Giff undressed and slid beneath the covers. He had a difficult time getting to sleep. He frequently did. Tonight he thought about Michael. Maybe Michael would have turned out better if Mom hadn't died. Or if Giff had done a better job raising him. The old man hadn't had time to raise him, not with working full time at the factory and putting food on the table. Giff had been selfish. He'd led his own life and hadn't paid much attention to either the old man or Michael. Which meant that Michael had been pretty much left alone since the time he was six years old.

Giff should have done a hell of a lot better by Michael than that.

Giff got the call at eight o'clock the next morning, just about the time he was waking up from his troubled sleep.

Mae. She was sobbing.

"The kids heard us arguing this morning, Giff," she said. "They know what Michael did. They were both crying. I could barely get them off to school. They think they'll never see their dad alive again."

"Did Michael go to work?"

"Yes."

"What time's he get off work?"

"Five."

"I'll be out there then."

"God, Giff, I'm so sorry you have to go through all this."

"He's my brother, Mae."

"I know, but—"

"I'll see you at five."

Giff ate a small breakfast of poached egg and unbuttered toast in the hotel restaurant. He read *The Cedar Rapids Gazette*. There was no mention of a body being discovered in a factory basement.

Later in the morning, he drove out to Jefferson High School, which was where he'd graduated. He always came out here when he came back to town. He wasn't ever quite sure why. He sat in the parking lot and looked at the big brick school. Two thousand, two hundred students these days. The day was overcast and cold. But in his mind the day was sunny and it was twenty-five years ago and his life was all ahead of him and he knew that someday he would lose this sadness he carried with him. He'd never known what the sadness was about, just that it was always with him.

But here was a seventeen-year-old Giff, just now coming out the side door of the school, wearing a tie-dyed shirt and bell bottoms, shoulder-length hair, and driving an old junker of a '61 Chevy. He was already doing favors for the nightclub crowd, where everything from drugs to abortions were dealt. But when Giff looked at his old self now, he saw an optimism on the kid's face. He wouldn't have this sadness much longer. Not much longer at all.

Sometimes, Giff wondered if he was the successful one, after all. For all his troubles, Michael had a good wife and a nice family.

Giff had girlfriends and fine cars. And the sadness.

On the drive back to the hotel, Giff heard on the radio that the man's body had been discovered and that the police surmised that they were dealing with a homicide. The victim's name wasn't given.

In his hotel room, Giff lay on the bed trying to nap but he couldn't. He just kept thinking of Mae and the kids and how awful it was going to be for them.

He slept for twenty minutes and then got up and went down to the hotel gym and worked out hard for half an hour, fifteen minutes on the weight machine, fifteen minutes on the treadmill. He went back upstairs and showered. Then it was time to go to Michael's.

□

When he got there, Mae answered the side door. No radio played. No TV blared.

In the living room, Amy and Karl sat silently on the couch. Their eyes were red from crying.

"You hear from Michael?" Giff said.

"Huh-uh. You want coffee?"

"Please."

Giff sat down in the armchair and looked at Amy and Karl. "This'll all work out, kids. Don't worry."

"He's going to prison, isn't he, Uncle Giff?" Amy said.

"They'll kill him in there," Karl said. "I know a kid, his dad was in Anamosa, and this guy killed him right in the cafeteria."

"Your dad's going to be fine," Giff said.

"He didn't mean to kill him, Uncle Giff," Amy said. "He really didn't."

"I know, honey."

"The guy just fell," Karl said, "and hit his head."

"The police'll believe him, won't they, Uncle Giff?" Amy said.

"I'm sure they will," Giff said. "I'm sure they will."

Mae brought his coffee. "Why don't you kids go out and play?" she said.

"It's not very nice out," Amy said.

"You'll be fine, honey," Mae said. "Uncle Giff and I need to talk."

"Talk about Dad, right?" Amy said.

"Right."

"He really didn't mean to kill him," Karl said. "He really didn't."

When they were gone, Mae said, "He isn't at work."

"When did you check?"

"Just now. In the kitchen. I phoned, I mean." Then: "Maybe he's running away."

"I don't think so. Most likely he's getting drunk somewhere."

"Oh, great. Drunk on top of everything else."

She went over to the couch and sat down. Tears were beyond her now. She looked angry and scared. "This wasn't enough for him. The kids weren't enough and the house wasn't enough and I wasn't enough."

"That's probably my fault," Giff said. "I didn't do a very good job of raising him. Neither did the old man. He spent a lot of time running with a bad crowd and we never really broke him of it."

"It's gonna kill those kids, if he has to go to prison, I mean."

"I know."

She had just finished speaking when they heard the car in the drive. Mae got up and went to a side window. "It's him."

"Good.

"He doesn't look drunk. He's walking fine."

"Great," Giff said.

Michael came in. He smelled of cold but he didn't smell of liquor. He carried his winter coat over to the front closet and hung it up. He didn't say anything. He came over and sat down next to Mae.

"I've been in church most of the afternoon," he said.

"Church?" Mae said.

"I made the Stations of the Cross and then I just sat there and prayed." Michael took Mae's hand and held it. "I'm not as scared as I was." He looked at Giff and smiled sadly. "Giff isn't a believer. I suppose this sounds crazy to him."

"Better than going to some bar," Giff said.

"I'm ready for when they come," Michael said. "I'm going to tell them the truth and whatever happens, happens. That's what I was praying for. Strength. I've never had it much before. Now I've got it. I can feel it." He tapped his chest dramatically. "Right in here."

"Maybe they won't ever connect you to him dying," Mae said.

Giff and Michael looked at each other. They knew she was just wishing out loud. But they didn't want to hurt her.

"Maybe," Giff said.

"Yeah," Michael said. "Maybe."

The kids came in. Amy went over and hugged Michael so tight she looked as if she was trying to crush him. Karl stood to the side and just looked at his father. Karl's eyes were damp and every few moments, his lower lip trembled.

Mae finally had to pry Amy away from her father. Mae took the kids down the hall. A door closed. You could hear Amy crying behind it.

Michael sat on the edge of the couch, very tense, and said, "I'm not even scared anymore. Going to church really helped me, Giff."

Giff could see that his little brother wanted to cry, too.

"I feel good in here, you know?" Michael said and tapped his chest again. Mae came out. "I'll put on some supper."

"Thanks, honey," Michael said.

"Will you stay and eat, Giff?"

"Sure. Thanks, Mae."

Mae went out to the kitchen.

"It'll be nice to have you here for dinner," Michael said. He still looked like he wanted to cry.

The car pulled into the driveway just as the CBS news came on the TV screen.

Giff heard the car. He glanced toward the front door.

Michael heard it, too. His whole body twitched violently. They both knew who was here.

Mae came out. "There's a black car in the driveway."

"Detectives," Michael said.

Just then, Amy started sobbing again.

"Giff, I'll wait here with Michael. Could you go in and just give her a hug? She really loves you, Giff."

"Sure," Giff said. Then, "You don't have to tell them anything, Michael."

"I know."

"I'm going to get you the best lawyer around here."

"Thanks, Giff." Michael's right arm was shaking. Mae's eyes

glistened. She made a sign of the cross as they heard two car doors slam.

Giff went into Amy's room. It was tiny and pink and fixed up prettily.

Amy lay face down on the bed, weeping. Karl sat next to her, rubbing her back.

"Come on, Amy. Come on, Amy." Karl said it over and over, like a prayer.

"He's going to prison," she said it every few seconds. "He's going to prison."

Karl looked up at his Uncle Giff. Giff nodded and Karl stood up and Giff sat down on the bed next to Amy.

He turned her over and lifted her up and sat her in his lap. She put her head on his shoulder, the way a small child would. Her face was warm and wet from her tears.

Karl nodded a goodbye and left the room.

"We won't ever see him again, will we, Uncle Giff?"

"We just have to wait and see what happens," Giff said. Then realized that didn't sound very optimistic. "Everything's going to be fine. It really is, Amy."

"I'm just so scared, Uncle Giff."

"I know you are, honey. But you've got to get hold of yourself, all right? Do you have some music?"

She looked up at him. "Music?"

"There. That radio. Why don't you turn it on and lie back and just try to relax a little."

"Karl said detectives are here."

"They are. But that doesn't mean anything."

"It doesn't?"

"Huh-uh. Detectives go places all the time and it doesn't mean anything."

She clung to him, hugging him almost to the point of pain for both of them. "I love you, Uncle Giff."

"I love you, too, Amy," Giff said, standing up and knowing what he had to do.

He went over and turned on the small cheap radio. Amy had it tuned to a rock station. He turned it up a little. "You like that song?" She nodded, sniffling tears.

"Just lie back and listen to it."

"I love you, Uncle Giff," she said again.

"I love you, too, honey," he said.

He went out to the living room.

Two big men in overcoats stood in the doorway. One of them had a little notebook in his left hand. They smelled of cigarettes and cold night air.

The bald one was saying, "We're just trying to interview everybody who was gambling in that basement last night."

Mae and Michael sat on the couch very close together. Holding hands. Giff almost had to smile. The way they clung so desperately together made it obvious that Michael had something to hide.

"I'm the man you're looking for," Giff said. "I went there after my brother lost a lot of money last night. I tried to get some of it back. I was sure the guy had cheated my brother. When I said this to the guy, he pushed me and I pushed him back. I guess I pushed him too hard. My brother didn't have anything to do with it."

As he was talking, Giff looked at Mae and Michael a few times. Michael would never survive prison. Somebody would kill him for sure. His family wouldn't survive, either. Giff knew what happened to a lot of families when the old man went to the slam.

Mae started to say something, then Michael started to say something, but Giff fixed them with a sharp look and they remained quiet.

Six, seven years max—maybe less if he didn't cause any friction in prison—and he'd be out.

Unlike Michael, Giff would be able to take care of himself in and out of prison.

"You're confessing this," the bald detective said. "You realize that, don't you?"

"We haven't even done his Miranda," the other detective said.

Mae was at his side, then, sliding her arm around him, whispering in his ear. She looked up at him and whispered, "You don't have to do this, Giff."

He smiled at her sadly and said, "Yeah, I do, Mae. Yeah, I do."

Then he looked back at the detectives and said, "Read me my rights and then let me get my lawyer on the phone. Then we'll all go down to the station together."

The detectives still looked surprised. Most things didn't come this easy.

The bald one read him his rights and then Giff said, "Can I go say goodbye to my niece? It's just down the hall."

The detectives glanced at each other and shrugged. "Sure."

Then the bald one said, "I'll follow you and wait outside the door." Giff went down the hall, knocked gently, and then went into the room. The bald detective lagged a couple of feet behind him.

Giff went over and picked up Amy and gave her a kiss. "Everything's going to be fine, Amy."

"They're not going to take him to prison?"

"No, they're not, honey."

He held her for a long, tender moment. Sometimes with Amy, he didn't feel his familiar sadness. So now, for just this moment, he clung to her as desperately as she'd clung to him a few minutes ago in this same room.

Then he set her down. "I've got to go now, honey."

He walked out of the room and the bald detective said, "Seems like your brother's got himself a real nice family here."

"Yeah," Giff said, "he sure does."

Rafferty's Comeback

by Ed Gorman and Robert Morrish

I was Rafferty's punishment. Mick Rafferty's. The only thing he liked more than shaking down speeders for twenty bucks was beating up folks who weren't white, Christian, heterosexual and submissive.

The Chief, the widely hated John F. O'Hallahan, got pissed at Rafferty for doing a little free-lancing on his own. Rafferty started shaking down a bar owner who was selling coke and smack out his back door. O'Hallahan wanted to be solely in charge of all corruption in this station. Him being the Chief and all, it was only proper.

So I became Rafferty's punishment. Gone was the Mick's crony-squad car-partner of twelve years. Replaced with somebody—i.e., me—who embodied two of Rafferty's least favorite attributes. I was black and I was a rookie.

Don't think Rafferty didn't bitch about it. He bitched to everybody in the station, even threatened to take his bitching higher. But then the Chief as well as the watch commander got scared that if Rafferty bitched to downtown, there just might be an investigation, and that just might mean that a few cops would wind up in prison.

Almost everybody's on the pad. That's how you keep people in line. Slip them two, three hundred extra a week for not ratting any of their fellow officers out, and they become felons themselves. No chance *they're* going to squeal.

First couple of weeks I rode the four-to-midnight shift with Rafferty, I found things in my locker. Little black dolls hanging from nooses. Ripped-out magazine photos (*National Geographic*, probably) of African natives with plates in their lips. And the masterpiece: a crime scene photo of a black kid lying bullet-riddled and bloody on a sidewalk. Somebody had pasted my photo over his face. Nobody had ever accused Rafferty of being subtle. But he certainly made his point.

What we had those first few weeks was like a Sunday morning political talk show. He accused blacks of being lazy, crooked, murderous, and able to get ahead only because of "all those fags in Washington and their fucking affirmative action bullshit." It so happened I didn't much like affirmative action, either. But that was about the only thing we agreed on. And I disliked myself for agreeing with him on even one subject.

Several times I had to haul him off people. He was one of those towering, beefy Irish guys with a bent nose and a scarred face—in his case, a perfectly formed piece of jagged lightning on his cheek. He had one of those nuclear tempers that make your bowels clench. You never knew when he was going to attack somebody with his billy. He never shared his speeder money, either. Most cops share with their partners. But I didn't care. The money I got handed in a white envelope at that station every week went into a Catholic halfway house where my brother was trying for the third time to re-enter society without resorting to heroin. I probably would've kept the graft money if so much of it hadn't come from drugs. I mean, I'm just as hypocritical as the next guy. And once you get a taste. . .

But in this case it was just too much. I still had to look at myself in the mirror.

Rafferty and I were in a race of sorts. It would be interesting to see which one of us drew first. I'd come home wasted from stress every night, shaking and angry and despondent. But not from the streets. From Rafferty.

The night it started was a rainy, chilly Tuesday in early October. Rafferty'd had a fight with his wife, who'd found lipstick on his white jockey shorts, he told me. He was using me, for the first time, not as a punching bag but as a confidant. I hated myself for playing along.

"You know what happened, don'tcha?" he said. "This hooker who always goes down on me, free gratis? She had this new lipstick on. This real smeary shit. And so it's all over my underwear. I'm not gonna hear the end of this for a while, you can count on that. You married, by the way?"

Bad guys should be made to sign a contract that stipulates they are never allowed to be out of character. Bad twenty-four hours a day, seven days a week.

Because when they go good on you—troubled, in need of a bud—they just confuse the issue. You know that as soon as they've used you they'll go right back to being pricks. And you'll just end up feeling foolish for having gone along.

"Yeah," I said. "A wife and two daughters."

At least he got the suspense over with quickly. He instantly reverted to type.

"She white?" he asked.

"White?"

"Your wife?"

"Oh. Right." I gave him my best watermelon-eating smile and said in my best raghead voice, "I sure wouldn't want to make the massah mad by messin' with no white woman. No, suh, I surely wouldn't."

"I just asked a civil question, asshole."

"First of all," I said, "it wasn't civil. It was racist. And second of all, I believe you're the asshole here, not me."

Thank God we got a call just then. A man was badly injured in a crosswalk. Ambulance was being dispatched.

For the next twenty minutes, there wasn't time to worry about how much Rafferty and I hated each other. There was a job to do. A lot of people think just because cops are on the take, they're worthless. Incompetent. But it doesn't work like that. You can be crooked as hell and still be a damned effective cop.

An upscale shopping area. Seen through the windshield, the lighted store windows and the crowd gathered on the corner were mottled with raindrops. No radio crackling at the moment. Just the lonely sound of the wipers slapping back and forth as we pulled to a halt.

As I got out and headed to the intersection, the ambulance came up, siren dying like a cry in the throat. Most of the crowd huddled beneath umbrellas, soggy beneath their giant black mushrooms. A woman was sobbing; a man was telling everybody to "move back, give him room!"

But as I reached the victim and knelt next to him, I could see that he was going to need a lot more than room. He was a middle-aged, prosperous-looking white man in a dark blue suit, light blue shirt and regimental-striped necktie. Two things tainted his otherwise nice-looking face, a large, crescent-shaped birthmark on his right cheek just below the eye, and a earthquake-like crack right down the center of his forehead. The former was an act of God. The latter was an act of a driver and car that didn't seem to be around.

The emergency boys took over from there. They worked quickly at first, making their preliminary examination and getting him onto the gurney. But they slowed by the time they were shoving him into the box-like opening at the rear of the ambulance. They knew he was dead. Everybody here knew he was dead. No reason to hurry now.

Rafferty and I divvied up the crowd. *Did you see him get hit?*

Did you see the car? Did you get a look at the driver? Do any of you know this man?

And many more questions, standing there in the drizzle of this early October evening, ambulance gone, the rain heavy enough to wash away the worst of the gore near the curb, traffic resuming at full speed again, gawkers gone, life goes on.

More cops. The store manager. Rafferty on the cell phone feeding the name and address of the dead man to the watch commander, who usually made the calls to the family.

"You know how much he had in his wallet?" Rafferty said when we were back in the car.

I shrugged, not particularly caring. Death always hits me the same way. Makes me think of my own wife getting a call from our watch commander. Seeing her face in those first terrible moments of understanding. Seeing the confusion and terror on the faces of my little girls. Raging against death. I took a couple years of community college. Our English professor said that the single most important line in all literature was from a French poet whose name I've forgotten: *Why are we born to suffer and die?* Not Bessie Smith, not Billie Holiday, not even Dr. King had the answer to that one.

"He had a couple grand. And every kinda credit card you can think of. Rich bastard is what he was."

"He was still a human being."

Rafferty laughed, a grisly sound. "That's what you say."

Over the next few months, the tension in the squad car eased somewhat. We still didn't like each other but at least Rafferty quit trying to "rattle the monkey cage" as he so eloquently put it. Our wives weren't exchanging recipes and our kids weren't getting together for movies at the mall. But Rafferty was civil most of the time and so was I.

In fact, the second time it happened, we'd just finished an evening pizza together and each of us had swigged down an illegal beer. Graft is fine and dandy at the station house; but over the past couple years, too many cops had piled up too many cars and downtown was on everybody's ass about drinking on the job. Even a beer.

"It's bullshit, you know, that no-drinkin' rule," Rafferty said. "I can drink a six-pack and be perfectly fine."

I didn't argue even though he was wrong.

"Hell, I bet I could drink a pint of Old Grandad and still be fine."

That one I probably would've challenged but before I could respond the call came in. Hit-and-run in one of the white ethnic neighborhoods that front on our turf.

Blocks and blocks of small brick houses. Blocks and blocks of trees just now shorn of summer leaves. A windy, chilly Friday night. High school football night. Made me sentimental for those days. Drums crisp and sharp on the air. Bright red marching band uniforms. Gladiator-like cheers when the home team scores. And some of the nicest, sweetest sex you'll ever see in the bodies of the cheerleaders as they jump up and thrust themselves against the night in those skimpy little skirts. I'd played a little but didn't start very often. Still and all it was enough to get me at least three of the many, many girls I'd wanted and secure a reasonably popular position on the totem pole of high school society.

No other official vehicles in sight. We swung out of our doors, both carrying flashlights because of the dark street that had been constructed back when working folks first started getting some money just before the Depression. We made our way quickly to where a small group of people stood looking down at the thing that had once been human. I'd never seen arms and legs broken into such ungainly positions. I'd never seen a head stove in quite so deep in the side.

The handful of watchers were old. Blanched, bone white, huddled into unraveled sweaters and threadbare coats, the men either pot-bellied or emaciated, the women hunched and arthritic or obese and clumsy when they moved. I could see the steeple of a Catholic church a block away. The priest there would at least occasionally say the mass in the language of the old country.

"What the hell," Rafferty said as I started asking the questions. He was behind me, hunched down next to the dead man, the man who looked very much as if he was of this neighborhood, decades of hard work and frugality having carved him into little more than bone.

"What?"

"C'mere a minute."

I went over. Bent down next to him.

"Look."

Rafferty shone his light on the man's face. On the right cheek. Just below the eye. The crescent-shaped birthmark.

"You see it?" he said.

"I see it."

"What the hell's that all about?"

"I don't know."

The ambulance had a wraith-like quality, white and glowing, as it wailed toward us like something that had just popped through from another dimension. Right behind it came the homicide detectives.

Different ambulance service. Different emergency personnel. The birthmark meant nothing to them. Weren't interested in the slightest. Once the corpse was inside the glowing box, they pulled away from the crowd.

I was asking an old woman to tell me again about the noise she'd heard when I glanced down the street, near the intersection, where the rusted monster of a gray and battered Buick sat just out of the circle of streetlight.

I felt cold when I saw it. Goosebumps. Chills. Those were the physical responses, anyway. But the fear ran deeper. I didn't know what the hell that Buick was all about but I knew instinctively that it had some bearing on this hit-and-run. Just as it had had on the other hit-and-run. Instinct.

There were three police vehicles in the street. The crowd had grown. Fourteen-and-fifteen-year-old boys now. Bored on a Friday night. All the cars and people served to give me cover to slip across the street and disappear into the shadows. I didn't run but I did double-time it up the street. I wanted to find out who was in the Buick.

When I was about halfway down the block, the huge grinding, throbbing, misfiring monster of the engine surged into shaky life and began to push the car away. I ran after it. But then the Buick's power kicked in and the rusted beast started moving fast.

I ran down the street after it, faster, faster so that I could get a look at its license plate. The Buick raced through a red light but not before I got what I wanted. A look at the plate. A glimpse of the driver and the passenger. Appeared to be a woman at the wheel. A black woman. At least I was sixty percent sure she was black. And next to her, a slumped-over white man. White hair.

"Where the hell you been?" Rafferty said when I got back to the accident scene.

"I had an idea."

"You don't do shit unless you talk to me first, capiche?"

He said it in the loudest and most abusive way possible. Maybe I had a butt-chewing coming. But he didn't have to make it public.

We got names, we got phone numbers, we got addresses, we got squat. These were elderly people. They only came out for emergencies and after it appeared that all the violence was over. What the hell's an atrophied old man using a walker going to do if some punk starts to hassle him? They had good reasons for not rushing outdoors. And so they made terrible witnesses.

"So what the hell were you doing when you were supposed to be helping me interview people?"

This was after the detectives basically kicked us out. Didn't we have anything better to do than stand around and waste the taxpayer's time and money when the heroic and legendary detectives have everything under control?

"I saw a car circle the block twice," I lied.

"What kinda car?"

"Teenagers, it turned out. I thought it might have been our hit-and-run."

"You looked at the grille and the fender."

"No, Rafferty, it never crossed my mind."

He glared at me. "You putting me on? You *didn't* look at the grille and the fender?"

"God, Rafferty, of *course* I'm putting you on."

He still glared. "You better be."

So I didn't tell him about the Buick. Maybe it meant nothing, anyway. But if there was any glory to be had—"Channel 6 has an exclusive interview with the city police officer who found and arrested the hit-and-run driver who recently killed two of our citizens"—if there was any glory to be had, I decided not to share it.

The following Monday was my day off. There was a drain spout I'd been promising to fix and leaves to rake and a wife to take to lunch. She was one of those housewives who managed to be beautiful while working seventy hours a week around the house. I made a point of taking her out to lunch at least once a week.

I was also doing something else. Or *not* doing something else. I wasn't checking out the Buick's license number. Instinct had told me it was important; now instinct was telling me to stay away, that maybe it was *too* important, if that makes any sense. I resisted until Tuesday of the following week and then I called a friend at the motor vehicle department and learned what I needed.

The address was in a small Jamaican ghetto. The name was Bovita Jombanta. I drove over there in my own vehicle, a two-year-old Ford. In that neighborhood, a black cop in a squad car is not exactly taken to the collective breast. He is, if anything, despised even more than white cops.

The streets there were just as dull and dreary as any other ghetto. Even the bright colors of the clothes and the happy Jamaican songs pouring from boom boxes and out open windows on this Indian summer morning were turned gray by their surroundings. The drunk lying face down on the sidewalk; the half-naked children, too many in number for anybody to give them the care they needed; the idle and infirm and unemployed on the corners and the stoops and leaning against the grim little stores that sold rancid meat and over-priced beer and liquor . . . a whole lot of people were to blame for this, from the folks who lived here themselves to the Congress that stuck to their old ways of dealing with poverty and ignorance. And the dealers, of course. They were everywhere, sly, furtive parasites, feeding off you as you fed off them.

I parked and went up to the empty stoop. I knew enough to hold my breath when I went inside. The smells would be toxic.

Inside it was what I expected. Scream of unhappy infant; thunder of arguing couple; rage of rap song. Two, three flights of filthy stairs running between walls that were a museum gallery of graffiti, sexual boasts, personal threats, sad angry doggerel as inane and inept as most rap lyrics. Feces on the steps—rat, cat, dog; one turd that might even have been human.

I knocked, slightly winded, on apartment door 3-C. And it was funny, like a gag in an old movie, the instant I knocked on that door the one directly across from it, behind me, opened, and a voice said, "She isn't home."

When I faced her, I saw a white woman of about twenty or so. Slender, blonde, attractive without being pretty, and blue blue of wily eye. She said, "Shouldn't you be in uniform?"

Her words had their desired effect. She'd startled me.

"You're a cop," she said.

"How do you know that?"

She nodded to 3-C. "Bovita taught me."

"Bovita is who I'm looking for."

"I know. But you're out of luck. Today's the day she spends in the cemetery."

The conversation was just unreal enough to make me nervous. The more I looked at the young woman in the white T-shirt with the nice swell of breast and the nice fill of Levi's, the more I felt guilty about being here. Instinct again: *This is your last chance to get away before it's too late.*

"I just made some coffee," she said.

"I guess I'll be going."

"I scared you, didn't I?"

"Scared me?"

"When I said you were a cop." She had an easy, friendly smile. "You should've seen your face."

This is your last chance to get away before it's too late.

But the sensible side of me was in control now. "I'll be back sometime. I'd appreciate it if you wouldn't mention my visit to Bovita."

"Oh, she's been expecting you."

"Expecting me?"

"You or somebody like you. Somebody official. Somebody who is starting to figure it out." The smile again. "That's quite a birthmark, isn't it? Right below his eye and everything?"

Then her phone was ringing and she said, "I need to get that. But I'm sure you'll be back."

She closed the door. I heard her hurried steps going to the phone. And then she was talking and I was gingerly stepping back down the stairs that had been mined with feces.

We never did get over our mutual anger from that night, Rafferty and I. He seemed to think it was a major offense that I had gone chasing after something without his permission and I was still sure that he shouldn't have ripped me apart in front of civilians. They were white. I didn't need my authority undermined any more than that.

I spent three days working through my brief encounter with

the girl across from Bovita's place. She could have just guessed I was a cop. I guess we begin to exude our occupation after a while. But there was no way she could have guessed about the birthmark. She knew something. Maybe she knew everything.

It rained that early Saturday afternoon—the same afternoon there was a good college football game on the tube—the afternoon I went back up to find Bovita.

The apartment house was even noisier. Kids home from school. Kids on every step it seemed; in every inch of hall space.

I knocked on Bovita's door. This time there was no answer. This time the door across the hall stayed closed.

That night we got the third one. Or the third one we knew about, anyway. An intersection. A light-skinned Negro with processed hair and a good, double-breasted tan suit. A van had hit him. This according to a witness. Didn't get the license number. Didn't see anybody in the van. Did, though, see some kind of junky old car pulling away down the street.

Rafferty kept the beam of his flashlight trained on the dead man's face. And the crescent-shaped scar under his right eye.

Two days later, I went back to Bovita's place again. This time was a repeat of the first time. I knocked on the door and the door on the other side of the hall opened.

The girl said, "You get out of here, man. And you tell your fucking friend, next time he touches me, I'm going to put a mojo on him. You see if I don't."

Her former poise was gone. She was angry and petulant. I didn't blame her. She had a black eye and you could see a large bruise across her pert little nose.

"I don't understand," I said. "'My friend?' Who're you talking about?"

"Who am I talking about? That fucking Mick cop you ride with. And I can call him a Mick because I'm Irish, too."

I smiled. "You're politically correct at a time like this?"

"Well, you still shouldn't call people names. I'll bet people've called *you* a few names in your time."

I nodded. "Yeah, I guess so."

"You tell him for me, all right. You tell him that if he ever comes around me again, I'm putting a curse on him. A bad one?"

"That's what a mojo is?"

"Yeah. What the hell did you think it was?"

Some kids wandered past. I waited until they were gone, then said, "I really need to talk to you."

"Oh, no. I'm not giving you a chance to push me around, too."

"Listen, I hate Rafferty as much as you do. I didn't even know he knew about Bovita."

"You didn't?"

"No. I kept it a secret. I not only hate him. I don't trust him."

She read my face. Not just looked at it. Read it, the way you read a page of a book. After a long time, she said, "You'll be sorry if you try anything rough."

"I won't. I promise."

She didn't belong in the apartment. Not with a two-hundred-dollar pair of Reeboks on her small feet. Not with a gold bracelet worth at least that much on her delicate little wrist. Not with the large screen TV in the corner of what looked to be a museum of voodoo artifacts. Not that I knew much about voodoo. But I'd seen enough bad TV movies to recognize some of the trappings.

"You want some coffee?"

"No, thanks. All I want is for you to sit down on the couch over there and tell me when Rafferty was here and what he wanted."

"He's spooky."

I glanced around. "So is this room."

"Not if you understand what everything means."

"I guess that's where Rafferty is different. The more you understand him, the spookier he is. So tell me what happened."

Four nights ago. She heard somebody in Bovita's place. Somebody bumping into things. Somebody who didn't belong there. She went across the hall, figuring it was a burglar. She took her cell phone, figuring she'd call 911. But it wasn't a burglar. It was something much worse. With a gun. And a badge.

He was big. He was threatening. And he hit her, more than a few times. So, against her will, with blood oozing from her cuts, hating him, hoping someday, somehow to destroy him . . . she tells him what he wants to know.

It started with Bovita's sixteen-year-old grandson, working uptown nights. Washing dishes. Jamaicans not exactly on the best career paths. Leaving work late, tired. Standing on the corner waiting for the night's last bus. When this new sports car jumps the curb and smashes the boy against a nearby light poll. Then backs up and squeals away. The driver so drunk he can barely control the car.

Bovita draws on all her psychic resources seeking out the driver–at least when she's not visiting the cemetery, which she does virtually every day. Eventually she finds the guy. His name is David Clendenon. A wealthy stockbroker. He's apparently in the clear.

At least until Bovita finds him. Then he sprouts a birthmark on his cheek and tire tracks across his chest.

Thing is, his death doesn't satisfy Bovita, doesn't make her pain go away. But it does give her a little taste. A taste of revenge, and for revenge.

And so, a few weeks later, when Bovita listens to her neighbor's tear-stained voice describing a guy who's molested her niece, a guy who's still walking the streets, scot-free . . . well, it doesn't take long for Bovita to connect point A to point B.

And Chester the molester's career is over, punctuated by the exclamation point on his cheek. Seems that Bonita chose the "birthmark" as a way to mark the tainted. And a way to sign her handiwork. And it seems she was just getting started.

I got the picture. A lot of people think just because someone's on a vigilante mission, their cause is just. Righteous. But it doesn't work like that. You can feel righteous as a saint, and still be so misguided that no map will ever set you straight.

I got the picture, all right. But what I didn't get was how she fit into all of it. So I asked her.

And she tells me the story of Lori Dayton, local university student majoring in anthropology. Lori Dayton, writing a paper on voodoo. An intermediary leading her to Bovita. A "psychically gifted elderly lady," or so Lori was assured. Lori spending four days and nights with Bovita, getting her story, and a whole lot more. Learning just how gifted Bovita really was. Getting somehow sucked into something she would never even have believed in just a few days earlier.

Then young and earnest Lori Dayton dropping out of college and moving into the apartment across from Bovita—despite the dangers for a young white girl of living in such a place—and becoming the old woman's acolyte.

I listened to her story without saying much. I can't say it made a whole lot of sense to me–a girl like her giving up everything she had the way she did. But I figured she'd gotten her own taste of something–power, could be, or maybe just a sense of being part of something mysterious–and she liked it.

And that's where Rafferty comes in. Literally. I'm about to make a stab at talking some sense into this nice UMC white girl when the door pops open—thanks to a handy little burglary device Rafferty carries—and there he stands in all his wild-eyed, sneering glory.

"Well, well," he said. "So our little college girl digs coons, does she?"

He came in and slammed the door. There was nothing to say, nothing to do. He had his Clint Eastwood pointed right at me.

"I've thought of havin' a little piece of that meat myself, partner," he said. "Guess I can't blame you for tryin', either."

"Don't let him touch me," Lori said.

"How're you going to explain killing us?" I said. "Not even the Chief could cover that up."

"I'm not thinkin' of killin' either one of you, <u>partner,</u>" he said. "I just want in on the action."

"What action?" I snapped.

"You didn't tell him?" he said to Lori.

She made a face. "He thinks he can get Bovita to do all kinds of things for him, make it easy for him to break into places. You know, figure out how to knock out alarm systems. Get into vaults. And—"

And I laughed. Right out loud. I couldn't help it. It was so crazy. Nobody had less imagination than Rafferty. He believed in what he could see, feel, touch, steal, pound, maim. And here he was . . .

"You believe all this stuff, Rafferty? No offense to Lori here, but this is all fantasy. Except for the killing part. I believe Bovita did that. But the rest—are you kidding me? Maybe I can't explain the birthmarks, but they sure weren't caused by any kind of 'magic.' There's a rational explanation for them. There has to be."

Lori frowned. "And I thought Rafferty was the dumb one. What other 'rational' explanation could there be?" She didn't sound scared any more. She sounded mad, and disgusted. "Why don't the two of you get out of here? I'm sick of both of you." She shook her head. "No wonder people call you 'pigs.'"

Rafferty looked stunned. You hold your Clint Eastwood on somebody, you expect a little respect, if not outright terror. "You see this, girlie? I'm in charge here. And I decide when I leave."

She flung her arms wide. Her breasts rose in a fetching way. "Then shoot me, Rafferty. Go ahead. C'mon, right now. Blow my brains out."

He glanced at me. "This bitch'z crazy, you know that?"

But he shoulder-holstered his weapon and walked sullenly over to the door like a chastised little boy. And I followed him out. I didn't know what else to do.

⬜

"What we've got here is a gold mine," Rafferty said when we were in the car later that night, patrolling the streets. Didn't matter he'd been pointing a gun at me earlier. We still had our jobs.

"What we've got here," I said, "are the delusions of three crazy people."

"Three? I thought there was just this Bovita broad and Lori in on it."

"And you. You've bought in as much as Lori has."

"Yeah? So what's your explanation for all those dead guys?"

"I don't know." I'd spent a little time on my daughters' computer earlier, trying to figure that out. "There are birthmarks that are common to people whose mothers had certain viruses when the kids were in the womb."

"So?"

"So maybe that's what we're dealing with here. Some weird kind of coincidence."

He snorted. "So you're saying you don't want in?"

"'In' what, Rafferty? There's nothing to be 'in' except voodoo bullshit. And that's all it is. Bullshit."

"These are your people, pal. I'd think you'd have a little more respect for them than this."

He was at it again. "'My' people? Because they're black? Believe it or not, Rafferty, I grew up in a nice, middle-class neighborhood. And unless they kept it hidden pretty well, nobody there was practicing any voodoo."

"Maybe in their basements," he said, "late at night. You know what I'm sayin'?"

Oh, I knew what he was saying, all right. I always knew what Rafferty was saying.

"You wait and see," he said. "That Bovita bitch is gonna help me get rich."

⬜

We didn't get much chance to argue it further. A couple days later, the state people and the *federales* showed up together at the station. Dark suits, men and women alike. Briefcases, men and women alike. Cell phones, men and women alike.

They went six deep in the command structure. The press had received advance warning. Chief O'Hallohan left in cuffs with his head so low I think he might have scraped his chin on the parking lot concrete. One of the *federales*—out here just this morning from DC—told us that it would be a while before they got around to the street cops. You didn't get any press for busting people like me. The Chief would get you headlines, and headlines would get you promotions.

A week later, Rafferty resigned by mail. He was three years short of his pension.

I actually tried to call him a couple of times but all I got was his machine. On one of my days off, I even drove out to his little suburban tract house. I think he was there but he didn't answer the door.

It was sort of funny. I hated him but I wanted to find out exactly why he'd quit so suddenly. Was he that scared of the investigation? Was he sick, maybe? Did he actually find somebody else who'd hire him?

I got a new partner. He was white but he didn't seem to have any particular problem with people of other races. He didn't seem to have any more affection for Rafferty than I did. In fact, he knew a lot of Rafferty bigot/sexist stories and told them well. Rafferty was a legend.

The months passed, and soon Rafferty wasn't much more than a bad memory.

Then one sunny spring day, a blood red Caddy convertible swept up alongside me as I parked my three-year-old Ford in the police lot.

"Bet my car can beat yours."

I almost didn't recognize him. The deep tan. The sun-bleached hair. The twenty-pound weight loss. The randy golden stubble on the sun-tanned cheeks. The expensive yellow sports shirt.

"How you doin', badge-boy?"

"Not as well as you," I told Rafferty, openly admiring his Caddy. "Those are some wheels."

"You think this'z something, you should see the new pad."

"You got pictures of it? You know, like baby pictures or anything?"

"Make jokes all you want. You ain't nothin' but jealous."

"You know what, Rafferty? You're right. I *am* just jealous." But what I was, mostly, was confused.

"I told you ol' Bovita would come through for me."

And then before I could say anything, he swept away, aiming his car at a buddy of his who was at the far end of the lot.

For the next few days and nights, I thought about calling Lori. Finding out if she knew what was really going on. But did I really *want* to know? Did I really want to get caught up in it—whatever "it" was? Did I maybe want my simple, rational view of the world to get turned upside down? I decided no. I'd rather have my little life than Rafferty's big one. Because big ones had a way of crashing down in very violent ways.

Rafferty died the next week. Hit-and-run. Leaving a trendy restaurant on the east side, he stepped off the curb and some unidentified citizen—probably with the same alcohol blood-level as Rafferty—ran him over in front of a half-dozen horrified revelers that Rafferty had been buying drinks for all evening.

The cops threw one of their funerals. All very formal. One of their own. I hope to have such a funeral myself someday. When I'm around 119 or so.

I went. I couldn't quite bring myself to think kind thoughts but I did hold off the worst sort of resentment and anger he'd always inspired in me. I figured the condition of his soul was up to God.

And I figured that whatever he'd been involved in, I was happy not to know. Ignorance is bliss, and all that.

Summer came. Camp for our girls. A three-day vacation at the lake for the wife and me. Softball games for our police team. Too many burgers and brews in our backyard. And then, as was its way, winter disguised as autumn was upon us, tearing away leaves and color and warm breezes. By mid-October, the temperature was already dipping into the twenties at night.

And then one early dusk—the twilight sky a winter rose, the dying sun seeming to go nova behind the skyscrapers—I stood in a dusting of snow and gaped at a dead man sprawled in the street.

Fleshy black middle-aged male. Good suit. Expensive shoes. And an even more expensive wristwatch.

But it was none of that that got my attention.

"You see that?" said my partner, shining his beam on the man's right cheek. Just under the eye. A jagged scar, just like a piece of lightning. "Just like Rafferty's. Ain't that weird?"

I called her the first chance I got. She'd moved, but it wasn't hard to track her down.

"I figured I'd hear from you sooner or later," Lori said.

"I saw Rafferty's scar last night, on a dead man."

"That wasn't just Rafferty's scar. That was Rafferty."

"The guy I saw was black. And besides, Rafferty's already dead."

"Rafferty's *body* is dead. But his soul isn't. I put it inside that guy last night. And made sure he got run down like a dog."

I thought about what she'd said, about putting Rafferty "inside" another man, and the rational part of me wanted to scoff. But then I thought about everything I'd seen, leading up to the latest dead man in the street, and I just said: "You killed an innocent man just to get back at Rafferty?"

She laughed. "I thought you didn't believe in all this."

"I don't. At least not completely." Truth was, I wasn't sure what I believed any more.

And so I just listened to what she told me. That the guy whose body Rafferty was in that night wasn't 'innocent.' That he couldn't be, because the gro-bon-ange–that's what she called the curse she used–had limitations. That a soul as dark as Rafferty's could only go into the body of someone who's just as evil, like a killer or a rapist. That she was going to keep putting Rafferty's soul in other bodies so that he'd keep dying over and over again. That every time, he'd have to go through the pain and the fear and the realization that he was dying. And that she was doing all this to Rafferty because he'd killed Bovita.

Not directly. But he'd kept pushing the old woman to help him steal more. He always wanted more. Every time took a lot out of Bovita. She kept getting weaker and weaker, but Rafferty wouldn't let up.

And the two of them couldn't do anything to Rafferty, since he'd tracked down Bovita's grand-daughter, beat her up; said if anything ever happened to him, he'd arranged for a acquaintance of his to kill the girl. Slowly.

But then he finally pushed Bovita too far. The old woman slipped into a coma. Two days later, she passed. That was it for Lori. She decided then and there that Rafferty had to suffer. Didn't matter what might happen to Bovita's grand-daughter. There was a toll to pay.

I stayed quiet for a long time after she finished her story. I still had some questions running through my mind, but I wasn't sure I wanted to hear the answers.

"I hope you appreciated the irony," she said.

"Irony?"

"Rafferty was such a bigot, I figured it'd serve him right to put him inside a black man. Pretty funny, when you think about it."

"Yeah," I said, just before I hung up, "pretty funny."

It's been a year now. I'm not sure when it's going to end. Or how many times Lori's killed Rafferty.

But I call my friend in the morgue to check out every hit-and-run in the city. So far, there've only been two with Rafferty's scar, both of them black. I suppose Lori doesn't want to draw too much attention to it. Maybe just wants to keep it as sort of an inside joke. Between her and me.

But I'm not calling her again to find out. She doesn't seem to be anybody I'd want to piss off. If you know what I'm saying.

That Day at Eagle's Point

The day was dark suddenly, even though it was only four in the afternoon, and lightning like silver spider's legs began to walk across the landscape of farm fields and county highways. It was summer, and kids would be playing near creeks and forests and old deserted barns, and their mothers would see the roiling sky and begin calling frantically for them, trying to be heard above the chill damp sudden wind.

The rains came, then, hard slanting Midwestern rains that made me feel snug inside my new Plymouth sedan, rain making noises on the hood and roof like the music of tin drums.

That was the funny thing, I told Marcie I was buying the Plymouth for her, and she even went down and picked out the model and the color all by herself, but even so, a couple of weeks later, she left. Got home one day and saw two suitcases sitting at the front door, and then came Marcie walking out of the bedroom, prettier than I'd seen her in years. "I'm going to do it, Earle," was all she said. And then there was a cab there, and he was honking, and then she was gone.

I didn't handle it so well at first. I just read and reread the letter she left, trying to divine things implied, or things written between the lines, sort of like those Dead Sea scholars spending their whole lives poring over only a few pages.

Her big hangup was Susan Finlay, and how I'd never really gotten over her, and how there was something sick about how I couldn't let go of that gal, and how she, Marcie, wanted somebody to really love her completely, the way I never could because of my lifelong "obsession" with Susan Finlay.

That was a year ago. She only called once, from a bar somewhere with a loud country-western jukebox, said she was drunk and missed me terribly but knew that for me there'd never be anybody but Susan, and she was sorry for both of us that I'd never been able to love her in the good and proper way she'd wanted.

Another thing she hadn't liked was my occupation. Over in Nam, I was with a medical unit, so when I got back to New Hope, the town where I was raised, I just naturally looked for work at the hospital. But the hospital per se wasn't hiring, so they put me in touch with the two fellows who ran the ambulance service. I became their night driver, four to midnight, six nights a week. The benefits were good, and I got to learn a lot about medicine. In the beginning, Marcie was proud of me, I think. At parties and family reunions, people always came up to me and wanted to know if I had any new ambulance stories. Old ladies seemed to have a particular fascination with the really grim ones. Marcie liked me being the one people sought out.

But then my novelty faded, and there I was just this Nam vet with the long hair and Mexican bandit mustache, and a little potbelly, and glasses as thick as Palomars, bad eyesight being a family curse. Forty-three years old, I was, time to get a real job, everybody said. But this was my real job, and it was likely to be my real job the rest of my life. . . .

I'd hoped to catch a good glimpse of the hills on the drive up this late afternoon. The hills were where David and Susan and I liked to play. This was Carstairs, the town I grew up in and lived in till the year before they shipped me off to New Hope. Dad got the lung disease, and Mom felt it was safer to live in New Hope where they had better hospital facilities.

But in my heart, Carstairs would always be my hometown, the town square with the bandstand and the pigeons sitting atop the Civil War monuments, and the old men playing checkers while the little kids splashed in the hot summer wading pool. If I tried hard enough, I could even smell the creosote on the railroad ties as Susan and David and I ran along the tracks looking for something to do.

The three of us grew up in the same apartment house, an old stucco thing with a gnarled and rusty TV antenna on the roof and a brown faded front lawn mined with dog turds. We were six years old the first time we ever played with each other.

We had identical lives. Our fathers were laborers, our mothers took whatever kinds of jobs they could find—dime store clerking, mostly—and we had too many brothers and too many sisters, and sometimes between the liquor and the poverty, our fathers would beat on our mothers for a time, and the "rich" kids at school—anybody who lived in an actual house was rich—the rich kids shunned us. Or shunned David and me, anyway. By the time Susan was ten, she started working her way through all the rich boys, breaking their hearts one at a time with that sad but fetching little face of hers.

But Susan had no interest in those boys, not really. Her only interest was in David and me. And David and I were interested only in Susan.

I was jealous of David. He had all the things I did not, looks, poise, mischievous charm, and curly black hair that Susan always seemed to find an excuse to touch.

I guess I started thinking about that when I was eleven or so. You always saw the older kids start pairing off about the time they reached fourteen. But who was going to pair off with Susan when we got to be fifteen—David or me? Sometimes she seemed to like David a little more than me; other times she seemed to like me a little more than David.

Then one day, when we were thirteen, I came late up to Eagle's Point, and when I got there, I saw them kissing. It looked kind of comic, actually, they didn't kiss the way movie stars did, they just kind of groped each other awkwardly. But it was enough to make me run over and tear him from her and push him back to the edge of the cliff. The fall would have killed him, and right then that was what I wanted to do, take his life. I pushed him out over the cliff, so he could get a good look at the asphalt below. All that kept him from falling was the grip I had on the sleeve of his shirt.

But then Susan was there, crying and screaming and pounding on me to pull him back before it was too late.

I'd never seen her that upset. She looked crazed. I pulled him back.

I didn't speak to either of them for a few months. I mostly stayed home and read science fiction novels. I'd discovered Ray Bradbury that spring.

School started again, and David could be seen in the halls with this cute new girl. I started hanging around Susan again. If she was sad about David, she never let on. She even asked me to go to the movies with her a couple of times. David kept hanging around the cute new girl.

In October, the jack-o'-lanterns on the porches already, I went to Susan's house one day. I kind of wanted to surprise her, have her go over town with me. Nobody answered my knock. Both the truck and the car her folks drove were gone. I tried the kitchen door. It was open. I figured I'd go in and call out her name. She slept in some Saturday mornings.

That's when I heard the noise. I guess I knew what it was, I mean it's pretty unmistakable, but I didn't want to admit it to myself.

I didn't want to sneak up the stairs, but I knew I had to. I had to know for absolutely sure.

And that's what happened. I found out. For absolutely sure.

They were making love. I tried not to think of it as "fucking" because I didn't want to think of Susan that way. I loved her too much.

"Oh, David, I love you so much," Susan said.

Susan's bedroom was very near the top of the stairs. Their words and gasps echoed down the stairs to me and stayed in my ears all the time I ran across the road and into the woods. No matter how fast I ran, their voices stayed with me. I smelled creek water and deep damp forest shadow and the sweetness of pine cone. And then I came to a clearing, the sunlight suddenly blinding me, to the edge of Eagle's Point. I watched the big hawks wheel down the sky. I wanted them to carry me away to the world Edgar Rice Burroughs described in his books, where beautiful princesses and fabled cities and fabulous caches of gold awaited me, and people like me were never brokenhearted.

What I'd always suspected, and had always feared, was true: she loved David, not me.

I stayed till dark, smoking one Pall Mall after another, feeling the chill of the dying day seep into my bones, and watching the birds sail down the tumbling vermilion clouds and the silver slice of moon just now coming clear.

In the coming days, I avoided them, and of course they were full of questions and hurt looks when I said I didn't have time for them anymore.

Dad died the autumn I was sixteen, the concrete truck he was driving sliding off the road because of a flash flood and plunging a few hundred feet straight down into a ravine. Mom had to worry about the two younger ones, which meant getting a job as a checkout lady at Slocum's Market and leaving me to worry about myself. I didn't mind. Mom was only forty-six but looked sixty. Hers had not been an easy life, and she looked so worn and faded these days that I just kept hugging her so she wouldn't collapse on the floor.

I saw Susan and David at school, of course, but they'd months ago given up trying to woo me back. Besides, a strange thing had happened. Even though they lived on the wrong side of town and had the wrong sort of parents, the wealthy kids in the class had sort of adopted them. I suppose they saw in Susan and David the sort of potential they'd soon enough realize, first at the state university, where they both graduated with honors, and then at law school, where honors were theirs once again.

I stayed around the house after college, working the part-time jobs I could get, hoping to work full-time eventually at the General Mills plant eighteen miles to the north. I dropped by the personnel department there a couple of times a month, just so they'd know how enthusiastic I was about working for them.

But by the time they were ready to hire me, Uncle Sam was downright insistent about having me. So they gave me an M-16 and a whole bunch of information about how to save your ass in case of emergency and then shipped me off with a few hundred other reluctant warriors and set us down in a place called Dan Tieng, from where we would be dispatched to our bunkers.

I've always wished I had some good war stories for the beer nights at the VFW and the Legion. But the truth is, I never did see anybody around me get killed, though I saw more than a few men being loaded into field hospitals and choppers; and so far as I know, I never killed anybody, either, though there was a guy from Kentucky I thought about fragging sometimes. I did not become an alcoholic, my respiratory system was not tainted by Agent Orange, I was not angry with those who elected not to go (I would not have gone, either, if I'd known how easy it was to slip through the net), and I never had any psychotic episodes, not even when I was drinking the Everclear that sometimes got passed around camp.

While I was there, Susan wrote me three times, each time telling me how heroic she thought I was, and how she and David both missed the old days when we'd all been good friends, and how she was recovering from a broken arm she got from falling down on the tennis court. Tennis, she said, had become a big thing in their lives. They'd both been accepted by a very prestigious old-line law firm and were both given privileges at the city's finest country club.

I wrote her back near the end of my tour in Nam, telling her that I'd decided to try golden California, the way so many Midwestern rubes do, and that I was planning on becoming a matinee idol and the husband of a rich and beautiful actress, ha ha. Her response, which I got a day before I left Nam, was that they were going to Jamaica for their vacation this year, where it would be nothing but "swimming swimming swimming." She also noted that they'd gotten married in a "teeny-tiny" civil ceremony a few weeks earlier. And that she'd been married in a "white dress and a black eye—clumsy me, I tripped against a door frame."

Well, I went to California, Long Beach, Laguna, San Pedro, Sherman Oaks . . . in three years, I lived five different places and held just about double that number of jobs. I tried real estate, stereo sales, management trainee at a 7-Eleven, and limo driver at a funeral home, the latter lasting only three weeks. I'd had to help bury a four-year-old girl dead of brain cancer. I didn't have it in me ever to do that again.

By the time I got back to New Hope, Mom was in a nursing home equidistant between New Hope and Carstairs. I saw her three times a week. Back then, they weren't so certain about their Alzheimer's diagnoses. But that's what she had. Some days she knew me, some not. I only broke down once, pulling her to me and letting myself cry. But she had no idea of our history, no idea of our bond, so it was like holding a stranger from the street, all stiff and formal and empty.

I met and married Marcie, I got my job at the ambulance company, I joined the VFW and the Legion, I became an auxiliary deputy because my Uncle Clement was the assistant county sheriff and he told me it was a good thing to do, and I made the mistake of running into a cousin of Susan's one day and getting Susan's address from her.

The funny thing is, I was never unfaithful to Marcie, not physically anyway. I had a few chances, too, but even though I knew I didn't love my wife, I felt that I owed her my honor. Bad enough that she had to hold me knowing that I wanted to be holding Susan; I didn't have to humiliate her publicly as well.

I never did write Susan, but I did call her. And then she called me a couple of times. And over the next six, seven years, we must have talked a couple of dozen times. Marcie didn't know, and neither did David. She told me about her life, and I told her how crazy she was and where it would all lead, but she didn't listen. She loved David too much to be reasonable. I made all kinds of proposals, of course, how I'd just sit down with Marcie and tell her the truth, that Susan and I were finally going to get together, and how I'd give Marcie the house and the newer of the cars and every cent in the savings account. One time, Susan laughed gently, as if she was embarrassed for me, and said, "Earle, you don't understand how successful a trial lawyer David is. He makes more in a month than you do in a year." Then her laugh got bitter. "You couldn't afford me, sweetheart. You really couldn't."

There were a few more conversations. She saw a shrink, she saw a priest, she saw this real good friend of hers who'd gone through the same thing. She was going to leave, she had the strength and courage and determination to leave now, or so she claimed, but she never did leave. She never did.

The prison was a WPA project back in the Depression. Stone was carried from a nearby quarry for the walls. The prison sits on a hill, as if it is being shown to local boys and girls as a warning.

You pass through three different electronically controlled gates before you come to the visitors' parking lot.

You pass the manufacturing building where the cool blue of welding torches can be seen, and the prison laundry where harsh detergent can be smelled, and the cafeteria that is noisy with preparations for the night's meal. I walked quickly past all these areas. The rain was still coming down hard.

You pass through two more electronic gates before you reach the administrative offices.

The inmates all knew who I was. I wouldn't say that there was hostility in their eyes when they saw me, but there was a kind of hard curiosity, as if I were a riddle to be solved.

The warden's office had been designed to look like any other office. But it didn't quite make it. The metal office furniture was not only out of date, it was a little bit grim in its gray way. And the receptionist was a sure disappointment for males visiting the warden: he was a bald older guy with his prison-blue shirtsleeves rolled up to reveal several faded and vaguely obscene tattoos. He knew who I was.

"The warden's on the phone."

"I'll just sit here."

He nodded and went back to his typing on a word processor. He worked with two fingers, and he worked fast.

I looked through a law enforcement magazine while I sat there.

The receptionist said, "You do anything special to get ready?"

I shrugged. "Not really."

He went back to typing. I went back to reading. After a time, he said, "It ever bother you?"

I sighed. "I suppose. Sometimes." I got into this five years ago when the state passed the capital punishment bill. MDs couldn't execute a man because of the Hippocratic oath. The state advertised for medical personnel. You had to take a lot of tests. I wondered if I could actually go through with it. The first couple times were rough. I just keep thinking of what the men had done. Most of them were animals. That helped a lot.

"It'd bother me." He went back to his typing again.

Then: "I mean, if you want my honest opinion, I think it'd bother most people."

I didn't respond, just watched him a moment, then went back to my magazine.

George Stabenow is a decent man always in a hurry. Pure unadulterated Type A.

He burst through his office door and said, "C'mon in. I'm running so late I can't believe it."

He was short, stout, and swathed in a brown three-piece suit. This was probably the kind of suit the press expected a proper warden to wear on a day like this.

He pointed to a chair, and I sat down.

"The frigging doctor had some sort of emergency," Stabenow said. "Can you believe it?"

"You getting another doctor?"

"No, no. But he won't be here for the run-through, which pisses me off. I mean, the run-through's critical for all of us." I nodded. He was right.

He walked over to his window and looked out on the grounds surrounding the prison.

"You see them on your way in?"

"Uh-huh."

"More than usual."

"Uh-huh."

"Maybe a hundred of them. If it's not this, it's some other goddamned thing. The environment or something."

"Uh-huh."

"That priest—that monsignor—you should've heard him this afternoon." He grinned. "He was wailing and flailing like some goddamned TV minister. Man, what a jackoff that guy is."

He came back to his desk. To his right was one of those plastic cubes you put photos of your family in. He had a nice-looking wife and a nice-looking daughter. "You eat?"

"I had a sandwich before I left New Hope," I said.

"I'm going to grab something in the cafeteria."

I smiled. "The food's not as bad as the inmates say, huh?"

"Bad? Shit, it's a hell of a lot better than you and I ever got in the goddamned Army, I'll tell you that." He shook his head in disgust. "Food's the easiest target of all for these jerkoffs—to get the public upset about, I mean. The public sees all these bullshit prison movies and think, they're for real. You know, cockroaches and everything crawling around in the chili? Hell, the state inspector checks out our kitchens and our food just the way he does all the other institutions. Even if we wanted cockroaches in the chili—" He smiled. "They wouldn't let us."

I said, "I need a badge."

"Oh, right."

He dug in his drawer and found me one and pushed it across his desk. I pinned it to my chambray shirt. The badge was "Highest Priority." All members of the team wear them.

"The rest of them here?"

"The team, you mean?"

"Uh-huh," I said.

"Everybody except the goddamned doc."

Before he could work up a lather again, I said, "Why don't I just walk over there, then, and say hi?"

"You've got twenty minutes yet. You sure you don't want a cup of coffee at least?"

"No, thanks."

He looked at me. "You know, I was kind of surprised that he requested you."

"Yeah."

"You sure you'll be all right?"

"I'll be all right."

"Some of the team, well, they had some doubts, too, said maybe it wasn't right. You knowing him and everything."

"I know. A couple of them called me."

"But I said, 'Hell, it's his decision. If he thinks he can handle it, let him.' Anyway, this is what the inmate wanted."

"I appreciate that."

"You're a pro, and pros do what they have to."

"Right."

He smiled. "I'm just glad Glen Wright has to handle the media. If it was up to me, I'd just tell them to go to hell."

He was going to upset himself again, and I wanted to get out of there before it happened. I stood up.

"You fellas used to carry little black bags," he said.

"Yeah."

"Just like doctors. Guess you don't need them anymore, huh? Now we provide everything."

"Right."

We shook hands, and I left.

There are six members on the team.

Five of us stood in the chamber and went through it all. You wouldn't think there'd be much to rehearse, but there is.

One of the men makes certain that the room is set up properly. We want to make sure that the curtains work, that's the first thing. When the press and the visitors come into the room outside the chamber, the curtains are drawn. Only when we're about to begin for real are the curtains drawn back.

Then the needles have to be checked. Sometimes you get a piston that doesn't work right, and that can play hell for everybody. They get three injections—the first to totally relax them, the second to paralyze them so they won't squirm around, and the third to kill them. In my training courses, I learned that only two things matter in this kind of work: to kill brain and heart function almost immediately. This way, the inmate doesn't suffer, and the witnesses don't get upset by how inhumane it might look otherwise.

After the needles are checked, the gurney is fixed into place. If it isn't anchored properly, a struggling guy might tear it free and make things even worse for himself.

Then we check the IV line and the EKG the doctor will use to determine heart death. Then we check the blade the doctor will use for the IV cutdown. We expose the inmate's vein so there's no chance of missing with the needle. That happened in Oregon. Took the man with the needle more than twenty minutes to find a vein. That wasn't pleasant for anybody.

Then I went through my little spiel to the man about to be executed. I'm always very polite. I tell him what he can expect and how it won't hurt in any way, especially if he cooperates. He generally has a few questions, and I always try to answer them.

During all this, everybody else is rechecking the equipment, and Assistant Warden Wright is out there patiently taking questions from the press. The press is always looking for some way to discredit what we do. That's not paranoia, that's simple fact.

We didn't time the first run-through, which was kind of ragged. But the second run-through, Wright used his stopwatch.

We came in a little longer than we should have.

In the courses I took, the professor suggested that fifty-one minutes is the desired time for most executions by lethal injection. This is from walking into the chamber to the prisoner being declared legally dead by the presiding doctor.

We came in at fifty-nine minutes, and Wright, properly, said that we needed to pick things up a little. The longer you're in the chamber, he said, the more likely you are to make mistakes. And the more mistakes you make, the more the press gets on your back. Speed and efficiency were everything, Wright said. That's what my instructors always said, too.

Finally, I checked out my own needles, went through the motions of injecting fluids. My timing was off till the third run-through. I picked up the pace then, and everything went pretty well. We hit fifty-three minutes. We needed to shave two more minutes. We'd take a break and then come back for one more run-through.

When we wrapped up, Wright said we could all have coffee and rolls if we wanted. There was a small room off the chamber that was used only by prison personnel. The rest of the team went there. I walked down the hall to another electronic gate and told him that I was the man the warden called him about. Even though visiting hours were over, I was to be admitted to see the prisoner.

The guard opened the gate for me, then another guard led me down the hall, stopping at a door at the far shadowy end. He opened the door, and I went inside.

⬜

The man was an impostor.

David Sawyer had gotten somebody to stand in for him at the execution. Last time I'd seen him was at the trial, years ago.

The sleek and handsome David Sawyer I remembered, the one with all the black curly hair that Susan had loved to run her fingers through, was gone. Had probably fled the country.

In his place was a balding, somewhat stoop-shouldered man with thick eyeglasses and a badly twitching left hand. He was dressed in gray prisoner clothing that only made his skin seem paler.

I must have struck him the same way, as an impostor, because at first he didn't seem to recognize me at all.

On the drive up, I tried to figure out how long it had been since I'd seen David Sawyer. Eighteen years, near as I could figure.

"Son of a bitch," he said. "You changed your mind. The warden didn't tell me that."

I guess what I'd expected was a frightened, depressed man eager to receive his first sedative so he wouldn't be aware of the next three hours. You saw guys like that.

But the old merry David was in the stride, in the quick embrace, in the standing-back and taking a look-at-you.

"You're a goddamned porker," he said. "How much weight have you put on?"

"Forty pounds," I said. "Or thereabouts."

He sensed that he might have hurt my feelings, so he slid right into his own shortcomings.

"Now you're supposed to say, 'What happened to your hair, asshole? And how come you're wearing trifocals? And how come you're all bent over like an old man?' C'mon, give me some shit. I can take it."

For a brief time there, he had me believing that his incongruous mood was for real. But as soon as he stopped talking, the fear was in his eyes. He glanced up at the wall clock three times in less than a minute.

And when he spoke, his voice was suddenly much quieter. "You pissed that I asked for you to do this?"

"More surprised than anything, David."

"You want some coffee? There's some over there."

"I'd appreciate that."

"You go sit down. I'll bring it over to you." Then the eyes went dreamy and faraway. "I was always like that at the parties we gave, Susan and I, I mean, and believe me, we gave some pissers. One night, we found the governor of this very state balling this stewardess in our walk-in closet. And I was always schlepping drinks back and forth, trying to make sure everybody was happy. I guess that's one problem with growing up the way we did—you never feel real secure about yourself. You always overdo the social bullshit so they'll like you more."

"You were pretty important. Full partner."

"That's what it said on the door," said the bald and stooped impostor. "But that's not what it said in here." He thumped his chest and looked almost intolerably sad for a moment, then went and got our coffee.

The first cup of coffee we spent catching up. I told him about Nam, and he told me about state capital politics and how one got ahead as a big-fee lawyer. Then we talked about New Hope, and I caught him up on some of the lives that interested him there.

We didn't get around to Susan for at least twenty minutes, and when we did, he jumped up and said, "I'll get us refills. But keep talking. I can hear you."

I'd just mentioned her name, and he was on his feet, going the opposite direction.

I suppose I didn't blame him. The courts had made him face what he'd done, now I was going to make him face it all over again.

"Did you know she used to write me sometimes?"

"You're kidding? When we were married?"

"Uh-huh."

He brought the coffee over, set down our cups. "You two weren't—"

I shook my head. "Strictly platonic. The way it'd always been with us. From her point of view, anyway. She was crazy about you, and she never got over it."

We didn't say anything for a time, just sat there with our respective memories, faded images without words, like a silent screen flickering with moments of our days.

"I always knew you never got over her," he said.

"No, I never did. That's why my wife left." I explained about that a little bit.

Then I said, "But I was pretty stupid. I didn't catch on for a long time."

"Catch on to what?" he said, peering at me from the glasses that made his eyes flit about like blue goldfish.

"All the 'accidents' she had. I didn't realize for a long time that it was you beating her up."

He sighed, stared off. "You can believe this or not," he said, "but I actually tried to get her to leave. Because I knew I couldn't stop myself."

"She loved you."

He put his head down. "The things I did to her—" He shook his head, then looked up. "You remember that day back on Eagle's Point when you almost pushed me off?"

"Yeah."

"You should've pushed me. You really should've. Then none of this would've happened." He put his head down again.

"You ever get help for your problem?" I said.

"No. Guess I was afraid it would leak out if I did. You know, some of those fucking shrinks tell their friends everything."

"I blame you for that, David."

His head was still down. He nodded. Then he looked up: "I had a lot of chicks on the side."

"That's what the DA said at the trial."

"She had a couple of men, too. I mean, don't sit there and think she was this saint."

"She wasn't a saint, David. She never claimed to be. And she probably wouldn't have slept with other men if you hadn't run around on her—and hadn't kept beating the shit out of her a couple of times a month."

He looked angry. "It was never that often," he said.

"Still."

"Yeah. Still." He got up and walked over to the window and looked out on the yard. The rain had brought a chill and early night. He said, "I've read where this doesn't always go so smooth."

"It'll go smooth tonight, David."

He stared out the window some more. He said, "You believe in any kind of afterlife?"

"I try to; I want to."

"That doesn't sound real convincing."

"It's not the kind of thing you can be real sure about, David."

"What if you had to bet, percentage-wise, I mean?"

"Sixty-forty, I guess."

"That there *is* an afterlife?"

"Yeah. That there is an afterlife."

Thunder rumbled. Rain hissed.

He turned around and looked at me. "I loved her."

"You killed her, David."

"She could have walked out that door any time she wanted to."

I just stared at him a long time then and said, "She loved you, David. She always believed you'd stop beating her someday. She thought you'd change."

He started sobbing then.

You see that sometimes.

No warning, I mean. The guy just breaks.

He just stood there, this bald squinty impostor, and cried.

I went over and took his coffee cup from him so it wouldn't smash on the floor, and then I slid my arm around his shoulder and led him over to the chair.

I had to get back. The team had one more run-through scheduled before the actual execution.

I got him in the chair, and he looked up and me and said, "I'm scared, man. I'm so scared, I don't even have the strength to walk." He cried some more and put his hand out.

I didn't want to touch his hand because that would feel as if I were betraying Susan.

But he was crying pretty bad, and I thought Susan, being Susan, would have taken his hand at such a moment. Susan forgave people for things I never could.

I took his hand for maybe thirty seconds, and that seemed to calm him down a little.

He looked at me, his face tear-streaked, his eyes sad and scared at the same time, and he said, "You really should've pushed me off that day at Eagle's Point."

"I've got to get back now," I said.

"If you'd pushed me off, none of this would've happened, Earle."

I walked over to the door.

"I loved her," he said. "I want you to know that. I loved her."

I nodded and then left the room and walked down the hall and went back out into the night and the rain.

The next run-through went perfectly. We hit the fifty-one-minute mark right on the button. Just the way the textbook says we should.

Such a Good Girl

NICOLE

Nicole Sanders went to the nurse's office during third hour and put on a pretty good imitation of a genteel seventeen-year-old girl down with the flu, genteel meaning a quiet, pretty girl who was still a virgin, had never tried drugs in any form, and read *Cousin Bette* for relaxation.

Of course, it helped that she was a good student (usually, a four point average), and generally perceived as a reliable girl. Nobody on the staff of Woodrow Wilson High School would suspect her of faking flu so she could get off from school. She had a near-perfect attendance record. She just wasn't the kind to lie.

But lie she did.

In the parking lot, she climbed into the sensible little forest green Toyota Gran had bought her for her seventeenth birthday last month. Gran was her best family friend now. Dad was off in California with his new wife. And Mom . . .

"I sure hate to see you come down with this stuff," the nurse said sweetly.

She headed home. This late in the morning, the expressway traffic was heavy. The sometimes foggy March rain didn't help, either.

Home was a nice Tudor in a small, upscale suburb of nice Tudors and nice Spanish styles and nice multi-level moderns. Mom had gotten the house in the divorce settlement. Dad made a lot of money at his law firm and he'd inherited quite a bit when his father died several years earlier.

Nicole didn't stop at her house. She went down to the end of the block and parked behind a stand of pin oaks that was part of a small park-like area.

The cop-show phrase for what she was doing was "stakeout." She'd heard her mother call in sick this morning—she was a far better actress than Nicole and had put on a breathtaking performance—and now Nicole wanted to see what her mother did all day. As she'd passed by the house, she'd seen her mother's car in the drive. So Mom hadn't gone anywhere. Yet. And if Mom did go somewhere, Nicole had a terrible feeling that she knew where it would be. . . .

MITCH

"I really think Mamet sold out. You know, when he went out to La-La-Land."

It was a good thing she had a lovely pair of breasts because otherwise Mitchell Carey would have kicked her ass out of the apartment as soon as he got done screwing her last night.

He'd picked her up at a cast party. A small theater group had put on an ancient Mamet one-act. It was the sort of theater group that attracted the worst kind of pretentious wannabes and the worst kind of cruising idle rich, the rich seeing theater groups (correctly) as being ripe with sex, drugs and just about any kind of octopus-like emotional entanglement a man or woman could want. It was from the idle rich, a few of whom were Mitch's customers, that he'd heard about the play; so, having made the club scene earlier in the evening, having played his role as the handsome, fortyish Jay Gatsby to the disco and angel dust crowd, he decided to pop in on the theater folk. He'd stayed only long enough to meet Paula and woo her back to his den, whereupon he'd defiled her with great desperate pleasure. He hadn't merely screwed her, he'd ravished her and it had been wonderful. Three times they'd made love before heating up the remnants of a Domino's pizza lurking in his refrigerator. Then they'd found a great old Lawrence Tierney B-movie flick on a cable channel, *San Quentin*, and only after it was over and they were back in bed again with the lights out, only then did she start talking about herself (age 39, born in Trenton, New Jersey, three husbands, worked as a street mime and part of a comedy group a la Second City, had in fact come here to Chicago to get into Second City but so far no luck, look at Jim Belushi, she said, only reason a no-talent like him ever got in was because of his brother and everybody knew it) but by then he'd put a finger in his ear and switched the HEARING button to OFF. By the time she got to voicing her plans to audition for the revival of *Cat on a Hot Tin Roof* at the Ivanhoe ("I lose a little weight, and wear violet contact lenses like Liz Taylor, and learn how to talk Southern, I think I'd make a great Maggie the Cat, don't you?") he was blissfully asleep.

But now it was morning and she was standing naked at the sink in the bathroom while he was toweling off from his shower. And she was talking about how Mamet had sold out. Like Mamet would really give a shit about her opinion.

Then he noticed the time on the face of his Rolex that he'd set down on the tiny hutch next to the towel closet. He bought the best, man. Noticed the time and remembered his appointment. He had a customer he needed to meet at eleven-thirty. And it was now a quarter to eleven.

"I've got to hurry," he said. "I just remembered an appointment."

She was putting on her lipstick. She had remarkable lips. "I hope we're going to do this again," she said, still drawing the blood tube across her mouth.

"Absolutely."

She glanced at him skeptically in the mirror. "For real?"

"For real."

"I hate bullshit promises. I'd rather have you say you won't be calling again than, you know, stringing me along."

"I'm not stringing you along."

"We did this Cole Porter show in Denver, you know? And anyway there was this guy and that's all he ever did. We spent one night humping like bunnies and the rest of the run, he'd call me to make a date and then call me back to break it. I guess I should be happy he at least called to tell me he was standing me up."

"You've sure had an interesting life."

She glanced at him in the mirror again to make sure that he wasn't putting her on. "Really?"

"Really."

She seemed satisfied. "You know, I wouldn't mind blowing you before we trundle off."

"That's all right. I really am late."

He could never figure out why he felt so good at night with them in the bed and so bad—and so sad—with them in the morning when they were getting ready to go.

What he needed was some kind of new kick. Ennui was the word he wanted. Ennui was what he was suffering from. He made a nice living, he got all the ass a reasonable man could want, and yet he was a little bored. Something new was what he needed.

But there wasn't any time for navel-contemplation this morning.

Had to hurry. He had an eleven-forty-five customer.

KATE

Thank God she'd been smart enough to take her watch along yesterday. Over noon, she'd hocked it. Place not far from the office where she worked in Lincoln Park. Guy with a glass eye and bad b.o. appraising both the watch and Kate herself. The watch he didn't have any problem with. Knew the exact market value. What he could pay out, what he could take in. The exact market value of the woman standing in front of him was another matter. Tall, elegant, beautiful in a nervous, vulnerable way. But going fast. Probably no more than forty-three, forty-four or so but going fast. He seemed to know why, too. Four-hundred, she got. Four-hundred.

Their house is shrinking. That's how she thinks of it. The last time after coming out of rehab and being a good little girl, the last time she fell off she hocked the TV, the stereo, the good china and the good silver. She'd had a good run. This was in the summer, Nicole visiting her father and his teenage-bride (Gwen is twenty-three, actually) for a month. Kate started hitting the clubs again, feeling good and young again. Sleeping around a little (always safe sex, of course), even developing a quick crush or two on younger men, the kind who used to be all over her, even when she was married, giving her ultra-conservative ex-husband one more reason to treat her like a whore. She could still remember the night that she'd told him about this little habit she had, which was where a lot of her household budget was going, and how he looked so dashed and doomed. It was almost comic, the way he looked right then, so shattered but self-righteous, too, as if it was impossible that anybody he'd even associate with could possibly be a junkie. A beautiful girl, the daughter of a powerful state senator, a Radcliffe grad, a suburban siren of stunning seductiveness, a coke head? There ensued years—she had to give him that, he hung in there for years—of one rehab program after another, trendy clinics and experimental programs all over the country. She'd gone as long as a year-and-a-half clean and sober, as they say. So much hope, so much anger, so much fear, so much despair, so much failure, hope-anger-fear-despair-failure, the same cycle over and over again. He never quite believed that she couldn't help herself. At least that was how she saw it. He never quite believed that she truly tried to kick once and for all. Poor sweet Nicole, she believed. That's why she was losing weight all the time and going into these terrible depressions (she'd been twelve when she took her first Prozac) and staying in her room practically every weekend when her mother was using. She could have joined her father in LA with his new bride but she feared for her mother, feared that if she went to California, her mother would die somehow. So she stayed. "You're such a good girl," her mother was always saying. Kate looked pretty good. The bones were the secret. She had good bones. Killer cheeks and a mouth that was erotic and just a wee bit petulant. Not enough to put men off. Just enough to intrigue. And the bod, even twelve pounds lighter than it should have been, the bod was good, too.

Four-hundred dollars in her purse and a day free of Mr. Cosgrove, her boss at the public relations agency, an egomaniacal twit who was always broadly hinting that she should go with him on one of his business trips east.

And on top of that, she would soon be seeing her old buddy Mitch Carrey.

Life was beautiful. Life was good.

NICOLE

In the daylight hours, the jazz clubs and the art galleries and the odd little shops of Lincoln Park lost some of their nocturnal allure. A wild wailing sax sounded better carried on the wings of neon than on the gritty breezes of daytime. And crumbling brick facades had no romance to offer even the dullest of tourists.

Nicole followed her mother to a restaurant called The Left Banke, the intentional misspelling too clever by half. Good student Nicole knew that the original Left Bank in Paris, home to the cubists and the impressionists, not to mention Ernest Hemingway and Gertrude Stein, had probably been pretentious but at least had spared its tourists coy restaurant names.

Mom was driving the four-year-old Buick. The last time she'd gone off, she'd been forced to sell the Mercedes-Benz station wagon to make house payments. Nicole never told her father any of these things. She got tired of his sanctimony. Her mother suffered enough. At the meetings Nicole attended a few years ago, she learned that she was probably what the social workers called an enabler; i.e., she helped her mother keep up her habit. But what was the choice? What would happen to her mother if Nicole didn't help her? Easy enough for them to say let your mother hit bottom and find her own way back up. But what if the bottom was death? How could Nicole live with herself? She had tried everything to get her mother to stop. A year ago, she'd even cut her own wrists and been rushed to the hospital and put in the psychiatric clinic for three days of observation. Now, she was working on her own last, desperate plan, a way to force her mother to turn herself back into rehab and this time—Oh please God, please God, let it work for her this time—start on a life without cocaine. But first she had to find one thing out. . . .

Her mother didn't get out of the Buick.

Just sat inside as the light rain started.

Slick new cars disgorged slick new people running in their Armani suits through the rain, laughing and swearing as they reached the canopied entrance.

And her mother just sat inside the Buick.

He drove an old red MG, the steering column on the right side. He wore a tweed jacket in honor of the MG. He even had a pipe stuck jauntily in the corner of his mouth. He looked like a soap opera's impression of a sensitive British novelist: dark, shaggy hair, and an angular face handsome but with a hint of cruelty in the eyes and mouth. He parked next to her mother and then quickly got out of the MG and hopped into the driver's side of the Buick.

KATE

"You look tired, Mrs. Sanders," Mitch said when he got in the Buick and looked over at her.

"I have a pusher who calls me 'Mrs. Sanders,'" Kate said, a touch of desperation in your voice. "Is my life fucked up or what?"

"You know," Mitch said, "this makes the third time I've had to warn you. And right now, with the rain and all, I'm in a pissy enough mood to just open this door and walk back to my car and not sell you anything at all."

"Oh, God," Kate said, genuinely scared. "I forgot. I used the P word, didn't I?"

"Yes, you did."

And he had indeed warned her before. About the P word. P for Pusher. He'd explained his circumstances. What he was: Mitchell Aaron Carey. What he hoped to be, with his looks and all, was an actor. And he'd tried hard for several years, too. All the humiliating auditions. All the even more humiliating little jobs around the various theaters (he'd actually scrubbed toilets at the Astor one weekend). Now he was just taking it easy. Doing "favors" for upscale people afraid of or put off by the usual array of street people who dealt drugs. How many pushers could give you twenty minutes on Aristotle's theory of drama? How many pushers had ever had a two-line part in a Woody Allen picture? How many pushers had Chagall prints hanging on their walls? He was no pusher. He was just an actor temporarily between gigs making a little jack on the side, and being very, very civilized about it.

"God, I'm sorry. I really am."

He smiled. "I guess I really don't feel like going back out into the rain right now."

"I brought the money."

"You're kind've strung out, huh?"

"Yeah. Yeah."

He was torturing her a little for having called him a pusher. "You thinking of maybe doing a line right here?"

"You wouldn't mind?"

He smiled again. "You're a good looking woman, Kate."

"Thank you." But it wasn't compliments she wanted. It was the stuff.

"In fact, I've been thinking about you a lot lately."

"You have?"

"Yeah," he said, and reached in the pocket of his stylish leather car coat. He took the stuff out and showed it to her. "Yeah. I've been thinking about you quite a bit lately."

NICOLE

She followed him home. Watched him park. Watched him go up to his apartment. Then went into the vestibule and checked his name on the mailbox. The only male name on the four mailboxes.

She didn't feel quite ready for it yet. Tomorrow. She'd sleep on it. Sleep on it and think it through and kind of rough out how she'd approach him. Tomorrow was Saturday. No school. Tomorrow would be better.

When she walked in the house, her mother was dusting the living room and actually humming a song.

Nicole got tears in her eyes. This was her mother of long ago, before she'd discovered cocaine at a Los Angeles party. She'd been there with her husband, visiting his relatives, and they'd ended up at a party in Malibu and she'd been drunk and up for just about anything—the party showing her just how much of her youth and adventurousness she'd had to give up as the wife of a neurosurgeon and so unbeknownst to Ken she'd tried it—and now she was happy only when she was stoned.

Dusting. And whistling. With the wonderful scent of a pot roast floating out of the kitchen.

She was Mom again. Nicole couldn't help herself. She flew to her and took her in her arms and suddenly they were both crying without a single word having been said, just holding each other. And then Mom said, "You're such a good girl, Nicole. And I love you so much."

Nicole didn't sleep well. She kept waking up and thinking about what she was going to say to Mitch Carey.

Her plan was simple. She would tell him that if he continued to sell her mother cocaine, she would turn him over to the police. She believed—hoped, was the more precise word—that if her mother was cut off from Mitch's supply, then she'd panic and turn herself back to rehab. And this time it would work. This time it had to work. Absolutely had to.

Carey would be pissed but what could he do? He certainly didn't want to go to jail.

Mom made pancakes for breakfast. Blueberry pancakes. The kind she'd made back when Nicole was a little girl, and Mom and Dad were happy.

"I guess I'll go study at the library," she said, after finishing breakfast and putting the dishes in the dishwasher.

"I'm going to do some more cleaning," Mom said. Then grinned. "It's kind of fun being a Stepford wife again. Now all I need is a Stepford husband."

Ninety-three minutes later, Nicole pulled her car into a slot behind Carey's apartment house. The interior stairs of the place smelled of rubber and paint. A new runner had been put on the steps and new paint on the walls. Whoever managed this place, they took care of it.

Carey answered the door out of breath and with a white nubby towel wrapped around his neck. He wore a tight white T-shirt and blue running shorts. A Stairmaster stood in the background. Classical music played. Carey had a strong, tight body.

"Yes?"

"I'm Nicole. Kate Sanders's daughter."

He looked surprised. "Is everything all right? Nothing happened to Kate did it?"

"No," Nicole said. "It's just that I'm thinking of turning you over to the police."

This time, he looked even more surprised. He grabbed her by the wrist and pulled her inside. "Hey, we don't have to invite the neighbors in on this, do we?" His nod indicated the three other apartment doors on this floor.

The apartment was impressive in a cold and calculated way. The furnishings were chrome and black leather, with a white and black tile floor and walls painted a brilliant flat white. The only touches of color belonged to the modernistic paintings on the walls. Nicole knew even less about painting than she did about classical music. This was the kind of room that intimidated her with her own ignorance.

Carey had quickly regained his composure. The panic and anger were gone from his eyes. He said, "Care for some wine?"

"No, thanks."

She had let two boys get their hands down her pants and play with her sex. At a ninth grade slumber party she had taken three drags on a joint. And she had looked at a couple of porno videos her Mom and Dad used to play when they thought she was upstairs asleep. This was the extent of her licentiousness. Drinking wine at this time of day was out of the question. Or any time of day. Wine always made her dizzy, and usually made her sick.

"Why don't you sit down over there on the couch and let me shut the machine off?"

He clipped off the Stairmaster and then wiped his face and neck again with the towel. He took the matching chair across from the couch. He sat on the edge. He kept pulling on both ends of the towel, biceps shaping as he did so. She knew this was for her benefit.

He said. "So you turn me over to the police, Nicole, and then what?"

"Then she gets so scared without her supply that she decides to try rehab again."

"I see."

"And this time she'll make it."

"So that's the plan, huh?" There was just a hint of a smirk on his mouth.

"That's the plan. I don't want you to sell her any more cocaine."

"What do I tell her when she calls?"

"Just tell her that you're not in the business any more. That you're scared of the police or something like that."

He looked at her and smiled. "If I ask you a question, will you answer it honestly?"

"If you'll turn down the music. It's pretty loud."

He was up and at the CD player in seconds. "Not a Debussy fan, eh?"

"Maybe some other time."

When he was seated again, he said, "Have you ever seen her happy when she wasn't doing coke?"

"Of course I have."

"I realize you think you're being honest. But think hard for a moment. And be honest with yourself."

She saw what he was getting at. Her mother was miserable when she was clean and sober. That, Nicole had to admit. She'd look at her mother and she'd look miserable. Tense, lost, angry, anxious. And late at night, she'd hear her mother sob. And there was almost never a smile. Or any expression of joy. Her life was simply a matter of *not* using cocaine. And she did not share the pride or the pleasure that others seemed to take in her *not* doing this.

His phone rang. "Think about it, kiddo." He reached over to a glass end table and picked up the phone. And said. "Hi. I've got company." He laughed. "Actually, yes, it is somebody you know. Your daughter." Then, "I take it you haven't told her." Pause. "Then that'll be my pleasure, I guess." Pause. "I'll call you in a while."

After hanging up, he said, "She said she hadn't had time to tell you yet. She wanted to wait for the right moment, I guess."

"Tell me what?"

"She's taking in a boarder."

"A what?"

"You know, a roomer."

"Who?"

He grinned. "Me. I'm going to be living with you for a while."

MITCH

In the first week, Nicole took all her meals in her room. She barely spoke to her mother, and she wouldn't speak to him at all. She spent several Friday and Saturday nights staying over at her friends' houses.

Mitch enjoyed the setup. He was tired of all the artistes and pretenders he'd hung out with the past ten years. It was enjoyable to get up in the morning and have a home-cooked meal and then spend a few hours "blocking out" a novel. That's what he called it, blocking out. Taking notes and filling up lined pages with blue ballpoint ink. Such and so would happen in Chapter Six, such and so would happen in Chapter Ten and so on. He liked to think he was editing a film, moving this scene from here to here. The writing itself, after all this preparation, was bound to be simple. Or so he told himself. Of course, in ten years, he'd actually never written a word of text. But what the hell. That really would be the easy part.

He stayed in a basement room that was fixed up for guests. He had his own bathroom and shower and TV set. He even had his own entrance, right on the side. His MG fit nicely into the third stall of the garage. He walked around the neighborhood on the sunny days. It was like being in a sitcom, all the neighbors tending their lawns and waving to him, the sounds of friendly dogs and driveway basketball, the aromas of backyard cookouts and fresh hung laundry on outdoor lines.

This was the change he needed. No doubt about it. He had business to tend to but that took two, three hours at most a day. Had to keep his hungry little junkies hungry, and had to resupply his own stash with his own wholesaler. He always liked to tell people he was in retail, and so he was. This was the change he needed. A new kind of lifestyle. He felt invigorated, young.

He went easy on the sex, mostly for the sake of Nicole. If she found her mother in bed with him, she'd freak. Absolutely freak. She was a very pious little thing, sweet Nicole. Kate said she got the self-righteousness from her father. She said that was one reason she was so glad their marriage was over, so she didn't have him in her face all the time dispersing rules with a ferocity that would have put Moses to shame.

One rainy Saturday night, with Nicole sleeping over at a friend's house, he nailed her. She was as hungry for sex as she was cocaine. She was damned good: knowing, patient, clever and seemingly tireless. At one point, he rolled off the bed and lay on the floor laughing and screaming "Call 911! I can't take it any more!" And then she'd started laughing, too, and jumped off the bed, landing right on top of him. They spent an hour on the floor violating every silky hot orifice in her body.

He kept her coked up, and she kept him sexed up. At first, the first three-four weeks, they were discreet. Wouldn't want little Nicole to find out now, would we? They waited until she was gone before they did anything. There were a lot of nooners, Kate rushing home from the office for a line or two of coke and a ripping good time in the sack.

One night, when Nicole was upstairs in her room doing homework, they decided to do it in his room in the basement. It was like high school, the sneaking around, Nicole the stern repressed Midwestern parent, and them the fuck-happy teen-agers. She didn't catch them. The next night and the next night and the next night and the next night, they did the same thing, Nicole working on her homework and them humping in the basement. God, it was great, and the danger made it just that much more delicious.

One Saturday afternoon, she caught them.

Nicole had come home early from the library, tired from a long day's studying. They didn't hear her. They were having too much fun in Kate's bedroom. But Nicole heard them. She flung the door open and stalked into the bedroom and went over to him and grabbed him by the long, dark hair. A handful came off in her grip. She pushed him off the bed and to the floor and shrieked, "I want you out of here! And I mean right now!"

Humiliated, enraged, Kate flew from the bed and slapped her daughter hard several times across the face, hard enough to draw blood.

Nicole spat at her, silver spittle hanging comically on the end of Kate's classical nose, and then stormed out of the bedroom, and out the house.

She didn't come home that night.

Kate started calling all her friends. None had seen her.

Mitch said that she was just punishing Kate, trying to scare her. Everything would be fine. He cooed, he cajoled, he caressed, and he finally got Kate back in bed. But the little bitch had spoiled his evening for him. Kate just wasn't there for him that night. Oh, they had sex all right, but there was none of her usual passion or ingenuity. It was like screwing a hooker who was having an off night. The little bitch really pissed him off. He was enjoying his suburban sojourn. He didn't want it ruined by all these mother-daughter politics.

She didn't come home until Monday after school. By then, even stoked up on coke, Kate was a nervous mess. Pacing. Biting her nails. Jumping every time the phone rang.

The little bitch.

She pulled in just as dusk was making it a better world.

She sat in her car in the garage a long time. Kate kept wanting to go out there. Mitch wouldn't let her. "That's what she wants you to do."

"I've been such a terrible mother to her, Mitch. I really have." She was begging him to let her go out to the garage. But by now, Mitch was genuinely resentful of the little prig. She resented him because he'd usurped her place as head of the family. Without him here, Nicole would be giving the orders. That's how it was in some junkie homes. The older kid took over and became the parent while the parent became a pathetic child. A power thing. Nicole had enjoyed the power. Now Mitch had the power. And he wasn't about to give it up.

She finally came in an hour later. She didn't say anything.

Didn't even look at them. She just went straight up to her room and quietly closed her door. Kate spent the night fluttering around Nicole's door like a moth around a summer night's streetlight. But it did no good. Nicole wouldn't acknowledge her in any way.

Kate wouldn't come down to the basement, not this night or the next or the next. Kate pleaded with Nicole to speak to her. But Nicole came in the door at night and went straight to her room and reappeared only the next morning, in time to go to school. She wouldn't even say goodbye.

Mitch took it for a week, feeling helpless and sorry for himself. He did not like being at the mercy of the little bitch. She was spoiling his time with middle America. But Mitch, failed artist, failed husband, failed father, failed son, was nothing if not ingenious.

Mitch had a plan.

NICOLE

She finally gave in, of course. Nicole.

Mitch was out somewhere. Mom was sitting in the kitchen. Drinking coffee. She looked great. The coke was killing her but it was a tradeoff. While she was dying, Kate looked better than she had in a long time, and was in a much better mood, too. Nicole poured herself a cup from Mr. Coffee and then came over and sat down at the kitchen table. The sunlight was bright and lazy in the air.

Neither of them said anything for a time. For this uneasy moment, they were strangers.

"You been all right, Nicole?"

"Yes. You?"

"This would be a very happy time for me if my daughter and I were getting along."

"Are you in love with him?"

Kate smiled. "God, no."

"But you sleep with him, anyway?"

"I enjoy him, honey. And part of that enjoyment is sex."

"And the drugs."

"Have you noticed how much happier I am? I mean, until you and I had our falling out?"

Nicole nodded.

"Have you noticed how much better I look?"

"I know what you're going to say, Mom. But you're wrong. The coke may make you feel better right now but it'll kill you eventually."

"Maybe that's not the worst thing, Nicole. To die, I mean. I enjoy the high, hon. I don't know how else to say it. When I'm high, I'm fine. And when I have my own pusher living right in my own home—" She smiled. "A junkie's dream."

"You shouldn't call yourself that, Mom."

"Well, that's what I am."

"You don't have to be."

"I'll never go back to another rehab program, Nicole. I don't want to be one of those zombies who just hangs on her whole life, trying to put off taking another line of coke. It's not a way to live. Especially since Mitch is right under my own roof."

"He doesn't care about you, Mom."

"And I don't care about him. Except that he keeps me happy with his drugs, and satisfied with his sex. You're old enough to understand that, Nicole."

"So I just live here with you?"

"You'll be leaving for college in California in four months. Then you won't have to worry about it anymore." Then, "Don't you want me to be happy, Nicole?"

"You know I do."

"Then let me live the way I want to, hon. Then you can go away to college and not have to worry about me anymore."

"Oh, right. I go away to college and then I magically never worry about you anymore? It doesn't work that way, Mom. In case you hadn't noticed."

"Just be civil to him. That's all I ask. He doesn't like the way you and I are carrying on. Just be civil so he can enjoy himself while he's here."

Nicole carried her cup to the sink, washed it out, put it in the washer.

Then she went over and slid her arms around her mother and they hugged each other and they both cried and Kate said. "I just want to be happy and feel good for a little while, honey. That's all."

Nicole held her and kissed her. Tears filled her eyes.

A few minutes later, she was in her car and headed to the library. She had things to do.

Two nights later, the three of them ate dinner together at the long, mahogany table in the dining room. Candlelight, of course. Lasagna with fresh peaches and Caesar salad, Nicole's favorite meal, lovingly prepared by Kate after work. Dinner was late, but the food was delicious.

"How was school today?" Mitch said.

Nicole looked at her mother. Her mother looked frightened.

"Mitch, I'm going to try and get along with you for Mom's sake, all right? But don't pretend you're my father. Or that you're interested in my life. All right? I mean, that's really a pain in the ass."

Mitch laughed. "I hate to disappoint you. But I'm not old enough to be your father, Nicole. I'm only fourteen or fifteen years older than you are."

"I thought you said you were thirty-nine," Kate said.

He patted her hand. "I only said that to make you feel more comfortable. I'm thirty-two."

"Maybe you're lying to make *Nicole* feel more comfortable," Kate said, not entirely pleased by this sudden turn in the conversation.

Mitch smiled. "Yes. Maybe I am."

And so it went. One week, two weeks. A family. That's what Kate pretended was happening, anyway. That the three of them were somehow bonding. Watching her like this made Nicole so sad she couldn't even cry. She'd just sit stunned for hours staring out the window of her bedroom at the dusk birds sailing down the salmon pink sky, arcing black shapes against the dying days, beings whose freedom Nicole could only envy.

MITCH

It was during Mitch's fourth week in the house that he cut Kate off. Unbeknownst to both Nicole and Kate, this was the plan he'd been working on for the past few weeks. He wanted to dominate his circumstances completely. And there was only one way to do that.

One afternoon, late, Kate came home from work tense and showing signs of needing her friend the white powder. Long day at work, the boss on her case, two of her coworkers in particularly grumpy moods. She related all this as she stripped out of her clothes and lay down on the bed with Mitch. Ordinarily, Mitch would have been right there with the coke. But not today.

When he didn't offer, she said, "I could really use a little boost, Mitch." That was her coy name for it. "Boost."

"You do for me, I do for you."

Her head had been on his naked chest. Now she rolled away from him and looked at his face. "Is something wrong?"

"You do for me, I do for you."

"I don't know what you're talking about." She was already getting a little shaky. "Please, Mitch, I don't mind playing games, but give me a little boost first, all right?"

He leaned over on an elbow and looked at her. "This is a good time for you, isn't it, Kate?"

"Yes. You know it is, Mitch."

"Me here. You getting a 'boost' whenever you need it. And the sex isn't bad, either."

"The sex is great."

"And you don't want it to end, do you?"

A flutter of fear in her eyes and her voice. "Don't want it to end? What're you talking about, Mitch? Why would it end?"

He hesitated. Went into one of his Acting 101 routines. Looked down at the nubby bedspread, looked up at her briefly, then looked down at the nubby bedspread again. Troubled young man. Searching for the right words. Pure ham. But most of the ladies loved it. He said, in barely a whisper. "I'm going to ask you to do me a favor and you're going to get all pissed off and self-righteous and probably throw me out."

"I'd never throw you out, Mitch. God, I wouldn't, I wouldn't."

Impish grin. "That's because I haven't asked you my favor yet."

"Just ask me, Mitch. Just ask me."

So he asked her.

"Oh, Mitch." she said. "I should've known you were pulling one of your jokes on me. Get me all scared the way you did."

"It isn't a joke, Kate."

"C'mon, now, Mitch. I know how you like to put me on."

"No put on, Kate. I'm very serious."

"But you can't be serious."

But then she saw that he was serious.

And she got all pissed off and self-righteous and demanded that he leave the house right now. And for good.

A number of the neighbors commented on the screeching, dish-throwing, foul-mouthed argument that ensued within the walls of the Sanders place but that could be heard as far as half a block away. It went on like this, grand-opera style, for at least an hour. The neighbors hadn't heard arguments like that since the good doctor, her ex-husband, had moved out. Things must be going badly with her live-in.

Things must be going very badly.

NICOLE

When Nicole got home that night, she found her mother at the kitchen table, her head down on her hands. Something was terribly wrong. She used to sense that when she was a little girl and her Dad was still living at home. She'd come home after school in the echoes of one of their arguments and her stomach would knot up and she'd feel alone and scared, scared that one of them might have killed the other, and she would start to shake and cry and say little prayers over and over again that everything would be all right.

A half-filled bottle of J&B Scotch sat on the table in front of her. One glass. No ice.

Kate looked up at her wildly in the wan glow of the kitchen stove light. She was inching back toward her bag-woman demeanor, the hair wild and ratty, the eyes sunk deep and rimmed with black circles, the mouth slack with sparkling spittle collected in the corners. She'd been at work today. How had she accomplished all this just since work?

She was sitting in her bra and panties, with her long, lovely legs crossed. She was swinging her right foot to a rhythm only she could hear.

Nicole sat across from her. "Where's Mitch?"

"You're late."

"I was over at Sherry's."

"You should've called."

"I want to know what's going on."

"Nothing's going on."

"Bullshit, Mom. Bullshit."

Kate sighed. "I kicked him out."

"Why?"

"Because he's an asshole."

"That isn't an answer, Mom."

"It is for me. I kicked him out because he's an asshole. That sums it up pretty damned well, I think."

"You're shaking all over. He didn't give you a boost?"

"Screw his boost. I don't need his boost."

Mitch's words came back to her. About how happy her mother had been when everything was going well between her and

Mitch. How she'd get all the boosts she wanted. How she kept herself looking great. How she was productive and happy. This was already like the old days. It was scary and sad. And not for the first time in her life did Nicole think of getting the gun out of her mother's dresser drawer and putting it in her mouth and killing herself. Many, many nights during the divorce, she'd thought of doing this.

"You want me to fix you something to eat?" Kate said.

Her words, her manner put a melancholy smile on Nicole's face. "Oh, yeah, Mom, you're in great shape to cook. One more drink of Scotch and you'll pass out."

"And that's just what I intend to do, too. And don't you try to stop me."

Nicole sat there with her and watched her take one more drink. A good, big one. All the while muttering about how much better her life would be now that the asshole was out of it.

Nicole managed to get her to the downstairs john before she started throwing up. Then she managed to get her upstairs and in bed. Kate started snoring immediately. Nicole clipped the light off and went back to the kitchen.

She fixed herself a tuna sandwich on toast and had a few chips and a diet Pepsi. She cleaned up the kitchen and went to bed. But she didn't sleep. She wondered what had gone wrong with Mitch and her mother.

The deterioration was pretty fast. Nicole could remember a time when it took her mother five or six days to get to the screaming, stomach-clutching, glass-smashing state in need of a boost.

This time, she made it in two days. She didn't go to work either one: the first day, she didn't even get out of bed. Nicole missed another day of school.

She got in her car and drove over to a section where she was sure she could find plenty of drugs. She'd taken three hundred out of the ATM machine. She wasn't sure how much drugs cost but she figured that three hundred would be enough to buy something.

The trouble was that the street people scared her. She was always seeing TV news stories about carjackings. Even with her doors locked, she didn't feel safe. She cruised the black streets but the angry curiosity of the faces—spoiled little white girl from the suburbs, what the fuck she doin' down here, fuckin' bitch—soon pushed her back onto the expressway.

She would have to convince her mother to go into the detox program run by one of the local hospitals.

But by the time she got back home, she found her mother drunk and belligerent. And the moment she brought up detox, her mother went into one of her violent frenzies.

Nicole stayed in her room all night.

The next morning, she called in sick to school and went to see Mitch.

He was using his Stairmaster again. Blue running shorts, white T-shirt. He didn't bother playing the suave host this time. He invited her in. He kept working out on the machine.

"Let me guess why you're here," he said. His tone was sardonic.

"You were right."

"I was? About what?" He was sweating and panting a little bit.

"My mother was very happy while you were there. The happiest I've seen her in a long, long time."

He smiled icily. "And you want me to come back."

"Yes."

He looked at her. "She tell you why I left?"

"No. Just that you'd had a fight. I thought maybe you'd tell me."

"I don't think so."

"I'd better let your mother tell you."

"I'm a big girl, Mitch. I can take it."

He smiled. "You go ask your mother."

"I want you to come back, Mitch. I'm sorry if I acted like a bitch. You made her happy."

He came off the machine so quickly, she was hardly aware of him at first. Sliding his arms around her back and waist, finding her mouth with his tongue, easing her against the wall so that she could feel his groin pressing against her.

She pushed against him but he was too strong. She tried bringing her knee up but he knew how to block it.

Finally, she bit his tongue. He fell back from her, cursing, dabbing his tongue with the tip of his finger. Then he laughed. "I knew you were a tough one, Nicole." He held up his finger. "Blood."

She walked to the door. Jerked it open. Walked out into the hallway. Slammed the door behind her.

When she came in the back door, she saw several empty glasses smashed on the floor. Mom had been on a rampage again, the need getting overwhelming.

She went upstairs. Sobbing sounds came from the large bedroom.

A weariness came over her. It was odd to be this young and yet be so worn out. She felt as if she were ninety. On the way over, she'd thought about Mitch grabbing her and kissing her. Then she'd thought about the argument Mitch and Mom had had. She had a pretty good idea now what it had been about.

She stood outside the door a long moment and listened to her mother cry. Only a few days ago, Mom had looked young and vital again. And was busy and productive. True, there were peaks and valleys in her mood and addiction level, but on balance life was good and happy again.

You couldn't beat having a live-in pusher, she thought. She went into the bedroom. Kate peeked at her from behind a hand that lay against her face. "Go away. I don't want you to see me like this."

"I need to talk to you a minute, Mom."

"I can't talk now, honey. I'm sick. My whole body. Sick. You go downstairs or something."

"I think I know what you and Mitch were arguing about." She sat down on the bed. Took her mother's hand. Held it to her own face. She could feel warm tears on the hand. "I want to thank you, Mom."

"For what, hon?"

"For not asking me to do it."

Kate didn't say anything.

Nicole said, "He wanted me to sleep with him, didn't he?"

Kate didn't say anything.

"That's what you had the argument about, wasn't it?"

Kate didn't say anything.

"If I agreed to sleep with him, then he'd stay and keep you in drugs. That way, when he got bored with you, he'd sleep with me."

"He isn't a bad person, sweetie. He just looks at sex different from how we do."

"He's a creep. He took advantage of you and now he wants to take advantage of me." She kissed her mother's hand. "Thanks for not asking me to do it."

"I knew how you'd feel about it, honey."

"I appreciate it." She gently put her Mom's hand back on the bed and said, "Why don't I make you a little soup?"

"I don't know if I could hold it down."

"At least, let's give it a try." She hesitated. "Then I want to talk to you some more about rehab, Mom. You can't go on like this."

Kate looked beyond exhaustion. Something had died in her. The gleaming eyes, the happy voice of a few days ago were gone. "Maybe that's what I need. Rehab, I mean." She spoke in a dazed voice, staring tearily out the window. "Maybe I should quit fighting it."

"Why don't you take a little nap? I'll bring the soup up in a half hour or so."

Kate held her arms out. Nicole slid into her sleep-warm embrace.

Nicole was watching the MTV Top Ten countdown. Eight of the songs were rap, with sneering black guys pushing their faces into the camera. Nicole was too romantic for rap. She liked the ballads, especially by the black girl groups, who were as romantic as the boys were unromantic.

She yawned. She was exhausted and looking forward to bed. Three hours ago, she'd served her mother chicken soup and a glass of skim milk. She'd tucked her into bed and turned on the electric blanket. When Kate was in withdrawal, she got the chills bad.

She was just about to click off the TV with the remote when the gunshot exploded and echoed.

Her first impression was that something had blown up. Stove. Or water heater. Something like that.

But in the next moment, she realized what had really happened. Gunshot. The gun from Mom's drawer. Upstairs. Mom.

Fear blinded her.

She took the steps two at a time, tripping on the last of the stairway, grabbing the banister to keep from falling over.

Mom Mom Mom, she kept thinking.

The master bedroom was empty.

The smaller bedroom was empty.

She ran into the bathroom.

Her mother, completely naked, vomit covering her chest and stomach, her head twisted drunkenly to see Nicole, sat on the edge of the bathtub, a gun in her right hand. The top of her head was dusted with plaster from the hole in the ceiling that the bullet had made. A half-full bottle of J&B lay at her feet.

Nicole could never remember her this far gone. She stared at Nicole but with no recognition whatsoever showing in her eyes. Huge goosebumps covered her arms and legs. "No more fucking detox, kiddo," she said to no one in particular. "No more fucking detox."

She raised the gun to her temple. Or tried to. The movement was jerky and imprecise and gave Nicole plenty of time to grab her mother's wrist and ease the gun from her hand.

Then her mother began sobbing. She slipped to the floor, reeking of her own vomit and urine, wild-eyed and aggrieved beyond Nicole's imagining, slumped trembling and dry-heaving and crying on the pink bathroom rug.

Nicole knelt next to her mother but it did no good. Kate wrenched herself away. "I fucking hate you, you little snotty bitch! You want to put me back in rehab! I fucking hate you!"

Nicole tried several times to console her mother but finally gave up. Her mother had slipped into a fetal position and started muttering to herself in a language and cadence only she could understand. If even she could comprehend it.

Only a few days ago, this had been a happy woman.

Nicole slipped quietly from the bathroom, and went and made a phone call.

They were in the kitchen. Nicole and her mother. At the table. Drinking coffee. This was six hours after the bathroom incident. Kate had showered, eaten half a sandwich, and begun drinking black coffee as fast as Mr. Coffee could turn it out.

And, most important of all, Mitch had given her a boost.

Nicole had called Mitch. He'd agreed to come over. He'd brought a large suitcase. He'd agreed to try it again, with Kate and all, for a few days.

Mitch was upstairs now, in the master bedroom, waiting for Nicole.

"You don't have to do this, you know," Kate said. "You really don't."

"It was my decision, mother."

"I mean, you know how appreciative I am. And he is very good in bed, honey. And he promised me he'd be very, very gentle and take his time. You could do a lot worse, your first time."

"I'd better get up there. He's waiting."

"He's really not a bad guy, hon. He's really not." Then, "What're you going to wear?"

"Just my pajamas, I guess."

"Too bad you never liked sleeping gowns."

"I like sloppy old pajamas, Mom. They're comfortable to sleep in."

"You're so pretty." Kate touched her daughter's cheek. "And you're such a good girl."

Nicole looked upstairs. "Well, I'd better go."

She was just leaving the kitchen when her mother said, "You really don't have to do this, you know."

He was in bed. Propped up against the headboard. No shirt. Glass of wine. Cigarette going in the ashtray. A PBS concert of some kind on the tube. This was a very nicely appointed bedroom.

He smiled at her. "You looked scared, Nicole. I'm not the boogeyman. I'm really not."

"I'm not sure what I'm supposed to do."

He raised his wineglass. "Well, first of all, I want you to chill out a little. You know what I mean? Relax. Believe it or not, you just might enjoy this. Kate tells me you're a virgin. Is that true?"

"More or less."

"Oh-oh. Was there something you never told your mother?" The smile firmly in place.

"I've never gone all the way, if that makes me a virgin."

"Well, that certainly makes you a virgin in *my* book." He patted the bed next to him. "Why don't you come over and sit down next to me. I want you to like me, Nicole. I really do. We could have a very nice relationship. We really could."

"The three of us, you mean?"

"Sure, the three of us. You and I would have one relationship, Kate and I would have another relationship. You see what I mean? And maybe sometime—" He paused.

"Maybe sometime what?"

"Oh, we'll talk about it later, maybe. For now, pour yourself some wine and sit down here and let's get to know each other a little better. All right?"

He was gentle.

A couple of times, she even found herself if not exactly enjoying it then not exactly *not* enjoying it.

She'd had all these preconceptions. That it would hurt a lot. That there would be a good deal of blood. That she would feel deeply changed by the experience.

None of these things happened to her.

They made love twice. They started on a third time but then he asked her gently if she'd mind doing him. The doing scared her more than the actual intercourse. She hated doing him and when she sensed he was going to come, she jerked him out of her mouth. She felt angry that he came all over her mother's bedspread.

He lay back and pulled her down to him, holding her. He lit a cigarette.

"So, do you hate me?"

"I don't want to talk about it."

"I tried to be gentle."

"You were gentle."

"I tried to be nice."

"You were nice."

"I was hoping you'd feel a little better about me, you know, after we'd done it and everything."

She said nothing.

"You hear what I said, Nicole?"

"I heard."

"So, do you feel any better about me?"

She said nothing.

"Guess you don't want to talk, huh?"

"I'd like to go to my own room now."

"Sure, if that's what you'd like." Then, "You know what *I'd* like?"

"What?"

"You remember when I said 'maybe sometime.'"

"Yes, I remember."

"Well, what I was thinking about was the three of us getting together all at the same time."

"My mom?"

"Yes."

"And me?"

"Uh-huh."

"Having sex with you?"

"It could be a lot of fun. I mean, I admit it sounds a little over-the-top at first. But when you think about it, it isn't all that raunchy. I mean I'm sure it's been done before."

She stood up. She felt sick.

It would probably happen, what he was talking about. Somehow they'd be able to convince her to get involved in it. Somehow.

"I'm going now."

"Just think about it, Nicole, all right? What I was talking about?"

She slipped out of the dark bedroom and went into her own bedroom.

In about half an hour, her mother came in. The bedroom was all shadow and silver moonlight. Nicole was under the covers.

"Nicole?"

No answer.

Her mom came over and knelt next to the bed. "Did it go all right?"

Nicole decided to answer. "Yes."

"Was he nice?"

"Yes."

"He didn't hurt you or anything?"

"No." Then, "Could we talk in the morning, Mom? I'm real tired."

She lay there for an hour trying to get to sleep. But all she could think of was what he'd suggested, about the three of them getting together.

She slept until late into the dark night. They woke her with their noises. Her first impression was that he was hurting Mom but then she realized it was just Mom's wild enjoyment she was hearing. Mom would go along with it when the time came. Not at first. Not without some convincing. But eventually, she'd go along.

She'd go along.

And so would Nicole.

Three different neighbors reported the shots. People on the nice, quiet, respectable block are up from their beds and out the door, arriving in pajamas and nightgowns and robes and slippers just about the time the first patrol car reaches the Sanders's driveway.

A heavyset cop knocks on the front door of the Sanders's home, pauses, and then knocks again.

This is when the side door of the house, the one that opens on the driveway, eases open and Nicole appears.

None of the neighbors have ever seen Nicole look like this. Hair unkempt, pajamas torn and blood-soaked, hands filthy with blood. Blood everywhere. Even in her hair. Even on her feet. Blood. No mistaking what it is. Blood. She stands in the headlights of the police car, moths and gnats and mosquitoes thick around the headlights (big motor throbbing unevenly, needing points and plugs), and that is where the neighbors get their first good look at the knife she used. Butcher knife. Long wooden handle. Good but not great steel. A knife she just grabbed from the silverware drawer before going upstairs.

A second prowl car. This one dispersing two cops. Man and woman. The man starts dealing with the crowd. Pushing them back. The woman goes directly to Nicole.

"I need to know your name, miss, and what happened here."

But Nicole is long gone.

The first cop comes down the steps. Says something to the female officer and then goes in the side door.

"What's your name, miss?" the female cop asks in a soft voice. "I want to help you. I really do."

The crowd has grown greatly in a few minutes. Two different TV stations are here now, one in a large van, the other in a muddy Plymouth station wagon.

The first cop is back from inside. Goes to the other male cop. "It's a mess in there. A man and woman. The woman looks like the girl there. She stabbed the hell out of them. Shot the guy, too. It's a frigging mess."

A few people in the crowd are close enough to hear this. A whisper like an undulating snake works its way through the crowd. Shock and sadness and yet a glee and excitement, too. The shock for the pitiful young girl standing blood-soaked in the headlights, her mind obviously gone; and yet glee and excitement, too. Every day life is so—everyday. No denying the excitement here. And didn't Kate Sanders think she was at least a little bit better than everybody else? And exactly who was that man who'd moved in a while ago? And now look at Nicole. Poor, poor Nicole.

The reporter from the van, having heard what the cop found inside, now gets his cameraman to follow him around as he gets statements from various neighbors.

"Well, Kate, the mother, she and her husband split up a few years ago."

"They were very quiet people, really, though I think everybody knew that Kate had quite a few personal problems."

The cameraman angles his machine up the driveway, letting his lens linger on the lovely, crazed, blood-spattered girl standing in the headlights, Ophelia of the suburbs, which will make great fucking TV, just this lone shot of this lone heart-breaking crazy fucking girl.

And (voice over) a neighbor lady saying into the microphone: "It's just so hard to believe. She was such a good girl; such a good girl."

About the Author

Ed Gorman has been writing full-time since 1984 after a career in advertising. Prolific in the mystery, dark suspense and western fields, he had written more than a hundred stories and many novels, including *Stranglehold*, due from St. Martin's this fall. His short fiction, distinctive for its emotional depth, has been reprinted in numerous anthologies, including *The Shamus Winners* (2010). This is his first book for Perfect Crime.